INTERNATIONAL PLAYER

LOUISE BAY

D0870164

Published by Louise Bay 2019

ISBN – 978-1-910747-57-5

ONE

Truly

If getting a kick from solving spreadsheet errors was wrong, I didn't want to be right. I lived for this stuff. My fingers didn't work as quickly as I wanted them to, and the numbers on my screen seemed to appear in slow motion. Clicking back to the original cell on my spreadsheet, the totals now balanced. A simple blunder made by one of my junior team members had just taken me an hour to fix. And I'd loved every minute of it—the challenge of turning disorder into order and then the neat numbers that now lined up. "Thank you," I said to myself, raising my hands in the air as if taking in applause from a crowd.

"You know you're a total geek, right?" my twin sister, Abi, asked from the doorway of my office.

I dropped my hands. "Jesus, how long have you been standing there watching me like a complete weirdo-stalker?"

"Actually, I said your name several times but you were in some geeky trance." Abigail kicked my office door closed behind her then stalked toward my desk, sliding one of the two salad boxes she was holding toward me. "I brought you lunch. I figured we could eat together."

I saved my now-accurate spreadsheet. "Since when are you free for lunch? Don't you have some donor to schmooze?" While I was all numbers and back-office stuff, Abigail was in charge of bringing in the money to the charitable foundation that my mother founded nearly forty years ago. I called her Chief Schmoozer or Director of Arse Kissing. She preferred CEO. Whatever.

"Not today, little sister." Abigail had been born six and a half minutes ahead of me and she never let me forget it. "Today, I get to have lunch with you." She plonked herself down on the chair in front of my desk, and from her handbag, she pulled out two drinks, her phone, and cutlery wrapped in napkins, then set them between us.

"Are you moving in?" I sighed. Lunch with Abigail was a complete time suck. I had a thousand things to do. "I'm really busy. I'm way behind getting the monthly reporting finished off and—"

"Thirty minutes, Truly." She emptied a pot of dressing onto her salad and began to stir. "You have to eat, and it will do you good to have a break. I keep telling you that you need more balance."

I groaned and grabbed the salad. I clearly wasn't getting rid of her. "Should you be having dressing on your salad?" I asked as I emptied my pot onto the chicken, herb, and cucumber bowl she'd brought me.

"Don't you start too. Rob has already turned into the food police. And the exercise police. And the breathing-in-and-out police."

I winced. "Well, it's understandable—it's your first baby. It's nice that he's being protective."

"As if I'm likely to be reckless. It's not like he wants this kid more than I do. I swear, it's like he's expecting me to announce that I'm going to sign up for a bungee jump or something."

"You should leave some brochures around the house, just to mess with him."

"If it wasn't likely to bring on a stroke, I might. Speaking of extreme sports, I have some interesting news."

I poked my fork into my salad. "About extreme sports?" The Harbury Foundation often had people fundraising throughout the UK by participating in sponsored sky dives or abseiling or other crazy stuff people were prepared to donate to.

"Kinda. Rob spoke to Noah last night."

Noah. Blood pounded in my ears, and I was sure if I glanced down, I'd see my heart beating out of my chest. I kept my chewing constant, as if the sound of his name had no effect on me whatsoever.

Abigail paused to finish her mouthful of food. I willed her to get on with it. To tell me whatever it was she didn't want to say about her husband's best friend.

"He's moving back."

I swallowed before my throat closed up and I choked to death on salad.

"Rob told him he can stay with us for a few weeks while he finds a flat—the last thing I need is a houseguest when I'm as big as a whale and working twenty hours a day trying to get things ready for when I go on maternity leave."

I closed the lid on my lunch, my appetite dead, and dumped it into the bin beside me. "That's not very considerate of him. Did you tell him no?"

"He knows I'm not happy. He didn't get any last night."

I hadn't seen Noah Jensen for four years, two months, and three weeks—not that I was counting.

"You used to be good friends with him, right?" Abi asked.

Good *friends*. Yeah. That's what we'd been. I'd been closer to him than any man I'd ever known, despite never having slept with him. I'd never told Abi about my crush on him. It felt silly and childish to long for someone so hopelessly out of my reach. I knew she suspected—she'd made a few comments about the time we spent together and the fact that we were both single. But I'd always just ignored her. "I doubt he even remembers my name, and I've forgotten what he looks like." That wasn't entirely true. Or even a little bit true. Noah was the best-looking man I'd ever laid eyes on. A six-foot-four Nordic god with a square jaw and eyes as blue as the ocean.

He looked like he belonged with my sister.

Despite being twins, Abigail and I were complete opposites. She worked hard but made it look easy. Was always perfectly put together but never seemed like she tried. With shiny, golden-blonde locks, she took after our mother, while I'd inherited my unruly dark hair from my father. It wasn't straight enough to be sleek or curly enough to be interesting. Abigail's pale skin and blue eyes gave her a captivating, regal air. My amber eyes and unremarkable coloring helped me melt into the background. She was married. I was terminally single. But despite our differences, we'd always been close. The one thing we had in common apart from DNA was our shared commitment to the foundation.

"Well, you'll get to catch up at lunch on Sunday."

Bloody hell, I'd forgotten about lunch. I hadn't seen Noah since . . . since the night before he went to New York. Since we almost kissed. Had we though? Was my memory playing tricks on me? I just knew that when he'd left, I'd missed him more than I should have, and I didn't want to put myself back into a position where I was pining after a man so obviously out of my league. I'd fallen into that trap once already. "I'll see about lunch. I'm really busy."

"Busy doing what? Anything that's work related can wait until Monday. And it's not like you actually have a social life or anything."

"Give me a break. I enjoy my work. And I'm good at it. And I enjoy being good at it. It's not like I'm just filling the pockets of corporate Britain. As you say so often in your speeches, the foundation makes a real difference."

"I didn't mean it that way, it's just that . . . work can't be the only thing in your life. I worry about you—I want you to be happy."

I rolled my eyes and prepared for the increasingly regular lecture I got about my lack of socializing. "I am happy and don't try to make out like I'm the only worka-holic Harbury sister. Are you sure *you* can make lunch on Sunday? Don't you have index cards to fill out or something?"

Abigail kept details of everyone she met on small white cards. She had thousands of them listing everything from the ages and genders of donor's children to what they liked to eat and the places they liked to holiday most. Before she went to an event or a meeting, she'd remind herself of every-thing she learned about a person. Then when she spoke with them, she'd appear invested and thoughtful, and that person would feel special that such a beautiful woman remembered their previous conversations so clearly.

"Index cards. Funny. At least I'm having sex."

My sister was way too invested in my love life. Or lack of it.

"I don't want to hear about you banging Rob."

"When's the last time you went on a date even?"

I dated. Not successfully and not for a while, but it happened from time to time. "Mr. Muscle, probably."

"The fact that you call him by the nickname my husband gave him makes me think that maybe you weren't that serious about him."

"You said date. You didn't mention being serious."

She sat back. "I just worry. Speaking of which, I need to figure out what we're going to do when this kid decides to join us. You don't have any more hours in the day." The question of who was going to cover Abigail's maternity leave had been hanging in the air since before she and Rob had even gotten pregnant. There was no one who could do what Abi did. No one who could command a room, give a speech, or tell the compelling stories of the children we helped like she could. Fundraising would stall while she was off, which meant the longer she was off, the fewer people we could help. The foundation wouldn't survive longer than a few weeks without her.

"You know you can't call him or her 'this kid' forever, right?"

She shrugged and I made a mental note to start a list of possible baby names in case she didn't. I got the list-making gene when they were dividing them up in the womb. "Rob is going to take three months off, and honestly, I'm good with that. I want to be back at my desk in six weeks. I love this job."

"I need you back as soon as possible. Six hours will be bad enough." I was being selfish. I should try to talk her into taking more time off. Six weeks didn't sound like a long time, but Abigail knew the foundation would falter without her. If I was having a baby, which was as likely as snow falling in July, they could replace me in a heartbeat. But Abigail was the heart of this place.

She was the beautiful, charming twin. The one who could sell ice to Icelanders. She was used to persuading middle-aged men, enamored by her witty conversation and easy charm, to part with their cash.

Thankfully, she wasn't due to go on maternity leave until mid-December. That meant she'd still be here for the busiest time of year. "Six weeks is manageable in January and the first week of February, since the New Year is always slow. Fundraising will fall through the floor while you're off, but at least you'll be around for the lead-up to the end of the year and the winter ball." What was it about dark, winter nights that made people want to give up their money?

"Yeah, I want to exceed our targets over the next five months. Then I'll feel better about taking those six weeks off. Especially with the children's rehab center in the picture."

The Harbury Foundation researched and picked the recipients of its support carefully. This year, I'd visited a local pediatric spinal injury unit and witnessed what hopelessness looked like. It had been horrifying. What little equipment they had was for adults or broken. The children had no chance, and the expressions on their faces seemed to suggest they knew that and had given up. With our help, it could be transformed from the place dreams go to die into the leading European center for the treatment of pediatric spinal cord injuries. "Twenty-five million is an aggressive goal, but it means we're going to make a difference to these kids for the rest of their lives. It will be one of the most rewarding things we've ever done." We both grinned like dummies at each other. We might be polar opposites in so many ways, but the foundation united us.

She leaned forward and held up her palm, and I pressed

mine against hers in a half high five, half reassuring hand hold. She held my gaze.

"By the time I push this kid out, we'll have the spinal cord center nailed, but I want you to promise me something." She adopted her older-by-six-and-a-half-minutes sister tone. "Don't make the center an excuse for not making an effort to have some kind of social life."

I groaned. "I'm perfectly happy."

"Alone and knee-deep in spreadsheets. You need . . . breadth. A hobby. A boyfriend. Maybe accompany me to a function every now and then."

"That's work, Abi. Or had you forgotten?" I was way out of my depth at those functions. I always felt so awkward wearing tight dresses, high heels, and red lipstick. It was like I was playing dress up in my mother's clothes while never knowing what to say. And if I was uncomfortable, I made everyone around me uncomfortable, and uncomfortable people didn't write big checks. I'd always been happy to have Abigail take the limelight while I sloped off into the corner with a book. It was why we rarely argued. We didn't fight for attention, we respected each other's strengths, and although I envied my sister in some ways, it didn't extend into jealousy. I understood I was happier when I stuck to what I was good at. But there was still a little niggling feeling in the back of my mind that if I was better at fundraising, at schmoozing, at delivering speeches, or just more charming, then maybe Abi would be able to take more time off. I pushed it to the side of my brain. No, she'd never be happy with that. She enjoyed what she did. We worked well together because our strengths didn't overlap, and I had enough to do.

"But at least you'd be meeting new people. At the

moment, you only interact with employees of the foundation and your dry cleaner."

"I leave my dry cleaning with my porter, and he collects it while I'm at work."

She arched an eyebrow at me. "Now you're just making my point for me. You're twenty-eight, not eighty. Maybe *you* should take up bungee jumping."

I was no more likely to bungee jump than I was to have a baby. My version of extreme sports was hunting down a first edition of a favorite book. "Your thirty minutes are up. What do I have to do to get your pregnant arse out of my office?"

"Say you'll come to lunch on Sunday. That way my conscience can rest easy that you're getting out enough."

"Fine. Stay here. I'll work from the conference room."

Abigail laughed but stood. "No excuses. You've got to eat. And even if you don't give a shit about socializing, it will be nice for Noah to feel like he has friends back in London."

If Noah was back in London, that meant I'd be running into him a lot. Maybe it was better to rip the plaster off and get seeing him for the first time over with. Perhaps the crush I'd had on him will have faded. Maybe he'd changed. Perhaps he'd have some explanation of why he'd not made any effort to keep in touch after he'd left for New York. Seeing him might stop me occasionally, on a Friday night when I was alone with a bottle of pinot noir, listening to the vinyl copy of *The Unforgettable Fire* that he'd brought around that night in September. Stop me from remembering how he'd insisted we sit in silence and listen to it from start to finish, then almost kissed me.

I'd wanted to forget about Noah Jensen. When he was in New York, it had been easy. But now that he was back in

London, I just wanted to make sure I didn't wind up back where I'd been four years ago—longing for a man who saw me only as a friend.

"I'll think about lunch on Sunday. But if I come, I want roast potatoes. None of that boiled stuff Rob came up with last weekend."

She lingered, her hand on the doorknob. "I'll tell Rob. And think about what I said. Breadth. A hobby. A night out at the cinema occasionally."

"Whatever." I turned back to my computer screen, itching to get back to work. And silently vowing to throw out that turntable Noah had bought. It had been taking up room in my flat for far too long.

TWO

Truly

I was an early riser but five thirty was pushing it, even for me. Crouching on the floor and using a pencil, I stabbed through the brown tape sealing the package that had been delivered yesterday. Jesus. Threaded tape? Who did that? Psychopaths, apparently. I'd need scissors.

Abigail might think an ordinary person didn't need a stationery cabinet in their home, but times like this proved her wrong. I didn't spend the next twenty minutes trying to find some scissors because I knew exactly where they were —alongside my notebooks (at least eight that had never been used), Post-its (every size and every color), envelopes (a selection of sizes and weight), paper (in ten different shades, *Bone Enamel* being my favorite), a hole punch, and shelves full of other neatly organized items that were or might be useful. I picked out one of two pairs of medium-sized scissors and sliced open the package.

Well, there was no excuse now. I had a brand-new pair of trainers, and I was wearing a sports bra. Time to start running. Working out counted as the *breadth* Abi said I needed. It wasn't work related, was a potential hobby (if I survived this morning), and it didn't involve thinking about Noah, which I'd been doing far too much of since Abi announced he was coming back. The fact that it didn't involve other people suited my introverted habits quite nicely. Abigail would be happy. I would be distracted. I was killing two birds with one stone.

The only problem was, I'd never run seriously before. But how hard could it be? It was just walking but faster.

I tied my brand-new Adidas laces and headed out into the July London morning. It was light enough to see where I was going and early enough for no one to be up to witness my potential humiliation. I was also hoping that while I was fighting for breath, I'd decide on whether or not to go to lunch at my sister's later that day.

I tightened my ponytail as I strode past the unoccupied porter's desk and paused outside the door. Which direction should I head in? I'd not planned my journey or anything, so I really wasn't prepared. Perhaps I should forget it for today and figure out a route for tomorrow? I could map out a manageable distance and head to a specific place, then work back. But I was here now, I might as well start.

I checked my watch and turned left out of my building toward the park, walking at first and then breaking into a light jog as I turned off my road. The streets were eerily quiet, and although cars passed me fairly regularly, it was almost as if I were in a different city. The dull roar of the motorway that I never normally noticed had disappeared, and I could even make out birdsong. Instead of dodging pedestrians, I had a chance to look around and examine the white stucco houses, mostly divided into flats, and wonder who lived beyond the glossy black front doors.

This wasn't so bad.

I just needed to keep my pace steady. Not push myself too hard, too fast. As I carried on along the empty streets, my breathing fell into a rhythm with my feet. I breathed in every two steps and pushed out again every two steps. The sensation of being so aware of my lungs emptying and filling brought my thoughts back to Noah.

And lunch. And how I wanted to see him, which clearly meant I shouldn't go. It had been four years. Why did my heart rate shift into a different gear when Abigail just mentioned his name? Why could I still remember how his arms felt around me and his beard scraped against my cheek when he greeted me?

I'd heard stories about Noah from Rob as he relived what he'd called his "glory days" at university, but our paths hadn't crossed until the wedding. Noah had just returned from working in Hong Kong or China or another faraway destination. Even then he'd stood out—all blond hair, white teeth, and long limbs. He'd grinned at me from across the aisle and I'd looked away. Confused by his attention, I'd done my best to ignore him through the rest of the ceremony.

When he'd tried to engage me in conversation during the pre-reception drinks, I'd tried to figure out why. Was he one of those uber-friendly people who just liked getting to know everyone, or did he feel obligated to make conversation because I was Abigail's sister? Or a bridesmaid?

When he'd asked me to dance the first time, I'd refused. The second time I'd offered him a deal—a fifty-pound contribution to the Harbury Foundation in return for three and a half minutes to Katy Perry's "California Gurls." He'd countered with two hundred pounds for five minutes and forty seconds of Spandau Ballet's "True."

I'd accepted.

For the first time ever, I'd been nervous to touch a man, for a man to hold me. Until Noah had slid his arms around my waist and breathed out a "Perfect" in my ear, his whiskers scraping my cheek. I'd melted into him, letting him press his hands against my back so there was no gap between us. Five minutes dissolved into just a few seconds where Noah had been the only person I'd been aware of in that marquee.

It was clear he was trouble.

And a player.

And well used to banging bridesmaids at weddings.

His intentions became all the more clear when I figured out we were the only two single people over eighteen at the wedding. So I challenged him to see me as a friend rather than a potential conquest. I told him that I wouldn't be sleeping with him, but we could hang out and I could steer him away from conversations with aunties who wore too much perfume and cousins who were ten years too young for him.

And that night something new had been born between us. I'd become the first ever woman he'd tried and failed to sleep with. He'd become the person I was closest to other than my sister. We'd become the best of friends.

He teased me for being a geek. I bollocked him for being a player.

He was always able to tempt me into doing things I thought I'd hate and ended up enjoying. I showed him how boys were not the only experts on comic books.

He'd once confessed how relieved he was that I'd rejected him at the wedding so we could be friends, and right then and there a line in the sand was drawn.

Noah turned out to be different to how I expected. He

wasn't just some handsome player. I liked him, respected him, thought he was clever and driven and humble, and somewhere along the way I'd developed a huge crush on him. At least he'd never known, and I'd been saved that embarrassment. I'd hidden it well. Under my geekdom, and firmly in the center of the *Friend Zone*.

And that was why I should avoid him. I didn't want my crush coming back and this time have him figure it out. He might have wanted to seduce me at a wedding because of a lack of other single women of a suitable age, but I wasn't the girl who was going to change his player ways, and I had no interest in being another notch on his bedpost. I should make an excuse about not being able to make lunch.

My thighs began to burn and a trickle of sweat ran from the back of my neck down my spine. I hadn't even reached the park yet, and I wanted to stop, give up, and turn back. But no. This was my chance to do something different. Prove to my sister that I had breadth and to myself that I'd changed and was no longer the girl who ran away from men who were far too attractive for their own good.

I wanted to see him again. I wanted my friend back. And I wanted to know if he remembered that night before he'd left for New York. That night when we'd shared a bottle of wine, listened to music, and we'd almost crossed that line that had been drawn in the sand between us.

Had he wanted me then?

Had he known how much I'd wanted him?

THREE

Truly

I bit down on the side of my thumbnail as I paced in front of the tidy, terraced Victorian villas. A ponytail looked casual enough, right? And everyone would be wearing jeans. But the blush and the eyeliner? On a Sunday? Abigail was bound to notice.

I should never have come.

The slate-gray front door of my sister's house swung open and I froze. "Truly?" my brother-in-law bellowed. "I thought that was you. What are you doing out there?"

"Sorry, just finishing up a call." I wasn't even holding my mobile, and anyway, who would I be calling on a Sunday? I really needed to work on my cover stories.

I lifted up on tiptoes and kissed Rob on the cheek. "Did you do roast potatoes?"

"I wouldn't dare do anything else." He scooped up the bottle of white wine in my hand. "Going for a change?" he asked, looking at the label. "You usually bring red."

"I just had it in my fridge."

"Along with some moldy cheese?"

And hummus, but I didn't say that. Instead I whacked his stomach with the back of my hand for daring to be right. A stocked fridge wasn't a priority. I usually ordered something in the office or bought two lunches and kept one in the communal fridge for later.

"Is that you, Truly?" my sister called from the kitchen.

I slipped past Rob and took a deep breath as I headed to the back of the house. The blush and eyeliner were just armor. Protection from Noah and his charms. I so desperately wanted to see him again and for him to have no effect on me. I didn't want to be the girl pining after some guy who didn't know she was alive or at least didn't see her as dating potential. It was sad and pathetic and that wasn't who I was. I pulled my shoulders back and turned left, expecting to see Noah for the first time in four years. But the only person in the large, airy room was my sister, who was at the hob, peering into a saucepan.

She spun around as Rob came in after me, looking guilty.

"Did you touch it?" he asked. Rob only agreed to cook on the basis Abigail left him to it and didn't interfere.

"I swear I didn't. I just looked. Because—"

"Don't pretend to be helping, Abigail. Pour the wine." He handed her the bottle he'd just taken from me.

"You're a cruel man, Robert Franklin, making a pregnant lady pour wine she can't drink."

I glanced around, noting that Noah was nowhere to be seen.

"You brought white?" Abigail asked as she kissed me on the cheek.

I shrugged, pushing my hands into my pockets as she took in my made-up face. She noticed, but at least she didn't say anything. Just like she didn't say anything about Noah's absence. Maybe I was off the hook. Maybe he'd had other plans. No doubt he had plenty of friends to catch up with, women to hang out with, things to do. That was who Noah was. He was *busy*. Always working toward one goal or another. Always on the go.

The footsteps thundering down the stairs told me I hadn't gotten off as lightly as I had hoped.

Abigail looked up at the ceiling. "I swear he's going to bring this house down."

Her voice faded out and all I could focus on was my breathing. It was as if my body had decided that it wasn't involuntary anymore, and if I wasn't careful, my lungs would empty and never refill.

I moved toward the glass doors to pull them open and suck in some more air.

"Hey, guys, sorry. I had to take that call." Noah's deep voice tumbled out from behind me, setting off goosebumps across my skin.

Slowly, I turned and took him in. All six foot four of him filled the doorway. I'd forgotten just how perfect he was in the flesh. My memory of him didn't paint him as vividly as he was in real life. It was as if the color had been turned up on him compared to the rest of the population. The high, chiseled cheekbones, the Nordic nose that looked like he just stepped off a long ship, and the dirty blond hair that was a little longer than he wore it all those years ago—it was all too perfect. His long, long legs were clad in denim and his broad chest was covered in what looked like gray cashmere. Jesus, no wonder this man had gotten over the desire to sleep with me and friend zoned me so quickly. He looked like he'd been designed for my sister—beautiful, graceful, and powerful.

He followed Abigail's glance toward me and as our eyes locked, I gave him a wave with both hands the way a five-year-old might.

"Truly," he said, his low voice echoing through my body.

His eyes lit up in the way they always did as a smile spread across his face. But his warm greeting wasn't reserved just for me. Or even people he liked. He simply had a way about him that made the people around him feel special. He strode over to me.

"So good to see you. It's been ages."

My body heated the closer he got, and as he bent, I inhaled that blend of citrus and warm skin I remembered. The scruff of his day-old beard caught my cheek as he pressed his face to mine. My heart began to pound, and I willed him to move away so he wouldn't feel it. "You look really well," he said, the pitch of his voice loud rather than intimate. He pressed his palms to my shoulders and held me at arm's length, then he glanced over at Rob and Abigail as if he wanted them to agree.

He released me, and as if he'd been holding me up, I had to step back to get my balance. I cleared my throat in the hope it would reset my pulse to a normal rhythm. "Welcome back," was all I could manage.

"Wine?" Abigail asked.

"I'd love a glass of pinot noir if you have it," Noah said.

Rob snorted. "You know we have plenty." He turned from the saucepan in front of him and rolled his eyes at me. "This guy turned up with six cases of it. And it is so *good*. You normally drink red; you want to try it?"

I shook my head. "Trying to keep a clear head, so I'll stick to white. I've got a busy week coming up."

"So how was the flat hunting?" Abi asked, then turned,

handing me a glass of the wine I'd brought. "He's been out all morning looking at places."

"Good. It's helping me narrow down what I want," Noah replied.

I slid onto one of the oak benches at the dining table so I faced the room. Resting my elbows on either side of my glass, I waited to hear all about Noah's life now. His future.

I was going to need *all* the wine.

"And what is it you want?" Abigail asked.

"A bachelor pad," Rob said, and I tried to keep my face neutral. "Somewhere that has mirrors on the bedroom ceiling."

"Something central," Noah said, ignoring Rob. "I want my commute to be short, but I need to be able to get out of the city quickly to get to the airport."

"Didn't you just sell your company?" Abigail asked as she poured the pinot noir into his glass. "Where are you commuting to? Are you going to get another job?"

Noah lifted one of his long, muscular legs over the bench and took a seat across from me at the kitchen table. "I'm still on the board, but I'm a non-exec, so I just have to go back to New York once a month."

"Wow, a job where you only show up once a month— must be nice to be you," Rob said over the clattering of the saucepans.

Rob knew as well as the rest of us that Noah worked hard. He might only have to show up in New York once a month, but Noah wasn't a guy who took it easy just because he could. He was always working toward something.

"I'm actively looking for my next business challenge. Taking my time and seeing what captures my interest. And I'm learning to fly."

"Flying? How?" I'd only been half listening while I'd been remembering the feel of his hot skin under my fingers.

Noah grinned. "I'm aiming for a full-on *Black Swan* moment. Until then, I'm going to work toward my pilot's license."

"Right," I mumbled, staring into my glass. Why had I asked such an inane question? This was why I was no good at the galas and the dinners that Abi navigated so effortlessly.

"Seriously? You're taking flying lessons?" Rob asked, glancing at Abi.

"Don't look at me as if you need my permission. I'm not your mother." Abi slid onto the bench beside me.

"Got my first one this week. I thought I might as well take advantage of having some free time. I'm going to do a skydiving course as well."

"Sounds like you," Rob said. "Action. Adventure. Is there anything you're afraid of?"

Noah just grinned. If the building was on fire, Noah would be the one organizing the evacuation and guiding everyone to safety. He was always in control, calm and sure of himself.

"Yeah, there's no way I can take flying lessons," Rob muttered. "Five and a half months until everything changes."

"So that's not long until you guys are parents. Are you terrified?" Noah asked.

"No." Rob placed the roast chicken on the table.

"Liar," Abigail replied.

"Okay, mildly terrified," Rob replied. "And of course, it doesn't help that Abigail is insisting she's going back to work the week after she gives birth."

"Six weeks after. And you know the demands of the foundation. I can't just abandon ship—baby or no baby."

Noah glanced at me, and I rolled my eyes as a thousand memories tumbled into my head and made my heart ache. Before he'd left for New York, this had been the pattern. Rob and Abigail would snipe, quarrel, and bicker, and Noah and I would look on amused, while trying to figure out who had won our bet.

How many times would Abigail accuse Rob of being a control freak?

How often would Rob ask for permission to do something that Abigail didn't like and then accuse her of being the control freak in the marriage?

How many bottles of wine would we get through?

Was he remembering all those things too?

"So apart from flying lessons, what's the plan?" Abigail asked.

As she and Noah chatted, Rob filled the table with a collection of different dishes and finally sat down. Then we began to eat, passing plates and sauces, scooping potatoes, and carving chicken.

How could it be this easy to sink back into a routine with this man who'd meant so much to me? It was a relief, but at the same time, so frustrating. If only Noah could have turned into some kind of arsehole, or gotten married. Or at the very least gone bald.

At least the anticipation was over now.

I had to accept that Noah was just the same as he ever was. It was me who needed to change. Me who needed not to fall for him again. He saw me as a friend, and that's the box I was going to keep him in—with the lid on tight.

FOUR

Noah

How long would the pounding in my chest, my burning cheeks, and the way my legs fizzed when I walked last? There was nothing like falling out of an airplane from fifteen thousand feet to throw your body for a loop. I pulled off my helmet, exhaled, then stripped out of my jumpsuit. As I pulled my jeans and t-shirt from the locker, Dave, one of the two instructors who'd jumped with me, entered the changing rooms.

"That was fucking fantastic," I said.

"Nothing like it."

"I enjoyed the tandem jump I did last year but this . . ."

"A much bigger adrenaline rush."

"Right." Did he still feel it? He'd confessed on the plane ride up that he'd jumped over three thousand times. I'd wanted to ask him if he ever got bored. I'd loved it, but surely the rush faded after so many jumps.

"Next week we *start* with a jump before the lesson so long as this weather holds," he said.

"Sounds good." I gave Dave a high five, then raked my fingers through my hair and headed out to the car park.

"Hey," I waved at Rob who was leaning against his car door as he waited for me.

"You're crazy." Rob shook his head as I approached. "I watched you come down. Isn't it easier—even safer—to develop a heroin habit rather than this?"

I chuckled as I slid into the passenger seat. "Nah, this is far more fun." The natural high from skydiving wasn't why I did it. I could see how that might be the driver for some people, but for me it was more that I didn't want to miss out on anything. Unless I didn't *want* to do something, everything was on the table. We were on this planet such a short amount of time—I wanted to fit in everything I could.

"Tell me honestly, did you nearly shit yourself?" Rob started the engine and backed out of the parking space.

"I wasn't scared at all." Before my accident, I would have been terrified, but not anymore. It probably should have been the other way around, but I wanted to make the most of what I had. Experience as many things as possible. "By the end of the summer, I'll come down on my own, without the instructors jumping by my side. Maybe that will be more frightening."

"I thought you were taking flying lessons, not *falling* lessons."

"You're funny," I replied sarcastically. "I'm doing the flying thing as well. The skydiving is less of a commitment. I thought I'd slot it in while I'm not working."

"I was going to ask if you ever just sit on the sofa and eat kettle chips, but I know you've never been a kettle-chips-and-chill kinda guy."

kettle chips had been Truly's thing. How had I forgotten that? I'd forgotten a lot of things about Truly, but that lunch on Sunday had brought it all whooshing back. I'd forgotten how much I liked being around her. How funny she was—sometimes intentionally and sometimes not. How it always felt like I might crush her if I wasn't careful when I wrapped my arms around her. The way she smelled of the coconut shampoo she said she used to tame her frizzy hair. Except, I'd never seen her hair frizzy, even when she'd run out of that shampoo. It was just soft. Wavy. Pretty.

"Thanks for helping me with this stuff. I could have hired someone, but I figured you'd appreciate a beer and a night out even it if did involve moving furniture," I said.

"I'm always up for a boys' night," Rob replied, fiddling with the radio and wincing when Britney Spears came on. "And we have a lot of them in the bank. Four years' worth. Anyway, I want to see your new place. I can't believe you ended up in Marylebone, you lucky fucker."

"Yeah, it's nice and central but has an easy path out of the city when I want to do stuff like this."

"A bachelor pad. Is Barry White playing on a constant loop?"

Married people were always far more interested in my sex life than anyone else. "Barry White? How old are you?"

Rob shut the radio off and shrugged. "Maybe that's what I did wrong when I was dating."

"Hey, you married Abigail. I don't see how that's getting it wrong." They were as close to the perfect couple as it was possible to be. Their bickering added to their charm. I knew Rob secretly enjoyed the attention. Witnessing that their dynamic hadn't changed over the last four years had been comforting.

"Yeah, she's a good girl. Maybe you should get yourself a wife."

I chuckled. "That's not really my thing."

"Are you still on a strict three-month cycle?"

"Fuck you. I don't have a cycle."

"You totally have a cycle. When's the last time you were with a girl for more than three months?"

I knew without having to think about it that there hadn't been anyone. Truly used to give me shit about it. Ironically, my friendship with her was the longest relationship I'd had with a woman, even though it hadn't been sexual. I'd done my best to seduce her the first time we met, and it had been the first time since school that a woman had knocked me back. "It's not like I plan it. It just works out that way."

"You don't think it would be nice to take a breath? Be still with a woman for a minute?"

"There was a time when I didn't think I'd be able to do anything but be still. So now I have a choice, I like to keep moving," I replied. I totally understood that some people, Rob included, would never get why I had the need to keep striving for more—to get faster, stronger, more successful.

"So, did you just finish your cycle or are you in the middle of one?"

"Are we talking about periods or women?" I didn't set a watch to my relationships. And I didn't cheat. I just didn't see myself in a long-term relationship or married, and I gravitated toward partners who were looking for the same. There were too many women that I hadn't met. I liked learning how a new body worked.

"Well if you're having a period, you definitely need to talk about it, but to a qualified medical professional and not me."

I grinned. I'd missed Rob. I'd seen him periodically since I'd moved to New York and kept in touch over email, but it hadn't been the same. Friendships made as teenagers were different from the relationships I'd formed once I'd started work. People I met now seemed to be more about networking than anything else. "No women. No one in particular anyway."

"No one in New York?"

"Turn right here," I said, indicating the turn off the Marylebone Road. I'd forgotten how bad the traffic was in London. "And then it's second on the left." I turned up the air conditioning a notch. "No one special." I'd been there four years and going by Rob's estimates that meant there should have been sixteen women . . . which sounded about right. Although not all of them had lasted three months—some of them I hadn't known for more than a few hours.

"Well, I'm sure you'll find someone soon enough."

"I'm not looking." I had a thousand things to focus on and a long list of things to do. Women weren't a priority. They never were.

"You're never looking but somehow the women always find you."

"Are you peanut butter and jealous?" I said with a grin.

"Have you seen my wife? I'm just saying maybe you should look rather than be found. You might discover someone who'll last longer than three months."

"I'm pretty happy focusing on the stuff that matters to me."

"Your problem is you want breadth not depth when it comes to relationships."

I chuckled. "Really? I don't see that as a problem."

"I'm just saying you don't know how good it can be with someone who knows you better than you know yourself. You never let anyone in long enough."

"Well I'll let you worry about that. And while you

ponder, I'll keep having fun and enjoying a *breadth* of women in London."

The car fell silent as Rob navigated crossing the traffic without running over the tourists who were filing out of Madame Tussauds.

"It was good to see Truly on Sunday," I said, wanting to change the subject from my love life. "She looked well. Happy," I stated, though I really wanted it to be a question.

Was she happy? She'd barely said anything about herself at lunch, and I hadn't wanted to ask in case it was . . . out of line. But she seemed just the same, looked just the same. Still beautiful in the same unassuming way. Still sheltering in the shadow of her older sister, who she'd always seen as more accomplished, more attractive. That was the thing that I liked best and least about Truly—she always underestimated herself.

"I guess," Rob said as he navigated the right turn. "What are all these things you've got planned? Are you going to spend all your time skydiving and taking flying lessons?"

"I've got a few things lined up. Meetings, introductions, that kind of thing. I want the next challenge to be as fulfilling as Concordance Tech was. But different." I pulled out a key fob and pointed it at the door. "The garage is just here on your right."

"Oh, you have parking. Nice." Rob said.

I was grateful he was easily distracted. It was the first time in my life I wasn't completely focused on a goal—learning to walk again, school, university, my business—and it made me uncomfortable. Untethered. So the goal for me was to find a goal, then the rest of life in London would fall into place.

"You don't have to work though, do you?" Rob asked. "You could just roll around in cash for the next decade?"

I pushed open my door. "I guess I don't have to work if I don't want to." The float of Concordance Tech had made me rich, and money brought freedom, but the thought of sitting on a yacht all day filled me with terror. Plus that was the playground of billionaires, not someone with a measly fifteen mil in the bank. It wasn't until I'd made money that I realized how much more everyone else had. "But I want to be constructive. I'm not sure about building another business." I gripped my keys and pressed the fob against the security pad by the door to the lifts. "You know that I don't like to do the same thing twice."

"Maybe a different kind of business?" Rob asked.

"Yeah. Maybe." I wasn't convinced. I had plenty to keep me busy. A list of things to do. But I wanted a purpose. An overarching challenge to consume me like building Concordance Tech had. I'd seen something on social media about an emergency fundraising the hospital that had looked after me after the accident were doing. I'd donated, but it didn't feel like enough. Maybe I could do something more. "I might do something entirely different. I'm not Bill Gates, but there are plenty of issues in the world that need time and attention."

"Don't joke about shit like that around Abi. She'll have you doing extreme sports to raise money for charity before you finish your sentence."

I paused before pressing my thumbprint into the ID panel in the lift and hitting P. "I might not mind that. What kind of extreme sports? I mean, I get that you might not want to learn to fly, but what about abseiling down one of London's iconic buildings—Tower Bridge, the Shard, or the

Gherkin, or somewhere? Wouldn't require much training, and it's for charity, no less. Why don't we both do it?"

Rob groaned. "I wish I'd never mentioned it. I can't wait for you to get a job so you'll stop this extreme-sport shit."

"It's not about the sport or having too much time on my hands. I just want to make sure I'm living life—squeezing out every last drop."

"I'm happy living my life on the ground."

"Yeah. I prefer the penthouse," I said, grinning as the lift doors slid open directly into my brand-new home. But in that way, I envied Rob. He was content with what he had. He wasn't always grasping for more, better, different.

I was used to having a thousand goals and going at them full throttle before moving on to the next one. It didn't matter if it was walking, exams, floating a business on the stock market—what drove me was a clear vision of what I wanted and a determination to succeed. But I was out of big ideas. I'd achieved the career goals I'd set for myself. Done everything I'd set out to do. But I wasn't content to sit back and enjoy the fruits of my labor. The view from the penthouse was nice, but it wasn't enough. I just wasn't sure what was next.

FIVE

Noah

I couldn't believe I was back here. If I'd known Abigail wanted to meet at the hospital where I'd formed so many unhappy memories, I wouldn't have come. I'd not been back since the day I was discharged. By then I'd been an outpatient for months, but it still dominated my life. I'd been so relieved when I'd left for the very last time.

I took a deep breath and opened the car door.

"I'm only going to say it once," Abigail said as she leaned against her car parked next to mine. "So this is your only chance to back out—just because we're friends, you shouldn't feel obligated to do this." Her hands on her hips, Abigail pinned me with her icy stare.

"I know. I don't feel obligated. I want to do the abseil."

When I'd called Abigail about doing an abseil— rappelling down a building—to help raise funds, she'd suggested I meet her at one of the causes they were supporting this year. She'd said she'd text me the details, which she'd only done last minute, giving me no chance to back out. What were the odds of her bringing me face-to-face with my past?

"I'm not trying to pressure you by bringing you to the hospital."

"I offered, Abi. Now are we going in or what?" It wasn't pressure I felt. It was dread. But I wasn't about to run and hide from anything. It wasn't who I was.

The automatic doors slid open and Truly walked out. Oblivious to everything around her, she had her head down and plowed straight into Abi and me.

"Shit," Truly said as she stepped back, swaying on her nonexistent heels, her amber eyes widening as she took us both in.

"How are you not dead?" Abigail asked. "What if you had walked into oncoming traffic?"

"How? There's no road here," Truly replied, pushing the sleeves of her oversized navy jumper back so they weren't hanging over the ends of her fingers.

Truly wasn't irrationally oblivious. She just blocked out stuff that didn't matter and was single-minded about things that did.

"What are you doing here, anyway?" Abigail asked.

"Just looking over their fundraising plan." She shook her head. "It's daunting. And heartbreaking. Why? What are you doing here?" Truly glanced between me and her sister.

"You better not have committed any solid figures," Abigail said.

"How could you suggest that?" Truly tilted her head as if genuinely hurt at the suggestion. "I'd never want to get these guys' hopes up. They have such a huge mountain to climb."

"I just don't want to let them down," Abi said, her tone flattening.

"Neither do I. But, honestly, I didn't even see Betty. I got some figures from Alistair and poked my head into the activity room. That's it."

"Sorry. I'm just on edge. Hormones, I guess." Abigail patted Truly's arm in apology. "You know you have a pencil holding your hair up, right?"

Truly glanced at me, then shrugged. "It's useful. Anyway, I need to get back to the office." She pulled out a huge set of keys from her pocket and moved past us toward the car park.

Abi and I stepped through the sliding doors and the familiar smell of the rehab room hit me as if I'd last been down this corridor last week, not nearly fourteen years ago. Nausea churned in my stomach. I turned right, following Abigail but knowing the way as we walked beneath a sign for the Children's Spinal Injuries Unit. I'd vowed never to come back. And I wasn't prepared now. I'd worked hard while I was here to walk again and even harder when I'd left to forget this place. The memories I made here I didn't want to relive.

"We won't go into the ward, but the activity room is what I want to show you anyway. You immediately see where the need is." Abigail led the way through two sets of double doors.

As we walked into the cavernous room, I glanced up to see the ceiling stained with chunks of plaster missing. "Wow." A thousand memories hit me like a sucker punch, and I found myself unable to speak. A dull ache coursed through my body like a scar deep within me was reminding me the pain was still there.

"I know. The place is a mess," Abi said from beside me. "The roof needs replacing—who am I kidding, the entire place needs replacing. They have a target of twenty-five million."

"They're trying to raise twenty-five-million pounds?" I asked, not sure if I'd heard her right. I knew they were trying to raise money but that was a tremendous amount.

"Yep. We're doing what we can but . . ." Abi shook her head. "It's a lot. And I know the building's a mess, but that's only the start of it."

I might have money but that was more than I was worth. I was a dick for thinking my check of five thousand would make a difference.

"The equipment is broken and there's just not enough of it to cope with the number of patients," Abi continued as we made our way further into the activity room, and as if to prove her point, we passed a broken set of parallel bars that looked like they'd not been replaced since *I* was using them.

The floor was divided into distinct areas centered around pieces of equipment, just like it had been when I'd been there. Physiotherapists, doctors, and other adults were interspersed between the children, some working with kids one on one and others in groups. It even looked like some kind of martial arts class was being taught at the far end of the room.

The place was noisy, which was how I remembered it, but it was gloomy and dull and lacked the energy and laughter I'd enjoyed while I was here. It hadn't all been pain and suffering during my stay. Underneath there'd been hope, an undercurrent of determination, and finally success.

To our left was a boy of about fifteen walking tentatively on a treadmill that was on the lowest speed. He could have been me—lanky and stumbling but with the tightness of his jaw suggesting a steel that I recognized.

"That's the only treadmill they have now. These two

are broken," Abi said as she caught me watching the boy gain confidence with the aid of the physio who was helping him.

"They struggle to recruit physios because the pay is so low. The ones who are here haven't had a raise in seven years."

"So what happened?" I asked. "It didn't used to be like this."

Abi shot me a confused look, and I realized I'd given too much away. I didn't want to answer any questions or become the focus of our visit.

"I mean, you can tell that at some point they had more resources." Most of the equipment had been new when I'd been here. And by the looks of it they'd had nothing since. How on earth did they manage?

"It's a combination of government cuts and some of the charities funding them moving their support to other, more-fashionable causes."

While I was here, I never thought about where the money was coming from to fund this place. I'd never felt lucky to be in the situation I was. But compared to what these kids had to work with, I'd been more than lucky.

"And then there's all this new stuff that the medical director wants to do but just can't. There's this thing called a spinal stimulation . . . something that they use in America and would make a big difference apparently."

I was pretty sure she meant epidural stimulation. I wasn't sure what made me keep up with developments in the area, but I did. I even had some shares in the company that had developed the epidural stimulation treatments. And given the success they'd had in other countries, there was no doubt they'd make a difference here.

"Let me show you over here," Abi said, guiding us past

the free weights that were set up in the left-hand corner, just like they had been while I was here, except the mats they sat on were badly frayed.

I followed, still a little dazed by the activity in front of me and how eerily familiar it all was.

"Rob mentioned that you had some kind of issue when you were young. Did you have to have rehab like this?"

I scraped my hand through my hair. "Yeah." I didn't mention the months of just lying in bed, staring at the ceiling, trying to block out the doctors who'd told me I'd never walk again. I didn't mention the hours and hours I'd spent in this very room.

"I wanted to show you what Emily's doing." Abi led the way over to the nearest set of parallel bars.

A woman in a track suit hovered in front of a young, blonde girl of about twelve who was taking slow but steady steps, her hands gripping the parallel bars.

"Girl, I can see that work you've done on your quads. It's really paying off," the physio said.

The blonde grinned through her grimace. "I wish it felt like it."

I understood. It was difficult to see incremental progress when you were constantly pushing yourself. But every now and then you'd hit a milestone where you'd know you were moving forward—the first time you stood, even if your legs weren't taking all the weight, the first step. I shook my head. Fuck, I'd forgotten this stuff. Deliberately. The struggle had been so difficult, had required everything I had. I didn't like to remember it. I preferred to concentrate on my future.

"Great job, Bethany," Abi said. "I can tell the difference from last time."

"You can?" Bethany asked.

"Totally. You look stronger. More confident."

Bethany beamed, and Abi pulled at my arm, leading me further into the room.

It hadn't just been my physical body that had been put back together here. My entire character had been formed in this place. I'd learnt what I was capable of. I'd developed my determination. My desire to succeed. It had made me the man I'd become.

"Let's go and check out the kung fu. It's my favorite at the moment. The *shifu*—the teacher—is the best. Like powerful or something. Inside." She pointed her fingers toward her solar plexus. "You know?"

I'd never done kung fu while I was here. The only experiences I'd had involved Bruce Lee. As we moved forward, I watched five children of differing ages moving gracefully, almost slow dancing, as they mirrored their teacher's movements. It was kinda mesmerizing. Concentration bore into the kids' expressions, more prominent on some than others as they went through the routine.

Abi leaned into me. "It teaches them strength. And balance. To manage pain—to understand it and harness it. It also shows them the path to acceptance."

"Acceptance?"

"Yeah. Some of them will never play the sports they did before or have the same movement. And even if they do, life will never go back to normal for these kids. What's happened to them changes them."

My throat constricted and I swallowed, trying to push down the squeezing sensation of memories threatening to burst from me.

"Truly really gets it; I just know it works. The kids love it but the shifu does it as a volunteer. They only have one class every two weeks."

It was as if this corner of the room was completely oblivious to anything else around it. As if hope existed here when it didn't elsewhere in the room. Perhaps I could pay the shifu to come in more regularly?

Taking a steadying breath, I slowly turned around, taking in the drab room filled with so many uncertain futures.

Kung fu wasn't going to cut it. My checkbook just wasn't big enough. And an abseil wasn't either.

Something more needed to be done.

SIX

Truly

"You must really love him," I said to Abigail as I glanced at the man fiddling with a microphone. The pub wasn't dingy —the walls were a fresh, pale gray, the chairs and stools were covered in brown leather, and the floor was a polished checkerboard. The place looked more like a hotel lobby than a traditional English pub. But my sister was more oysters and champagne than chips and a Coke. She wasn't a pub quiz kind of girl.

"Well, I see it as a way of building up credit. I go to this, which he loves, and he cooks, which I love because it means I don't have to." We found an empty table by the window and took a seat. "And actually, it's not bad. They carry Cloudy Bay and have table service."

I chuckled. "A Hampstead-style pub quiz then."

"Exactly. Anyway, I dragged you along because you like trivia—and because you're the cleverest person I know."

Abigail beckoned over one of the waiters, ordering a bottle of pinot noir and a virgin mojito.

"I hope Rob will drink most of that bottle, because it'll be a lot too much for me," I said.

"Yeah. And Noah probably will too."

My heart sank. "Noah?"

"I told you he was coming, didn't I?"

She'd barreled into my office at six, insisted I take the evening off, then practically pulled me by the hair out to the car. She'd not even told me where we were going until my seatbelt was on and she'd turned onto the main road.

"It's not a problem, is it?"

"No. Why would it be?" I'd coped on Sunday. Even seeing him earlier in the week when I'd run into him outside the hospital had been okay. It had been fleeting, and I'd found that thoughts of him had faded faster than they had after lunch. But that was enough. I didn't want to keep running into him. I knew how vulnerable I was around him, and I didn't want to wade into the feelings I'd once had for him again. I just wanted Noah to disappear back to New York where all this stuff was three thousand miles away, instead of constantly bobbing to the surface of my brain.

"If I didn't think Rob would completely lose it, I'd have half a glass of wine myself—they say it's completely safe, and I could use it. I went over my calendar with Lisa today and the things I have to do before going on maternity leave are really starting to stack up. Just looking at it freaked me out a little."

It wasn't like Abigail to get overwhelmed. We both tended to overpromise, but this time Abigail was working with a timetable that had a fixed end date and zero flexibility—the baby couldn't be rescheduled.

"You okay?" I'd offer to help, but there was nothing I could do and we both knew it. There was no overlap in our jobs. Abigail was the face of the foundation, and I needed her. "I get it, there's still loads to do. But the main thing is to pace yourself. You have five months before this baby comes." I hadn't noticed before, but dark half circles sat below her eyes and tension ghosted across her face. She didn't normally wear her stress so obviously.

"God, now that I'm about to be a mother, I wonder how Mum did it."

"Have you seen her?" I asked.

"Yeah. Rob and I went on Monday for an hour—she had no clue who I was."

My stomach churned. Our mother might be still alive but the vibrant, determined woman who'd started and run the Harbury Foundation had been lost to dementia a long time ago.

"Last time I was there, I gave her an update on some of the fundraising figures. You know how much she liked the detail. I thought it might reach her in some way."

"Anything?" Abigail asked.

I couldn't answer. I just shook my head.

"She'd love what we were doing for the rehab center this year."

"Hey, girls," Rob called, stopping the conversation from getting any sadder. "You got good seats, well done. With you two on the team, we're bound to win this week."

I couldn't help but smile. Rob was delightfully upbeat ninety-nine percent of the time. I blew out a breath, and avoided glancing at Noah, whose heat radiated from him, while Abigail wiped her eyes.

Rob frowned. "You two okay? Did I say something?"

I patted one of the two empty chairs between me and Abigail. "No, sit down. We've ordered some wine."

Noah kissed Abigail on the cheek and slid onto the chair next to me, then leaned over to kiss me, too. It was almost too much. He was too close. His scent, his warmth, his hard body was almost overwhelming. This was precisely why I needed to avoid him wherever possible.

"Hey," he said. "I didn't know you were going to be here."

"Me neither. I mean, I hadn't planned to come, and I didn't realize you would be here." Jesus, I should just write it all down for him, just to be clear. How did he have me so nervous? "Abigail dragged me by the hair. Sometimes it's easier not to argue."

Noah chuckled. "As Rob likes to remind me, I'm unemployed so I have no good excuse to say no."

The waiter arrived, and Abigail didn't even let her mojito touch the table before she'd ordered another.

"It's true," Rob said, pouring the wine between the three glasses. "Jobless. Unemployed. A statistic." Rob shook his head as if disappointed. "I hope you're not claiming benefits. I don't want my taxes going toward—"

"I'm staying plenty busy," Noah said, shutting Rob down.

"Anything exciting on the horizon?" I asked, watching as he turned a coaster over in his hand. There was always more going on below the surface with Noah, which you had to dig to discover. It was one of the things I liked about him best.

"I'm going to invest in startups—I'd like to give businesses I believe in a chance like the one someone gave me and Concordance Tech. And I'm looking into a few other things as well—I just need to figure out—"

"Don't think you're getting out of that abseil," Abigail said. "I've already set up your fundraising page."

"I'm looking forward to it," he replied.

Noah wasn't the type to go back on his word. I wouldn't

have developed a crush on any man that did. And he'd always loved to push himself in everything. It wasn't just extreme sports, either. It was as if every part of him dared me to fall for him.

A tap of the microphone brought our attention to the front as one of the barmen distributed blank answer sheets.

"We need to think of a name," Rob said, pointing his pencil at the blank space at the top of the sheet. "Last time we were the Bulls."

"That's a terrible name," Noah said.

"It's because—"

"I don't care about the reason," he replied. "It's a shit name. What about Quizteama Aguilera?"

I giggled. "Or the Quizzard of Oz," I suggested.

Noah grinned, and I tried not to enjoy the fact that I'd amused him.

"Or Les Quizerables," Noah countered. "Or Trivia Newton-John?"

I laughed out loud. "Let's get Quizzical." I expected Abigail to laugh, but when I glanced over, her gaze was fixed on the bar.

Rob looked irritated but scribbled down Les Quizerables at the top of the sheet. "Come on, guys. We have to take this seriously." He nodded at Noah and me. "With you two brainiacs we could win this week."

"Oh, we'll win," Noah said with such authority that he left no room for doubt. "But it doesn't mean we can't have fun."

"Round one," the man at the front with the microphone announced. "General knowledge. Granadilla is another name for which fruit?"

Noah and I answered at the same time, "Passionfruit."

I glanced at Noah, who grinned right at me.

Rob narrowed his eyes in suspicion, but he knew better than to question what we were saying and he wrote down the answer.

I tentatively looked over at Abigail but she had her eyes shut. When she grimaced, I reached over and patted her hand. "Hey, are you okay?" I asked.

She plastered on a smile. "Of course. I think maybe I need to eat something. I'll go and order some snacks."

"Pudong, meaning 'east bank', is the financial district of which city?"

"Easy," Noah said, lifting his chin in a challenge he aimed at me.

"Shanghai," I replied with a little shake of my head.

He rolled his eyes—he knew I was right. God, I'd missed how good Noah always made me feel—like being the clever sister was okay. He didn't seem to look at me as some brainiac but as an equal.

I glanced over at Abigail, who was chatting to the barman about the menu.

"Name the fictional Welsh fishing village that features in the play *Under Milk Wood*?"

I rolled my eyes. Everyone knew this.

"I've read it but never heard it, so best I can do is spell it," Noah said. "L-l-a-r-e-g-g-u-b."

"How the fuck do you remember how to spell that?" Rob asked.

"It's bugger all, backward," I explained.

Rob underlined that answer as if we got extra points for that question or something. "Shit, we're definitely going to win tonight."

"No doubt," Noah said, holding my gaze and grinning in that way he had that made me feel that I was the only woman in his world.

Noah was affable and charming, made everyone feel like he was their friend, but underneath it all was a determination, a steel that I imagined could make him ruthless when he wanted to be, a tough negotiator, a hard decision maker. The combination had made him successful, allowed him to sleep with women and walk away without a second thought, and made him my personal kryptonite.

Abigail looked a little pale as she made her way back from the bar. "Do you need some fresh air?" I asked.

She stopped and blinked at me several times in quick succession. My heart began to pound. Something was wrong. I reached for her just as she collapsed.

"Rob!" I screamed as I gripped her arm. She was conscious, but it was as if her legs weren't working. I crouched down. "It's okay. Just sit. Don't try to get up." I glanced up when Rob appeared on her other side.

"Ambulance," Noah said into his phone. "She's pregnant and has collapsed. At the Crown and Horses on Haverstock Hill. Hurry!"

SEVEN

Truly

Rob emerged through the double doors and into the waiting area, his eyes downcast and his pallor as gray as the linoleum floors.

I jerked out of my seat. "What? What did they say?"

He shook his head. "They're still running tests. Her blood pressure is insanely high. They've got her lying in some weird position to take the pressure off the baby, which I don't really understand. They think it's pre-eclampsia."

"But she's going to be okay?" I needed certainty. Facts. What tests? What the fuck was pre-eclampsia?

"She's conscious and has a little more color back. They've given her a sedative and she's on a drip."

"I knew she was doing too much, putting too much pressure on herself." My nails bit into my palms as I fisted my hands.

"You know that's her nature. I'd told her a thousand times to slow down, but she seemed to be doing more rather than less." Rob pressed his fingers into his temples as if he needed to find a solution. "She doesn't listen to me. She wanted things in place for when the baby was born. She's been worried about the foundation and the rehab center— she takes too much on." He scrubbed his hands over his face.

This was my fault. If I'd been able to ease her burden, if the fundraising didn't all fall on her, she wouldn't be in this position. "She knows donations will grind to a halt when she leaves," I said, mumbling. "I'm completely incompetent at her job."

"You're hardly incompetent," Noah said from beside me.

"I am. All I can do is the numbers. Abi is the heart of the foundation."

"Well, after this, I'm prying the baton out of her hands and handing it to you." Rob paused, fixed his lips in a thin, straight line, and glanced at the floor as if he were stopping himself from saying more.

I swallowed.

"If, God willing, she and the baby are okay, things have got to change. She has to do less." He sounded almost angry with me, but I understood. I hadn't done enough to ensure Abigail was taking it easy. I should have insisted she cut back her hours, but then what? Who would do the stuff she was so good at? Especially running into the prime season for fundraising.

"Let's just focus on Abigail right now," Noah said. "It's good that she's conscious and she's in the best place to help her. All we can do is stay calm and wait."

"Can I see her?" I asked.

Rob shoved his hands in his pockets. "The doctors said no. Just me. They're trying to keep her stable."

I wanted to look at my beautiful twin sister, have her tell

me she was fine and it was all a big overreaction. I needed things to go back to the way they were. Her telling me she was older and knew better. And it might only be by six and a half minutes but somehow, over the years, those extra seconds counted for a lot. She was the one who plowed the path in front of us while I followed. I couldn't survive without her. I'd wither and die without her constant sunshine and smiles.

"I'm going back in there," Rob said. "You might as well go home. I'll call with any news."

I collapsed back into my chair. "I'm not going anywhere. Let me know as soon as you hear anything."

Rob and Noah exchanged a few words, none of which I could hear from where I was, then Rob headed back to Abigail, and Noah slid into the chair next to mine, his arm snaking around my back and pulling me into him.

"He blames me," I said. "I know I should have done more."

"He doesn't blame you. He's just worried. You both are. Let's just see how the tests work out."

"Do you think she's going to be okay?" I asked, glancing up at him.

"I think the doctors deal with stressed, pregnant women all the time. You'll know more soon."

It was an honest answer even if it wasn't particularly reassuring, but Noah knew that's what I needed—facts. Honesty.

"I'm going to grab some coffee. Do you want to come with me?" he asked.

I shook my head and pushed away from his chest. I couldn't leave. Abigail and I never left each other. We'd been together since conception. I wasn't about to leave her now when she needed me most. What if something happened? "No thanks."

"Nothing bad is going to happen, Truly. I wouldn't leave you if I thought it was going to, you hear me?" It was as if the man could read my every thought.

I nodded and though his words were comforting and I almost believed him, I still wasn't moving. I just couldn't risk it.

"I'll bring you one back. You want something to eat?"

I couldn't think of anyone I'd ever known who I'd want by my side more than Noah. He was calm, thoughtful, and focused, and it was almost as if just being near him made me a bit more of all those things.

But as much as his presence was soothing, I should have told him to leave and go home. Shouldn't have been comforted or pleased he was with me. Because he wasn't with me. And he never would be. I had no one in my life but my sister.

THREE DAYS PASSED in a blur of worry and anxiety. I'd spent most of that time at the hospital, going home just to shower and collect things for Rob and Abigail. Noah had left early on Friday, and I hated that I hadn't wanted him to go. I didn't like the fact that his proximity brought me so much comfort. I'd hoped that by now Abigail would have been given the all clear and things would be back to normal. But it was Sunday night and instead of ribbing Rob about his culinary skills, we were listening to my sister's prognosis.

"Bed rest? Don't be ridiculous. We're not in the sixteenth century; I'm not going into confinement," my sister snapped at the doctor. Her sedative had clearly worn off, and Rob thrust his hands through his hair in exasperation. If she wasn't listening to the doctor, Rob had no chance.

Abigail seemed to be back to normal the next morning and since then had been irritable about having to stay in the hospital while they waited for test results and monitored her.

"Will you just listen to the doctor? You need to take this seriously, Abi," I snapped back. I wasn't sure if she was scared or frustrated, but either way, she needed to hear what was being said.

The doctor cleared his throat. "It's not confinement. I'm not worried about you coming into contact with other people. It's about controlling your blood pressure—"

"And your temper," I added.

"And you need to be on your left side to ensure the baby isn't—" The doctor tried to continue.

"For twenty weeks? You can't be serious."

"Abigail." Rob sighed. "Please let the man finish."

"I'm afraid I'm very serious. You can ignore what I say, but if you do, I'll be seeing you back in this ward very shortly and the outcome next time might be very different. We've caught this early, but we can't be complacent."

"But I'll go crazy! Twenty weeks of being in bed? What if I stayed off my feet most of the day? Surely I could go out to dinner or pop out at lunch to give a presentation or a speech or something?"

"Abi, the foundation will be fine," I said, lying through my teeth. "No speeches or presentations for you."

"In my *medical* opinion, you can go to the bathroom, have a shower—even take a walk around the garden a couple of times a day as long as you're feeling up to it. But that's it."

My sister's eyes filled with tears. "But what about the spinal center—"

Rob turned to Abigail. "You need to listen to him. This is serious stuff. You can't be risking your life and the life of our child because you want to go to some fucking awards dinner."

The doctor raised his eyebrows, and I patted Rob on the arm, trying to calm him. "It's okay," I said. "Abigail is going to do exactly what the doctor said, aren't you?" I grabbed my sister's hand. "I'll handle the foundation."

I didn't know what I was going to do or how I was going to do it, but I knew Abigail wasn't part of the solution. "And anyway, you've been telling me I need to broaden my horizons—this will be the perfect opportunity. If I didn't know better, I'd say you planned this." I squeezed her hand.

"Are you sure?" she asked, her voice wobbling—vulnerability breaking through her tough exterior.

My stomach flipped as I realized she'd been waiting for someone else to be stronger, for me to step in, take the burden from her, be the older twin. "I'm surer than sure." I wasn't certain about anything other than I wanted my sister and her baby to be better. But for the first time in my life, I had to be the one who led the way for Abigail and me. I had to show her there was nothing to be worried about.

"Thanks, Truly," Rob said, shooting me a relieved smile. We were all on the same side. All wanted the same outcome. We just needed to remember it. And I needed to push down the rising panic at the thought of having to handle donors, presentations, lunches and dinners. What choice did I have? People were counting on me. As I thought about the task in front of me, it was as if an anvil was weighing down on my chest and every time I breathed it got a little heavier. I pressed the heel of my hand against my breast bone, trying to relieve the weight.

"The nurse will take you through your medication schedule and you can leave as soon as they've discharged you, but any change in blood pressure, dizziness, sudden bloating, or pain, I want you to come straight back."

"My own bed," Abigail said. "Thank heaven for small mercies." She looked up at me, worry darting across her face.

"Everything's going to be just fine," I said, assuring both of us. Because I might be about to have a panic attack, but as long as Abigail was okay then nothing else mattered.

EIGHT

Noah

"Thanks for the other night. Calling the ambulance, coming to the hospital. Means a lot," Rob said, handing me a beer from the fridge. I'd dropped around after my meetings had finished for the day to check on Abigail. Three days out of hospital and she was still in bed, adjusting to her new normal.

"I didn't do anything."

"I think you kept us all calm." He blew out a breath and slumped on the sofa at the far end of the kitchen.

"How is she?" I asked before tipping back my beer.

"She tells me fine, but I never really know. I think she got a scare and she's behaving herself at the moment. But I don't want to get my hopes up that she's going to stay in bed for five months."

"She'll do what's best for the baby, I'm sure."

A bang at the bottom of the stairs caught our attention, and we both snapped our heads around.

"Are you okay?" Rob called out.

"Yeah, I just tripped," Truly said as she came through the door, her hair wet. She was carrying a pair of scissors and a comb. I hadn't realized she was here, and maybe I was imagining it, but it seemed as though she was avoiding meeting my eyes.

When I'd returned from the US, I hadn't imagined her as part of the picture back in London as I had Rob and Abigail. It was as if she disappeared from the world, from my brain, while I'd been in New York, but now she was back and I remembered all the time we'd spent together since the wedding and before I'd gone to New York. I should have made more of an effort to keep in touch. I liked her. She was clever and funny and passionate about things she believed in. As well as being warm and thoughtful— someone I enjoyed listening to and sharing my deepest thoughts with.

How could I have forgotten all of that? And why hadn't I tried harder to keep our connection?

"Oh, hi," she said.

I smiled and tipped my beer at her. She pulled back her hair, which showed off her almond-shaped eyes and perfect, full mouth. A memory flashed into my head of her laughing on her sofa as we both ate Chinese takeaway. She'd been my first and only woman friend. She always captured my interest in a way I never quite understood.

"Why is your hair wet?" Rob asked.

"I have to cut it—it's easier this way."

"You're going to cut your own hair?" I asked. Truly had never taken much notice of how she looked. I appreciated that she preferred not to wear makeup. It was one of her many quirks that drew me to her.

"I have a donor lunch tomorrow and my hair is just . . .

Rob, will you do it? Just straight along the bottom. My hands are shaking and I have to go through these." She pulled a bunch of index cards from her back pocket.

"No fucking way," Rob replied. "Why don't you go to a hairdresser?"

"I have no time, and anyway, I always cut my own hair." She grabbed an oak stool from the breakfast bar and placed it in front of us. "Please. It's just a straight line."

Rob rolled his eyes. "I'm three beers in. You'll end up with a scalping. Noah will do it. He just arrived."

"Fine," she said, dumping the scissors and comb next to me on the sofa and hopping onto the stool.

I slid my beer onto the coffee table and grabbed the comb and scissors. I was no hairdresser, but at least I hadn't finished my first beer.

As I moved closer, she kept her eyes studiously fixed on the cards in front of her. "Ian Chance. CEO of Langham Foods. Total donation of thirty thousand pounds, and last year they had a charity bake off to raise money." She held up the card to show Rob as if he were going to call her out if she was wrong. "Three daughters, Chelsea, Marian, and Elizabeth—"

"This is one of the people at lunch tomorrow?" I asked as I hovered behind her. Her hair was almost down to her waist, ebony black and silky smooth despite the curls beginning to reform and reshape. I paused. Somehow it felt odd to be this close. Inappropriate. Intimate.

"Yeah. Abi has all their details on index cards, and I need to memorize them. I've done four. I have another six to do." She shuffled on her stool.

"Have you met this guy?" I asked, pulling the comb through her hair, the scent of coconut wrapping around me.

"No, I rarely meet donors. That's all Abigail."

"Then why would Ian expect you to know personal details like his daughters' names? You're not going to pretend to be Abigail. Dress up like her. You just need to do her job."

She turned on her stool to face me, a grin spreading over her face. "Good point. I need to know the professional stuff, but not things only Abi would know." The huge, warm grin on her face created a mixture of pride and fear in my gut. But fear of what? I wasn't afraid of anything. Not anymore. Not since the accident.

I stepped back. I really shouldn't be cutting her hair. I was going to end up fucking it up or something.

I pulled my phone from my pocket.

"Hey," she said, nodding at the comb in my free hand.

"Just a second. I have a solution." I pulled up the number of the woman I used in New York to sort out my wardrobe. I hated shopping, and Veronica ensured I never had to do it. "Veronica, it's Noah. I need a hairdresser." I told her it was for a woman, gave her Rob and Abi's address, and she assured me she'd have someone around within the hour.

I hung up and headed back to the sofa, scooping up my beer on the way.

"What just happened?" Truly asked.

"Oh, I've arranged a hairdresser. I think it's better for you to have a professional cut your hair."

She smoothed her hand over her head. "And what? You just ordered a hairdresser at eight at night? Just like that?"

"He's rich now," Rob said. "That's what happens. Everyone is at his beck and call."

"It's not like that," I said, though I supposed it was a little like that. "I just made a call. It's no big deal." Money made a lot of things about being in London different this time—where I lived, what I wore, the fact I could get a hairdresser at eight at night. But not who I was.

"Is this an ex-girlfriend of yours who's going to show up brandishing sharp objects?" Truly asked, her face entirely serious.

I grinned. "No. I called someone in New York. She has contacts." There was no way I was going to admit I had a stylist—Rob wouldn't let me hear the end of it. The fact was, I'd gotten pretty comfortable with my money, but I wasn't sure how comfortable those who knew me before my success would be with it. So, I hadn't employed a driver and I'd *just* taken on a personal assistant. And although my flat was a penthouse in one of the best parts of London, I'd been careful not to buy anything too big or extravagant.

"Right," Truly said, turning away from me. "Someone in New York. At least my hair will look okay. I still don't have anything to wear. I presume not a jumper, right?"

Jesus, she was out of her depth. "Definitely not a jumper. Do you have a dress and jacket?"

She looked at me as if I'd just asked her to down a pint of camel's blood. "You think I need a dress and jacket?" She slipped off the stool and began to pace in front of us. "I have black trousers. And I thought I'd wear them with a shirt. I have a white one that's fairly new." She grimaced. "Although that one might have a curry stain on it. *Shit*. I don't think I can do this." She balled her hands into fists. "I'm just not prepared. I'm going to have to cancel or call in sick or something—"

"Do you have a jacket?" I asked. "That would go with the trousers."

She grimaced. "Rob, Abigail will have stuff in her

wardrobe. I'm going to have to raid it. And perhaps she can help me shop for some stuff online."

"No!" Rob slammed his beer bottle on the coffee table in front of him. "There's no way that's going to happen. I don't want her thinking about work or worrying that you're not going to cope. You're just going to have to handle it."

Truly stopped pacing and rubbed her hands over her face. "Mason and Kelly will have to take over. Tomorrow they'll have to pick up as many of Abi's engagements as possible but—"

"Wait, what?" I asked before I could think about what I was saying. This was none of my business, but those kids at the rehab center deserved the chance I'd gotten, and getting others to fill in was not the way to raise twenty-five-million pounds.

"Mason and Kelly. You don't know them, but they're outgoing and upbeat and they can handle most of this social stuff."

"But this isn't social stuff." I shuffled forward in my seat. "It's business. Big donors, big supporters of the foundation are going to want to see someone at the top. Someone with the Harbury name."

"But I just have too much to do, and I'm not good at this stuff. I don't even have a smart outfit for tomorrow—"

"There's no point in having a fantastic back office if you have no money to count or spend."

She perched on her stool and then stood up again. "You think donors won't write checks if I'm not at the lunch or dinner or whatever?"

"I'm saying you won't even get them in the door—they'll cancel."

"I hate to say it but I think he has a point," Rob replied, taking another swig of beer. "I think Abigail would prefer you to be at these things rather than . . . whoever you said. But you can't ask—she's off limits. All she needs to know is that everything's fine and it's all being handled."

"But it's still the same foundation, the same good causes. Who could argue with the rehab center? You've both been there, right? They're desperate."

Truly was the cleverest woman I'd ever met, but she was also one of the most naïve. It was times like this that I thought maybe it was deliberate. She shut herself away so she didn't have to face stuff. "This isn't about good causes. Tell me why you don't go to work in yoga pants and a Star Wars t-shirt?"

She blushed. "Well, I want to appear professional. I mean, a little more than having Yoda on my chest. I know I don't dress like Abigail in the office—"

"But it shouldn't matter what you wear, should it? I mean, you're still Truly—whip smart and a tough negotiator, at least when dealing with your sister."

"So, you're saying it's about appearances?"

"You know that people don't make decisions based on logic and reason. People give money to charity to make themselves feel good. They want to feel special and appreciated—like they matter. If you fob them off on some junior member of the team, they'll just move on to the next charity who'll treat them like they just cured cancer."

Her shoulders slumped as she assimilated what I was saying. "I can't do two jobs. It's just impossible. And Mason and—"

"Forget about Mason and whoever the fuck else you've lined up." My beer landed on the table with a slam I hadn't intended. Truly jumped, but I wasn't backing off until I'd said what I felt. I knew how important the foundation was to her and Abi, and I didn't want her making a gigantic mistake that would jeopardize it. "You're going to have to do every meeting, presentation, or dinner that Abi had lined up. Delegate the financial stuff—recruit someone."

"But no one knows those systems and—"

"No one's going to run that department like you would. You have to accept that."

"Yes, but if I delegate the fundraising piece to people who would be better at it, the whole thing won't collapse in five months just because Mason and—"

"Are you prepared to take that risk? Put everything you, Abi, and your mother worked for on the line because you would prefer to hide behind your computer or be at home with a book? Make those kids at the rehab center suffer because you can't be bothered to go and buy some new clothes?"

She stared at her toes, finally out of excuses. I'd gone too far and I knew it. This wasn't my business. I had no stake in the Harbury Foundation. I should have left it, but I knew what those kids were going through. I knew how easy it would be for them to give up.

I could almost hear her heartbeat racing as her anxiety built.

"You know the perfect solution is staring you both in the face," Rob said. "Noah, you should help her."

"What?" Truly and I said in unison.

"It's perfect. You don't have anything to do at the moment." He raised his palm when I began to refute his statement. "I mean, it's not like you're running a business or trying to make something work. You have more free time than usual."

I couldn't argue with that, but it was hardly like I spent my days in bed watching soaps. I had a series of flying lessons planned, skydiving, and now that I'd recruited an assistant, I was going to start looking for office space.

"You've earned all this money. This would be a way of you giving back. Instead of writing a big check, you could actually do something. Be her consultant. You've done the schmoozing thing. You know how big business works—you know what the donors will be thinking and what will make them donate. Coach her a little."

"Truly can cope on her own; she just doesn't want to." Why was I giving her such a hard time about this? I should just relax, enjoy my beer, and leave her to get it together. Or not. "She doesn't need me." I glanced over at Truly to take in her reaction.

"You're right. I can cope," she said, but the worry skating across her eyes said differently. "Thank you for the business advice. I appreciate it." Her words wobbled as she finished her sentence.

"You're going to be fine," I assured her. "You've just had a lot to think about. I'm sorry to lay into you like that. I was being a twat. And so was Rob."

"Don't be sorry," she said, breaking our gaze and glancing over at voices coming from the hallway.

I got to my feet and realized Rob was with someone. Shit, the hairdresser. "Are you ready?" I asked Truly.

"Yes, it's good. I need a haircut. And a personality transplant. So, if you could just dial up one of your New York contacts and arrange that, I'd be very grateful." She gave me a small smile and I chuckled.

I wished I could help her. The foundation's plan for the rehab center was admirable and those kids needed the help, and I didn't like seeing Truly so out of her depth. It wasn't who she was. Shouldn't I help if I could? Rob suggesting that I accompany her to functions wasn't so ridiculous.

We'd once been good friends. And anyway, this was business, the best for the foundation. Twenty weeks would pass in a blur, and I'd be giving kids the opportunity that I was once given.

How could I say no?

NINE

Truly

What Noah had said the night before was right—big donors wanted to feel special, to deal with someone with the Harbury name. He just didn't know how difficult it would be for me, how anxiety-inducing it was. I'd almost slipped into a panic attack, but the hairdresser arriving had distracted me just in time. I hadn't had an attack in years—not since my short-lived membership of the debate society at university. Even now I was having to concentrate on my breathing. I knew sending Kelly or Mason was potentially destructive, but fear bubbled to the surface every time I thought about having to do what my beautiful, charming sister did so effortlessly. I wasn't her. I'd never be her. I played to my strengths, which were few and far between. Abigail played to hers, and she could do almost everything.

And the idea of turning my team over to someone else? I hated the thought. The likelihood was that I'd fail at schmoozing donors and the back-office departments I was in charge of would collapse. Abigail would come back, and I'd have burned the place to the ground.

I couldn't help it, my breathing became choppy and uneven and I pushed my chair out from my desk and leaned forward, resting my head between my knees. I had just about managed to get through lunch today. But presentations? Galas? Lunches and dinners with more people? Disaster was lurking behind every corner.

My phone buzzed and I ignored it. I needed a moment.

I tried to pull in a breath for three counts like I'd seen in films.

In, two, three, out, two. Shit. I tried again. *In, two, three, out, two, three.* It wasn't helping. My heart was hammering against my chest, my palms were sweaty, and images of hundreds and hundreds of faces staring at me flashed into my head.

I ignored the knock on my office door. I was too concerned about what was happening to me. Was it possible to have a heart attack at twenty-eight?

"Truly," a familiar, male voice called.

I couldn't look up. Couldn't even open my eyes.

Warm hands covered my knees and body heat radiated in front of me. "Are you okay? Take a breath."

What was Noah doing here?

I nodded, still counting my breath. As if he was familiar with the technique, he began counting along with me. "Out, two, three. In, two, three. Out, two, three."

His voice was calming. The counting hadn't worked when I'd done it alone, but hearing him counting too helped me settle into a rhythm.

Eventually, his hands slid from my knees, and I sat up and opened my eyes, right into his.

"Are you okay?" he asked, his brow furrowed.

I was such an idiot. A mess. And this was why Noah and I had only ever been friends. He was used to seeing me in no makeup with a smear of kung pao chicken on my face. And now I was panicking about a meeting that he would think nothing of. Yes, Noah only ever saw me at my absolute worst.

"What are you doing here?" I asked. I didn't want him to see me like this.

"Do you want some water?" He stood and poured me a glass of sparkling water from the bottle on my desk.

"Thanks." I took a sip and sat back in my chair.

"I came to talk to you. Apologize if I seemed harsh last night. I'm sorry if I made this worse, Truly."

I cleared my throat. "I'm fine. Just a little . . ." I watched as he slid into the chair opposite my desk, his long legs unfurling in front of him. "I just have a lot to do."

He nodded, steepling his fingers. "And I'm here to help."

I stared over his shoulder, trying to figure out how to respond. I thought he might forget about Rob's suggestion of being my personal consultant. At least I was hoping he would. The last thing I wanted was to be forced to spend time with someone who I found impossibly attractive. "I'll be fine. I just need to adjust."

"I totally agree," he said.

"Oh. Well, that's settled. Thank you for your offer."

"But until you are fine, until you adjust, perhaps I could help."

I groaned. "That's really nice of you, Noah, but Rob shouldn't have asked you—this isn't your problem."

"Rob wasn't wrong. I do have a little more time than usual as I ramp up my next project, so I have the capacity to do this."

"I don't know what you think '*this*' is, but we have it handled. It's all going to be fine." Perhaps one of the girls in the office could help me with clothes for future events. And although I was sure Noah would be helpful in lots of circumstances, I didn't want to spend any more time with him than absolutely necessary. I was a grown woman. I didn't have time for crushes.

"Truly, I just walked in to find you having a panic attack. Please—let me help you."

As much as I wanted to say yes, I didn't want to fall for him all over again, knowing I would only ever be a friend to him. It was too painful. Too much of a reminder that I would never be enough. I'd always be the less pretty, the less charming, the less loveable twin. "It's really nice of you to offer but really, you—"

"I can come to some of the meetings where you don't know the donors, help you work on your presentations, attend the dinners with you. Just until you feel more confident."

"I don't think that's a good idea. And anyway, since when are you the guru when it comes to charitable foundations?"

He blew out a breath. "Okay. Cards on the table. I'm not really giving you a choice. I'm going to help you and you need to get used to the idea. Remember, I know how business people think. I've done thousands of corporate presentations, dinners, and lunches. I know the rules. Understand how to play the game. And if I don't have any other credentials, I've at least proven I can calm you down."

"What do you mean, you're not giving me a choice?"

He stood. "I can work from Abigail's office, I presume? And I'll need an assistant."

This time I stood up. "Hey, wait a minute, you can't just come in here and . . . You're not the boss around here."

He raised a single eyebrow. "But someone needs to be, so I suggest you step up, stop being so stubborn, accept my help, and let's get on with the job."

My heart was beating through my chest. I rarely saw this side of Noah. He was usually so laid back and affable. I guess this was him in work mode and it was . . . kinda hot.

"I have a tendency to want to . . . fix things," Noah said, thrusting his hands in his pockets. "And seeing those kids at the rehab center? It just brought back some stuff. I need to do my best for them, Truly."

Shit, of course, his accident would make the rehab center's funding so personal for him. I rounded my desk until we stood just a foot apart, tilted my head up, and our eyes met.

"I'd not made the connection. Were you at the same hospital?" I asked.

He nodded, looking away. "I don't like to dwell on the past. You know, besides Rob, you are the only person I've ever talked with about the accident who wasn't around at the time. But, I don't know, this feels like I would be doing something positive for the future. It feels right."

How could I possibly not let him help if that's what he wanted to do? He needed this. The center needed him. Turning him down would be selfish. I'd just have to visualize someone else when I looked at him—Ricky Gervais or Steve Buscemi instead of the blond-haired, blue-eyed, six-foot Viking in front of me. "I'm sorry. I'm being an idiot. It would be good to have you help."

When the chips were down, those kids should be the only thing that mattered. Noah was more comfortable charming people and making small talk than I was, and he was good at calming me down. "It's business. Right?" I needed to see things in a different way. Use him for my own ends. Squeeze out all his knowledge and know-how. Not focus on his hard abs or the way he could make me laugh, calm me down, make me cry.

TEN

Noah

Truly shifted from one foot to the other in the boardroom of the foundation, and she craned her neck to see the screen behind her.

"No, don't look behind you. Look at the people in front of you. You're the one they have to buy into." We were about twenty minutes into our presentation prep, and the look in Truly's eyes suggested she already wanted to kill me. She'd get over it.

It was good to have a focus, a goal, my teeth buried in something I believed in.

"It's too much to remember. The screen, the clicker, what I'm saying." She slumped into her seat and tossed the remote across the table.

"You're right. This isn't working."

She gave me the side-eye.

"I mean it. I want to change things up. We don't need to turn you into Abigail, just a version of yourself that's the most attractive to donors." It was up to me to show her how to be her best and convince her that was more than enough.

She rolled her eyes. "You want me to show them my boobs?"

I chuckled.

"I swear, I'll do it. It's a whole lot easier than remembering all this stuff that I'm not good at."

"As much as I'm sure you have very nice boobs, I'm not sure that's the answer." I was pretty sure the money would roll in, but wasn't sure the Harbury Foundation's reputation would recover. "Let's abandon the screen and use printouts. It's not like it's a presentation to an auditorium. It's how many? Five?"

"Maybe six."

"Perfect. So you'll all be around a table. You can get hard copies of the presentation for everyone and just take them through it."

"What, just like I do for the board?"

"I guess. I'm not sure what you—"

"I sit and talk everyone through the slide pack. Abigail always does her bit standing up, but I never do. It freaks me out."

"Exactly. So, this way will be better." I glanced down at the paper copy of the slides I had in front of me. "And I want you to take out this slide." I drew a diagonal line through slide three. "It doesn't make sense the way you're talking about it."

"But Abigail—"

"I don't care. Slide three goes. I think you should replace it with testimonials from recipients of the foundation's help."

Truly frowned but tentatively drew a cross through slide three and scribbled down some notes.

"And we can work on your greeting, add in some of your humor and passion, and you're going to nail it." There was nothing Truly couldn't do if she set her mind to it. She just needed to believe in herself. My eyes dipped to her worried mouth. "We have a whole twenty-four hours before you give this presentation. You know all the material. We just need to make it work for you and then practice."

"And you'll be there, right?" She leafed through her slides. I'd never seen her so uncertain, so questioning of herself. She was usually so confident in her opinions and decisions. This more vulnerable side of her was new, and I found it drew me to her, motivated me to ensure she was completely prepared to take on this new role.

"You want me to come into the presentation with you?"

"Of course. You can't just send me into the lion's den on my own."

I chuckled. "It's hardly the lion's den." She glanced up, concern crossing her face. "But if that's what you need then sure. It's at three tomorrow, right?"

"Yeah."

"Once you've done one of these, the rest will get easier. It's always the same content, right?"

"Mostly. We have variations for new donors and repeat, then we tailor those to high net-worth individuals versus corporations."

"Good. Once you nail the first one, it'll only get easier. So make sure you wear something you're comfortable in and—"

She groaned. "I tried to get that curry stain out and it didn't work. And I found a hole in my good pair of black trousers."

"So, shopping is a priority for you."

"Shopping is *never* a priority for me."

Truly had the exact same attitude about clothes that I did. They were functional. Something you put on so you weren't cold or naked. "I can make a call. Have a stylist pick out some outfits for you."

"Oh God, a stylist? They'll have me wearing jumpsuits, blue lipstick, and over-the-thigh boots."

"Thigh-high boots might not be such a bad thing." I grinned at her. She'd look fucking phenomenal in a short skirt, red lips, and boots that hit mid-thigh.

She scrunched up a piece of paper and threw it at me.

"What? I'm a straight guy with a pulse. You put it out there."

"Seriously. Stylists just want you to spend a lot of money you don't have and dress you in things that are fashionable on the hanger but look ridiculous in real life."

"Truly," I growled. "I told you, you need to trust me. I'll get her to call you, and she can arrange something for tomorrow and then going forward, we'll go and see her together to put a working wardrobe together. I'll be honest and tell you if I think it doesn't suit you."

She paused, as if she didn't know whether or not she was going to accept. "I could really use your help, but I don't know how I can repay you. First, you were there to help with Abi, and now with this. It seems like each time I have a problem, you come and unknot it."

I didn't understand why that was an issue. "That's what I'm here for. And, yes, the rehab center is important to me too but . . . I want to help you."

She groaned, as if my response was the last thing she wanted to hear, and headed to the door.

"I'll let you know about the stylist."

She nodded and forced a smile. "Thanks. I do really

appreciate all this. It's just . . . a lot. The speech. The clothes. You." She shook her head. "Anyway. Thanks."

She swept out, leaving me in the meeting room, not quite understanding what had just happened. Why had she mentioned *me* as one of the things worrying her?

I pulled out my phone and dialed Veronica's number. Truly was right—I was here, unknotting her problems. But that's what I was good at. She needed my help. Those kids at the rehab center needed my help.

Truly liked to stay in her comfort zone, but I'd never realized how uncomfortable she was accepting assistance. She'd have to get over it. I wasn't going anywhere until that twenty-five-million-pound target was met, and Truly knew she was more than capable of filling her sister's shoes.

ELEVEN

Truly

I never understood people who said their hands shook with nerves. It had never happened to me. Until today. I held out my arms, palms down, and then snatched them back and sat on them, not wanting to see how they shook in front of me. There was so much resting on today. The future of the foundation—all those kids at the rehab center. It was like a mountain of pressure and expectation bearing down on my chest.

"Come in," I yelled at a knock on my office door. I usually kept it open, but I hadn't wanted anyone to witness my freaking out.

Noah appeared in the doorway and I exhaled, instantly feeling a little better. And then I groaned. Seeing Noah shouldn't make me feel better. I was trying not to fall down that particular rabbit hole. He was insanely good-looking in his navy suit and a dark-pink tie. Jesus, he never looked like anything other than male model material, but couldn't he have toned it down for today rather than turn up the volume? For my sake? The blue brought out his eyes and his crisp white shirt emphasized his long, tan neck. He looked like he should be making deals in New York City, not helping out in some tumbledown office in Shepherd's Bush.

"How are you doing? Do you need a paper bag?"

"No, but if you have a glass of wine, I'll take it. Seriously, Noah, I don't think I can go through with this."

"It's too late to back out now." He glanced at his watch. "People will be arriving any minute."

"Those kids at the rehab center really need our help. If I mess this up—"

"Those kids are the reason you're not going to mess this up. They're the reason we went through the presentation a thousand times yesterday. Stop trying to find a way out. Focus on how much preparation you've done, and how you know this place better than anyone in that room will. You have it down." He grinned, and the pulsing in my ears relented and the corners of my mouth turned up. How did he do that?

"Right, I got this," I whispered.

"You're going to have to do better than that," he said.

"Better than what?"

"That sad little smile. These donors want happy, upbeat, and smiley."

I rolled my eyes. "In other words, they want my sister."

"I've never understood why you always think Abigail is more capable than you at everything."

Wasn't it obvious? "Because she is. We are the exact opposites. She's—"

"Yeah, you're very different. But you're not worse than her at everything."

It was obvious that he was trying to boost my confidence, build me up. But he wasn't going to talk me out of knowing how my sister and I compared. I had a lifetime's evidence to fall back on. "No, you're right. I have an affinity for spreadsheets that she doesn't share, and I can wipe the floor with her in a pub quiz as long as it doesn't have too many reality TV questions."

"You really don't get it, do you?"

That was the point. I got it and I was fine with it. "Can we just focus on this meeting?"

He took a chair opposite my desk. "Do you have the printouts?" he asked.

I tapped the stack of papers at the end of my desk.

"So, you're focused on your five goals for today?" His tone was stern and authoritative, and if I hadn't been so nervous, I might have let my mind wander to whether or not he was like that in bed.

"Smile and eye contact," I said, reciting the first thing Noah was having me concentrate on. "That really should be two. Because they are completely different things. You can smile without eye contact and make eye contact without—"

"Truly," he growled as my voice climbed higher and higher. "Be calm. What's next?"

"Don't choke."

He chuckled but I was serious. "And you're in the meeting, why?" I asked.

"To make sure you don't choke."

"Funny. But seriously, how are we going to explain why you're in the room?" I checked the time. People should be arriving any minute.

"We should just be honest."

"You think we should tell them that because I'm incompetent at dealing with people, you're sitting in on the meeting in case I have an anxiety attack?"

"Get up," he said, as he stood and rounded my desk.

I frowned but did as he asked. He kicked my chair away and walked behind me. "Great outfit," he said, and I'd have sworn, if I didn't know better, he was checking out my arse. "Is this what the stylist sent over?"

This pencil skirt seemed far too tight and the shirt—I mean the green silk was beautiful. But it was far clingier than I was used to. I was sure to spill something down it before the end of the day. "I feel like I'm dressing up in someone else's clothes. Do I look ridiculous?"

"Anything but. You look great." He swept my hair in front of my shoulders, and I tried not to shudder. Touching me wasn't part of our deal. What was he doing? He brought his hands to my neck. "Christ, you're as tight as a drum," he said as he began kneading his fingers into my bunched muscles.

"What are you doing?" His touch had me stiffening instead of relaxing. He didn't touch me. That wasn't the kind of friends we were. Was he trying to force me further out of my comfort zone?

He pressed my shoulders down. "Just relax and let me loosen some of this tension."

"I really don't think . . ." I sighed. His fingers felt good. They were distracting and firm, and as he worked, the scent of fresh laundry and lemon body wash hovered around me and I gave in. My shoulders dropped and my mind washed free of anxiety. I shouldn't be letting him touch me. I was supposed to be keeping him at arm's length, not allowing myself to think of him as anything but a colleague. I didn't want to go backward and be that girl with an unrequited crush. But right now, I was saving my fight for the boardroom.

We stood in silence as he continued to knead the knots he found.

"When you let yourself relax," he whispered into my ear, his warm breath floating against my skin, "you're better able to focus."

Noah released my neck and slowly smoothed his hands down my arms when someone knocked on my door. "You're going to be great."

Great? I'd be happy to get out alive, but I was so dizzy from Noah's touch that I'd forgotten to be anxious.

"Remember, you know this foundation inside out and back to front. You understand the charities you help and you care about them deeply. Just be yourself."

As he spoke, I still felt the echo of his hands, and the noise in my head continued to remain at a distance and my breathing stayed even. Maybe this meeting would be okay.

My assistant popped her head in. "They're starting to arrive. I've shown them into the boardroom."

"Thanks, Lisa. We're coming. Are the refreshments in there?"

"Yep, everything's set up."

"Okay," I said, taking a deep breath. "Let's do this."

I'd started to stride out when Noah called me. "Don't you want the presentations? And your notes?"

I winced and headed back to my desk, collecting everything I needed. We headed down the corridor, but as I paused to knock on the boardroom door, Noah grabbed my wrist. "This is *your* foundation. You don't knock."

Shit. Right.

"You have nothing to be nervous about." His tone was so calm and authoritative, he sounded so sure, it was easy to believe him. I exhaled. "Head up. Smile."

I lifted my chin and plastered on a grin before walking into the room.

Here we go.

THIRTY MINUTES LATER, I was done. After making chitchat with the donors, I went through my presentation. No one had interrupted, and I hadn't passed out, but I had barely drawn breath or looked up.

"Is it possible to get an electronic copy of the slides?" one donor asked.

"Of course," I replied, scribbling down a note for myself. "I'll send everyone a copy."

"It's impressive how you do so much with what you have," another donor said.

I smiled, my shoulders dropping as I drew a deep breath. I closed my pack of slides, grateful that I had finished the meeting before passing out. "Just drop me an email if you think of any questions later on," I said and stood. "And if I don't see you all before, then I'll no doubt see you at the winter ball."

After a couple of awkward goodbyes, I saw everyone out. And just as I shook hands with the last donor, I realized what I'd done—or hadn't.

My legs were weak and my mouth was dry as I stumbled back into the boardroom where Noah was waiting. "Oh, God—I didn't ask them to commit to funding next year," I said, leaning back on the closed door. "How could I have forgotten?"

Noah coaxed me over to sit next to him. "I think it was fine. You made the presentation and connected with the group. That was the hardest part, and you nailed it. Now you can follow up with a personalized email, thanking them for coming and asking them to let you know what they are planning to donate next year."

I let the heat of his body warm me, and everything seemed a little bit better. "You think I can do that? That's not what Abigail does."

"But you're not Abigail. You're Truly. You don't have to be a carbon copy of your sister to do this job."

"I hate being so crap at this stuff. Abigail is just so—"

"Abigail's been doing it a long time. Everything gets easier with practice."

"Well, I'd rather just stick to what I'm good at."

"Really?" he asked. "Where's the challenge in that? Don't you want to master new things?"

"It's not what comes naturally to me. Numbers come naturally. They never did to Abigail."

He paused. "So you can only be good at something if Abigail isn't?"

"That's not what I'm saying." I'd enjoyed arguing and debating with Noah when we were friends before. But our discussions usually centered on politics or science. I couldn't remember it ever being personal before. I wasn't used to him, or anyone, focusing on me and challenging me in such a personal way. "I'm saying, she's naturally better than me at some things, so it makes sense for her to focus on that stuff. I'm never going to be good at this public-speaking thing, so why force it? If I can't be exceptional at something, why not put my efforts somewhere where I know I can be the best?"

"Maybe you avoid public speaking because you don't want people to compare you and Abigail?"

"That's not fair, Noah. I've known Abigail since before we were born. I love my sister, and I have no hang-ups about her being beautiful and confident. People are drawn to her and so am I. I hate to be the center of attention, but she flowers under people's scrutiny."

"I know you love your sister. That's not what I'm saying. I'm asking why you compare yourself so negatively to her."

"Have you met Abi, Noah?"

He shrugged. "She has her talents and you have yours. You're both brilliant, beautiful, highly successful women. I don't understand why you see yourself as being less than her. To an outsider, it makes no sense."

Beautiful? Did he just call me *beautiful?*

"And if you keep comparing yourself to her," he continued. "You might miss out on new experiences if you don't accept that you might not be great at everything you try."

"I started running," I blurted out. "I'm terrible at it. But I tried it."

"Good for you," Noah said, nodding his head.

"And I'm going to keep doing it too, so I can get better. But at the same time, I do think it's possible to spread yourself too thinly."

"Maybe that's true," he said, his brow furrowed and his eyes fixed to the wall. "I just think you have a lot to offer the world. We all have more inside than we realize, and sometimes it takes something like your sister being ill or . . . my accident to bring that out. This is your chance to rewrite and reinvent yourself a little. You might find you're better at this stuff than you think."

"Your accident? You think that changed you?"

"It reframed things for me. It showed me the impossible was possible."

God, here I was whining about giving a presentation when Noah had had to overcome much worse just to be able to walk again. I needed to accept that the next few months were going to be hard, but that with Noah's help, I'd get to that finish line. "I'm not sure I'll ever be good at giving presentations and speeches, but for the next few months, I need to accept my fate and get on with it."

"You'll relax and improve. Given how nervous you were just a few minutes before you went in today, I think you did just fine."

"Despite the fuck-up at the end?" My shoulders sagged. "It was a lackluster performance. I need to do better."

"You're being way too hard on yourself. This was a major milestone."

"Next time is going to be a hell of a lot more pressure."

"The awards speech?"

I sighed. "Exactly. First, I have to stand up. Second, I have to wear an evening gown—I look completely ridiculous dressed up like that. Then I have to give a speech in front of two hundred and fifty people. I can barely manage a seated presentation in front of six people." My heart began to race at the thought of all those faces staring up at me, all that attention. Perhaps I could break my own leg with a hammer or something.

"These are people who love the foundation. They give up their free time to volunteer and fundraise. They start off on your side."

"But they don't know me."

"They will by the end of the evening. Do you have something to wear? Because we're not seeing the stylist until afterwards."

"I can wear what I wore to the winter ball last year," I mumbled, then glanced up. "But thank you. I couldn't have done this without you here today. I'm not sure I would have even made it to the boardroom. You've been a counterbalance for the voice inside my head telling me I'm useless."

"If only you had a little more faith in yourself."

"I mean it. I really owe you."

"Let's get through this, and I can think up ways you can pay me back." He pulsed his eyebrows and chuckled.

How did he always stay so relaxed and laid back? "In the meantime, I have a ton of new experiences to look forward to, whether or not I'm ready."

"You're more than ready. And I'll be right here alongside you."

That's all I'd ever wanted from Noah—for him to be by my side—eating Chinese takeaway or beating me at video games, but he was too restless for that to keep him happy for long. Our time together was temporary. It always would be. He wanted new and exciting. He liked a different girl every few months. Always focused on a new goal as soon as the last one was mastered.

Noah was always ten steps ahead, looking to the horizon, while I was happy staying in one spot, staring at my feet.

TWELVE

Noah

I closed the door of my newly purchased Range Rover and headed to the door of Truly's building in my tux. It seemed strange that she still lived in the same flat. Since I'd last been here, I'd moved between continents, built a business, and was now on my third apartment in that time. It was almost as if we were exact opposites in so many ways but then again, sometimes when we talked I'd never felt so similar to someone.

I pressed the buzzer. No answer.

I waited a few moments, but when I didn't see her coming down the stairs through the partially glazed doors, I buzzed again. I'd never known her to be late for anything.

"I feel ridiculous," she replied through the intercom.

I had to bite back a grin. "Do you want me to come up?"

"No, I'm on my way. Will you tell me if I look like a crazy person?"

"Truly, you're not going to look ridiculous." Truly was an attractive girl, and although she rarely made the most of herself, I was sure she looked perfectly fine as long as the dress was appropriate. "Get down here or I'm coming up and we'll be late."

She blew out a deep breath and the intercom went dead.

Instead of waiting in the car, I hovered at the door. Perhaps she'd changed her mind about wearing the dress she had worn to the winter ball and had decided to wear something a bit mental.

I cupped my hand over my eyes and peered through the glass. The lift doors opened and Truly stepped out.

I barely recognized her. She wasn't just attractive, she was a complete bombshell. The breath left my lungs. She looked incredible. The red dress perfectly showed off her hourglass figure, and her dark brown hair fell in glossy waves around her shoulders.

Jesus, was this what she was covering up with baggy jumpers and yoga pants? I'd always known she was attractive. I'd hit on her when I'd first met her—and I'd gotten a hint of it when she wore that pencil skirt at the presentation —but I hadn't realized quite how gorgeous she was until now. Or I'd forgotten, if that was possible.

She grinned at me through the glass, a wide, unselfconscious smile I knew was genuine. One she reserved for the people in her life she really liked. I felt like the luckiest guy on earth.

The lock released and I opened the door. "You look beautiful," I said, wanting her to believe it.

"Noah," she admonished, dipping her gaze to the floor.

"I mean it. Really beautiful."

"Well," she said, glancing at me. "You don't scrub up so bad yourself." She lifted her hand as if she was going to touch me, then snatched it away.

"We should get going," she said. "We don't want to be late."

I guided her down the stone steps to the car, my hand in the small of her back. As I touched her, she glanced at me. "Truly stunning."

I needed to remember this wasn't a date. She wasn't *my* date. We were friends. I was just helping her out. I was here to calm her nerves and nothing more.

I held open the car door and took her hand as she climbed in.

"Oh, hi," I heard her say to the driver.

I rounded the boot and took a seat next to her. "This is Bruce." The London traffic was a nightmare, so I'd given in and hired a driver.

"We've just met. Are you just working for Noah for the evening?" she asked.

I tried not to wince.

"No, Miss, I started full time last week," Bruce said as he pulled out.

Truly nodded and her gaze flitted to me. "You have a full-time driver?"

I shrugged. "It makes sense."

"Will you marry me?" She giggled. "It's a complete dream not to have to deal with public transport in London. What else can you opt out of now that you're rich? Do you have to stand in line at the bank with us muggles or can you hire someone to do that, too?"

She was teasing but frankly, wasn't far off base. My assistant would probably be the person who queued up for something. "If only you knew—you'd want to do more than marry me."

She blushed and pushed at my shoulders. "You're meant to be helping me focus."

"I'm distracting you. Stopping you from freaking out."
In truth, she was distracting me. She'd always thrown me a
little off guard—the way she'd turned me down at the
wedding, the way we'd hung out together as friends before
I'd left for New York. She'd had no expectations or demands
of me, and the way she was so open and honest was like
oxygen.

Truly was so unlike any woman I'd ever spent time
with. Apart from anything else, I wasn't sleeping with her.
Maybe our lack of physical relationship was the reason I
liked her so much. I couldn't help but wonder whether she'd
be more guarded in bed than she was during our conversations. I'd like to think she would be like she always was, like
clear, fresh water—honest, refreshing and completely
genuine. "Although I mean it, you look beautiful tonight.
That dress is . . ." Her soft breasts peeked over the top of the
bodice, and as she sat, light layers of fabric parted to reveal
her bronzed thigh. Jesus, that dress had magic powers.

"Abigail made me buy it."

"Well, I'm glad she did."

A little ridge appeared between her eyes as she
frowned. Was she as confused as I was? When I'd first laid
eyes on Truly, we'd been in church at Rob and Abigail's
wedding. She seemed to glide in, unaware of all the eyes on
her, as if she'd just assumed everyone would be totally
focused on her sister. Perhaps that was why she'd been so
unbothered by the attention. Truly didn't seem to realize
that however attractive Abigail was, she was just as beautiful. More so because she was so unaware of it. Abigail was a
thousand women I'd met in London and New York—confident, well groomed, gym fit, and totally aware of the effect
she had on men. Truly was just as beautiful but unique and
completely unaware of how gorgeous she was. She was also

completely and utterly . . . interesting. It was a quality I'd never seen as sexy until meeting Truly.

"Here we are," Bruce said as he pulled up to the hotel where the awards were taking place.

"Ready?" I asked, turning to Truly.

"Not even a little bit. Can we skip this part and go and do tequila shots in some twenty-four hour bar in the City?"

"Nope."

Her entire body sagged as if she'd really been thinking I'd say yes. Then she giggled and the sound connected right to my cock.

"I tell you what, I'll take you for tequila shots afterward if you make it through without a panic attack."

She shrugged. "Sounds fair, although you know that technically it will be one tequila shot. You know I can't drink. But it's incentive enough. Let's do this."

By the time I'd reached her side of the car, she was already halfway out. "Let me take your bag at least," I said as she refused my hand while trying to negotiate the step down.

"Thanks," she said. "These shoes are . . ."

"Sexy?" I suggested as she stepped onto the road.

"What is with you tonight?" she asked, nudging me in the arm with her evening bag. "Stop it with your plan to distract me so I don't get nervous."

I tucked a strand of hair behind her ear. "Okay, no more distracting you." Distraction hadn't been in my plan. I'd just forgotten how beautiful she was, how attracted to her I was, and it was showing. I liked the way her brain worked, how she didn't miss anything that was going on around her, and I especially liked how she never held back how she felt.

"It's working." She smiled. "But knock it off." She scooped up the front of her dress and walked toward the hotel lobby. "I have to stay focused or I'm going to forget the bloody speech."

I chuckled, and we made our way, side by side, to the venue room.

Volunteers greeted us as we headed toward our seats. We'd barely get two steps at a time before someone else greeted Truly with a hug and a smile and some piece of news they wanted to share or a question they'd been dying to ask her. They acted as if they knew Truly, even if she was convinced they didn't. They told her how pleased they were to see her and asked after Abigail. It was nice to see her have so much attention. The spotlight looked good on her.

"This is our table," I said as we arrived. "Right at the front." I pulled out her chair and she took a seat.

"That was exhausting," she said. "All those people talking to me. I didn't recognize half of them."

"It's nice. They care about the foundation and your family."

She nodded and reached for the water, her wrist so delicate, I wanted to wrap my fingers around it to give her strength.

"Let me," I said, taking the bottle before she could and pouring her a glass. "No wine?"

"God, no, can you imagine? My speech is right at the end. I'll have one to calm my nerves and before you know it, I'll be funneling alcohol into my mouth."

"Interesting image and doesn't exactly sound like you."

She laughed. "Maybe no alcohol now, but I'm going to hold you to tequila. I'll have earned it if I survive this."

"You're going to do more than survive," I said, completely sure of that. The thing I didn't understand was the way I couldn't take my eyes off her and how my hands were hot with a need to touch her.

That wasn't who we were.

We were friends. She was my best friend's sister-in-law. And I was here for the children of the rehab center. Truly wasn't a girl I wanted in my life for a standard three-month cycle, which was why I needed to get myself under control. Sure, she was beautiful. And funny. And clever and great to spend time with. But that wasn't why I was here.

THIRTEEN

Truly

I glanced up from the podium, locking eyes with Noah, as people applauded the Volunteer of the Year winner. Noah's expression was bright and encouraging, and it was easy to imagine that he was here as my date. He'd been so attentive. Flirtatious even. It was so easy to get sucked in by his charm and those blue eyes. Which was exactly why I'd wanted to avoid spending time with him. I was way too old for crushes.

Adrenaline coursed through my body. The speech had gone off without a hitch. People had laughed at a couple of my jokes, and I'd even managed to look up into the crowd. The fact that I'd written in red pen "LOOK UP" at the end of every paragraph had helped.

I took a breath and looked away as the winner took the stage. I passed over the envelope containing the spa certificate. Vivian was one of our longest serving volunteers, and someone I'd known since I was a kid.

"Congratulations," I whispered into her ear as I kissed her on the cheek. "And thank you for all you do."

She pulled me into a big bear hug and began to cry.

She mumbled a few thank yous into the microphone and then I led her off stage to rapturous applause.

Noah was at the bottom of the stairs and took both our hands as we negotiated the steps in our high heels.

"You were wonderful," he whispered as he led me to the table. "Let's get out of here."

He scooped up my evening bag and led us to the exit.

"Hey, what about the dancing?" I'd been sure he'd make me stay for the dancing part of the evening because it was the exact opposite of what I wanted to do.

He paused and looked back at me. "You want to stay?"

"No, of course not, I just thought—"

He took my hand. "We have tequila to drink."

Noah. Tequila. Me. It seemed like a bad combination. A dangerous one. But before I had a chance to object, he pulled me through the crowd. His determination, the way he gripped my hand tightly, it was as if I was his responsibility, his to keep safe.

The car was idling outside when we pushed through the hotel's revolving doors. Noah helped me in before going around to his side.

"Did you find somewhere?" he asked Bruce.

"Certainly did, sir. It's just a few minutes away."

Noah nodded and sat back, not letting go of my hand, like we were on a date. He was just being friendly and supportive but it was too easy to enjoy. "You were astonishing tonight."

"Astonishing? Because I didn't have a full-blown panic attack on stage?" I poked him in his arm, trying to remind myself that we were friends. That the touching was just . . . nothing.

"Don't give me that. You know you did well."

I grinned at him. "I'm pleased with how it went. Did you notice they even laughed at my jokes?"

"I did. And you stayed connected to the audience, glancing up all the time. I'm proud of you." He tightened his grip on my hand.

"Thank you. You deserve the credit, too. You helped me with the speech, calmed me down before the event, gave me confidence. And you being here? It means a lot, Noah. I know you have plenty of other things you could be doing."

"There's nothing I'd rather be doing." He held my gaze and swept his thumb across my palm.

This was why I'd first developed my crush on this man. It was as if he didn't know how *not* to flirt. Unwittingly, he always knew how to press my buttons, what undid me, what pulled me under. I should slide my hand away, tell him to turn the car around and to drop me off at home. I had meant to be avoiding unnecessary time with him. I was supposed to stop falling back into the habit of enjoying this man's company so much that our friendship blurred into something more. For me.

But I couldn't stop myself. I wasn't ready for my time with him to be over.

Bruce pulled to the curb, and Noah glanced out the window. "Just here?" he asked.

"Yep. It's open until four."

"We can drink plenty of tequila in that time," he said.

"You know that more than one shot and I'll be a mess."

"We'll see." He held my gaze for a beat too long and warmth coursed through my body. This was my opportunity to say no. To ask Bruce to turn around. I should go home—to my books and my bed. Tequila shouldn't be an option.

Noah slid out of the car before me, then helped me out after him.

As he shut the door I asked, "Bruce isn't going to wait, is he?"

"That's what I pay him to do." He took my hand again and we walked into the dimly lit bar.

"All these people at your beck and call—aren't you worried it'll change you?"

His stare pressed against me as I glanced around at the dark room. There were brown leather semi-circular booths on the outside of the room and a few tables in the middle. Soft eighties music played in the background rather than the ubiquitous dance music that seemed to surround me whenever I found myself out at night. And there wasn't one type of person here—not all office workers trying to forget the stress of their week or hipsters figuring out how they were going to change the world. It was a place anyone could blend into, which was the perfect place for me. Had Noah known or was this the closest spot open?

"Do you think it's changed me?" he asked as he led us deeper into the bar. A waitress stopped us, and when Noah gave her his name, she led us to one of the round booths.

"I don't know," I said honestly. "Has it?"

I took a seat, and Noah followed, sliding so close that his leg pressed against mine, his body heat seeping through to my skin. What was with him tonight?

"I think I'm still adjusting, but the money gives me freedoms I didn't have before."

"Freedom to not work? Help me?"

"To figure out what I really want."

My pulse thudded in my ears. His words seemed heavy. Important. And it seemed like we were skirting around the edges of something. Like we were about to cross a line from which there was no going back.

The waitress returned with the tequila and two shot glasses. As she went to open it, Noah held out his hand. "Thanks, I'll do it."

He took the alcohol, unscrewed the cap of the ornately decorated bottle, and tipped the amber liquid into the two glasses in front of us. "You said tequila. No going back now."

I hoped I didn't regret my request. I struggled to handle more than a glass of wine.

"To you, Truly," he said, raising his glass. "And to experiencing new things."

I picked up my glass, chinked it against his, and watched as he took a sip. "It's really too good to shoot. Have a taste."

I moistened my lips and lifted the glass. The alcohol coated my mouth like slippery, wet heat and I swallowed, the fire snaking down my throat.

"Good, right?" he asked.

"Yeah. Surprisingly so."

I watched as he took another sip, his Adam's apple bobbing in his long, tan neck. I held back my urge to press my fingers against his exposed skin and trace the liquid down, down, down.

I needed to snap out of it, remind myself how miserable I'd been pining after him when he'd left. I was never going to be the girl who got this guy. That wasn't how the world worked. I needed to stop looking for signs of affection that didn't exist. I needed not to hope for something that was never going to happen. "So, have you figured it out yet?"

"What?" he asked as he leaned back.

"What you want?"

"Right now?" He slid his arm behind my shoulders, his fingers skirting my hair, so it rested on the back of our seats.

Had he ever touched me like this? It was as if he didn't want to break our connection, as if he couldn't *not* touch me. Why were alarm bells ringing in my ears?

"Right now"—he swept his thumb across my bottom lip —"right now I want to kiss you." He held my gaze, waiting for some kind of answer.

The room fell silent; the only sound left was the breath leaving my lungs. I had a thousand responses but they all started and ended with *I want you to kiss me, too.*

The only thing I could see was Noah watching me.

The only thing I could remember was how he'd almost kissed me once before.

How was this happening again? I knew I shouldn't let it but I didn't want to stop it.

And of course, he saw my weakness in my expression and leaned into me, pressing his lips on mine. What was left of my resolve disappeared.

He cupped my face and I dissolved under his touch. Despite being in a room full of strangers, the moment seemed so private, so intimate, as if it was my first kiss and I'd just entered a new world. A small moan escaped my throat and Noah smiled against my lips.

"You taste so good." His low timbre rumbled through my entire body as his lips left mine and he finally released my face.

I pressed my palm to his chest. I needed some room to breathe, time, space. I had to think. That wasn't an *almost-*

kiss. It had actually happened this time. And it had been . . .

"We shouldn't," I said. I knew how deep my feelings for him had run, how long it had taken to get over him. I didn't want to open myself up again.

He picked up his shot glass and took another sip, this one bigger than the others. The glass was nearly empty.

"You're so beautiful, Truly," he said. "And I really like spending time with you." His hand dipped under my hair to the back of my neck, his thumb tracing the outline of my jaw.

How was this so easy for him? Was it because it was nothing? Was this what he was like with other women?

I didn't want to be just one of those girls who floated into his world for a few months and then disappeared. He meant too much.

"Noah?" I said.

"You want to leave?" he asked, a flash of disappointment crossing his face.

"No," I said, trying to slow everything down and regain control. But he leaned forward and kissed me, more urgently this time. The sweep of his tongue, the press of his fingers—it was all just *more* than before. Intense, passionate, powerful.

I pulled away. "But that's the problem, Noah. What are we doing?"

As if my words pierced his skin, his brow furrowed. "Kissing, Truly."

"But why?" None of this made sense. Was he just drunk or horny? I just didn't understand how we were here. Kissing.

He exhaled, his eyes shutting in a long blink. "I just can't not."

I sighed, and he brought his forehead to mine. "You're so beautiful, so kind and good . . . Do you not want me to kiss you?"

I slid my hands over his and tilted my head up. It was what I'd wanted since I'd met him.

He pressed his lips against mine again and the question faded into the background. All I could think about was how his body felt, how his skin was as smooth as I'd always imagined, and how he smelled—like lemons and the beach.

His tongue grew more insistent, and he twined his fingers into my hair. How was it possible that this beautiful man wanted to kiss me?

No matter how hard I tried, there was no way I could ever resist him.

The music changed from sultry to upbeat, and I melted further into his kiss.

Noah was the only man I'd ever wanted to see me as sexy, but all these years had gone by where we'd just been friends. What had changed? The hunger in Noah's eyes, the way he looked like he wanted to devour me, could almost make me believe that he wanted me. Almost.

He dipped the tip of his finger into his glass, then painted the alcohol across my lips before ghosting his tongue along the same path.

"I never knew drinking tequila could be this sexy," I said, copying him by coating my index finger in my drink and sweeping it across his lips. I paused for a second, and he leaned toward me, encouraging me, inviting me. I couldn't help myself; I leaned forward and licked him clean.

He groaned and caught my tongue with his, pressing and pushing, taking and giving. My breathing came out ragged and uneven, and heat rose between my thighs. How could a public kiss be this hot? What was I doing, giving in to the kisses of a man who could only ever hurt me?

Playing with fire.

Setting myself up for a fall.

Opening my heart to someone I knew couldn't give me what I needed.

But I didn't care. Not right then. It was just kissing. It was just tonight.

FOURTEEN

Noah

We had only kissed last night but it felt like more. As I sat facing the changing rooms at the office of the stylist, a tray of champagne on the table in front of me, it *still* felt like more.

Despite resolving to keep things about the foundation, last night something had snapped within me. Seeing her up on that stage, it was as if her devotion to all the good causes, her commitment, her desire to do right by so many people had all reached a crescendo. Seeing her on stage, giving a speech, dressed in an evening gown that left me speechless and unable to take my eyes off her, I was proud, overcome —defeated.

I'd wanted her.

And then her heat, the way she tasted and softened last night under my touch? It was passion and purity all wrapped up in one.

I should have held back, but I'd selfishly taken what I wanted without a thought for the consequences. I'd almost done the same just before I left for New York. But this time was different. There were even more reasons I should have held back. This time I wasn't going anywhere. We were friends, our lives entangled, and that made things complicated.

"There's no way," Truly mumbled through the door to the changing room.

"Come out and let me see," I called. "You're hungover. You're in no place to judge."

The girl still couldn't drink, which was why last night had stopped at kissing.

I grinned as I remembered carrying Truly up the stairs to her flat. She'd insisted she could sleep in the bar. In the Range Rover. Or on the pavement—wherever it was that we were on route back to her place.

"Shall I come in?" asked Natalie, the stylist Veronica had set me up with.

"It doesn't fit. I can't see where this arm is meant to go," Truly muttered.

Natalie shot me a smile, knocked on the door, and went in to help.

I'd always liked Truly, thought she was gorgeous from the first moment I saw her, but since she'd turned me down at the wedding, I'd backed off. Become the friend she insisted we should remain, but whatever attraction I'd felt for her in the beginning had been magnified last night. I'd felt it a thousand times stronger than I ever remembered.

So I'd kissed her. And kissed her again. It seemed like it had gone on for hours. And even now, sitting here with my hangover, all I could think about was her half-dressed on the other side of that door.

I needed to get a grip.

I pulled out my phone and checked my messages. My new assistant had arranged for an IT system to be installed at the office, and I now had a business email address. I knew I wanted part of my job to be investing in up-and-coming entrepreneurs, but seeing the state of the rehab center and helping the foundation had made me want to do more—really make a difference.

Natalie burst through the door, a huge grin on her face, then turned and held her hand out, coaxing Truly out of the changing room.

"It's not very me, is it?"

I couldn't focus on her question because I was mesmerized by her. And her outfit. "Well, it's certainly very . . ." It wasn't that it showed a lot of flesh—or any, for that matter. It was a one-shouldered black jumpsuit that teased with every curve it hid. The material flared out at the waist and clung to her arse.

"I knew it. I look ridiculous."

"You really don't. You look sexy as hell. Turn around." It was conservative and obscene at the same time. "I think you should get it."

"You do?" She looked at me as if she thought I was losing my mind. "It's super expensive."

"You look great. How does it feel?"

She avoided my question. "It's not the sort of thing I'd wear in the office. Or at a ball."

"No," Natalie said. "It's an evening outfit. Perfect for a date night. Or cocktails."

Truly scoffed. "I'm not really a cocktails kind of girl."

She was so cute. So bloody adorable. Drunk or sober. In jeans or an evening gown. Last night or now.

"Dates, then?" Natalie asked.

Truly cleared her throat. "I think I'd prefer to focus on things I know I'll wear."

Did she date? Was she dating? The thought of her with another man had my jaw tight and my fists clenched.

"The next couple of outfits are perfect for the office," Natalie said.

Truly exhaled. "Let's try those."

Natalie was right; the next couple of things were perfect work wear. A dark green dress that made her hair look black as night and a pair of trousers that had me asking her to spin around twice so I could check out her arse and then wondering whether I wanted other people to see her look so incredible.

What was happening? I might have been able to convince myself that my attraction to Truly last night had been courtesy of the tequila and her red dress, but today, no matter what she tried on, I couldn't help but imagine her out of it.

At the bar, I'd not thought through kissing her. I'd just acted on instinct and alcohol, but the same desire I had last night seemed to have seeped through into today. What had changed? Why had I kissed her last night when until then I'd been content with being friends?

I knew I enjoyed spending time with Truly. I looked forward to it, felt lucky that she gave me some of her hard-won attention. Truly was special. Rare. I liked her relentless honesty, the way my money didn't impact the way she was with me. I liked the way I knew that although she looked hotter than Hades in a tight dress and high heels, she looked just as sexy in a Batman t-shirt and pajama bottoms. I liked the fact that she worked so hard and was exceptional at what she did. And I liked that I couldn't outsmart her in a pub quiz or over a conversation about the economy of China.

But none of those things meant that kissing her had

been a good idea. My relationship with Rob and Abigail meant there was more at stake than usual. My friendship with Truly hung in the balance. After not seeing her for so long, I realized how much I valued our friendship, and I didn't want to lose that again.

What was happening to me? I groaned, uncomfortable at the unfamiliar, shifting ground beneath me.

"Are you bored?" Truly asked from the other side of the changing room.

"No, just trying to get my email to work."

"Are you sure?"

I was anything but bored when I was with Truly, which was something I couldn't say that about most of the women I spent time with. Maybe it was because I wasn't sleeping with Truly that she was more interesting to me. "I promise I'm not bored."

My phone buzzed. "Hey, I just got a message from Rob inviting me over for dinner."

A ping followed by a giggle suggested Truly'd just received the same message. "Yeah, me too. But that's weird for a Saturday, especially with Abigail in bed."

My phone buzzed again at the same time as a ping rang out from the other side of the dressing room door.

"Ahhh. That's nice," Truly said. "We're going to have dinner in their bedroom to help Abigail feel less stir-crazy. My sister doesn't do well without lots of noise and people around her."

"Can you make it?" I asked.

"Sure. It's Saturday night—not like I have anything better to do." The rustle of fabric filled the silence. "Can *you* make it?"

"Yeah, I can make it." I wasn't sure there was anything

better to do than have dinner with old friends. And Truly. "We can go straight after this."

Truly appeared in the door to the changing room. "Does this say winter ball to you?"

I swallowed, glancing down from her neckline where her breasts threatened to spill over the top of the navy-blue velvet. The bodice was fitted, and made it look as if I could wrap my hands around her waist. Because I couldn't form the words to tell her how incredible she looked, or how I wanted to push her back into the changing room, burrow under her skirt, and taste her, I just nodded.

"You hate it?" she asked, disappointment heavy on her face.

I shook my head. "I think it's perfect." I wasn't sure if I was talking about the outfit or her.

A smile crept over her face. "Really?"

"You know it."

She leaned forward, peering left as if to check if anyone was around. Natalie was at the other end of the store looking at accessories. "It's not easy to get in and out of."

I slid my phone onto the table in front of me and stood. "You need a hand?" I asked, my heart pounding.

She paused and our eyes locked. "Just with the zip."

I nodded and stalked toward her as she backed up into the changing room.

She turned and swept her hair up so I could reach the fastening.

I inched it down as slow as I could stand, tracing my finger above the seam, then down as the fabric revealed the smooth skin of her back. All I could hear was the heavy thud of my heart against my ribcage and the way she tried to keep her breathing even. When she tilted her head to one side and let out a little sigh, I couldn't resist pressing a kiss against the curve of her neck.

The zip undone, I slid my hands around her waist and held her, wanting to stay as we were for just a few minutes.

"How was that?" Natalie called.

I released Truly and stepped back as she shooed me out of the room. "It's hard to get in and out of," she replied. "But I kind of love it."

I grinned. I kinda loved that dress, too.

As Truly changed into the next outfit, I got to my feet and pulled Natalie aside. "Can you put the jumpsuit on my account and have it delivered to me?" I knew Truly would never spend the money herself if she couldn't wear it to work. But even if she never wore it, Truly should own that jumpsuit. And she *should* wear it. For cocktails. Or dates.

With me.

FIFTEEN

Truly

As I waited at the red lights, I skirted my fingers across my neck where Noah had kissed me, remembering how he'd taken such an excruciatingly long time to unzip my dress. It was as if he'd been savoring every moment we were so close.

I'd expected last night's tequila-induced kissing to be easy to sweep under the carpet. But as soon as I'd seen Noah this afternoon, all the feelings I'd been trying to push down had risen to the surface. It was becoming more and more difficult to pretend they weren't there. Lying to myself wasn't working. Then the way he'd looked at me, the way he'd touched me? He was shooting holes in every defense I had. I was supposed to be being sensible. Keeping my distance.

A car honked and I moved forward, then around the corner. We'd traveled to the stylist separately. It gave me some time to breathe. But I still didn't have any answers. Just a few seconds later I was pulling in to Rob and Abigail's drive about to face him again.

Noah's car was already there. No surprise, as I'd stopped for wine for the three of us and macarons for my sister.

I knocked and let myself in.

"Just turn it slightly," I heard Rob say, his voice strained.

"It's only me." I started up the stairs and came face-to-face with Noah's broad back and perfect arse.

"You need to shift it to you," Noah said.

"Why are you guys moving furniture?" I asked.

"We need to make our bedroom more social," Rob replied. "The sofa from the study will fit and give people somewhere comfortable to sit"—he heaved as they came to another tricky maneuver at the top of the stairs—"when they come visit," he finished as Noah reached the top step.

"I'll go and get some glasses," I said.

"Bring a bottle of that pinot noir that Noah brought. It's in the wine fridge."

I padded down the stairs, stuck the considerably cheaper bottle that I'd brought with me in the wine fridge and took out one of the ones I recognized from lunch a couple of weeks ago. I stuck the box of macarons under my arm, forked my fingers through the glasses, and scooped up the wine.

"Do you need a hand?" Rob called from upstairs.

"No, I'm on my way."

As I reached the doorway to Rob and Abigail's bedroom, I paused, watching the three of them chat. This was all so familiar. So comfortable and one of the many reasons why Noah and I shouldn't have kissed last night. In the completely impossible scenario that we started dating, what happened when it was over? I might be able to imagine us growing old and gray together, but that wasn't the way Noah operated. He'd soon get bored, end things, and then evenings like this wouldn't ever happen. I'd avoid lunch. He'd make excuses for not coming over for drinks. And I'd lose him as a friend. It wasn't worth it.

"Hey," I said. "I've brought wine and treats for the pregnant lady."

"Tell me the treats are macarons," Abi said.

"Of course." I caught Noah grinning at me out of the corner of my eye.

Abi reached out her arms for the sugar like a toddler.

"Hang on." Noah jumped up and took the wine and the glasses.

"Thanks," I said, catching his eye and giving him a small smile.

I pulled the box of macarons from under my arm and held them up. "These are the ones, right?"

Abigail glanced between Noah and me without looking at the box.

"Abi?" I said.

She frowned and held out her hand. "Sure. They're great. So, tell me, Noah, how's Truly doing? Did last night go well? Truly didn't send me a single photograph or even message me to let me know."

"Sorry, I totally forgot," I replied while Noah smirked, knowing why I'd forgotten.

"Did something dreadful happen?" Abi sat straight up, horror unfolding across her face. "Oh my God." She flopped back down dramatically. "Were you drunk on stage? Is there video?"

"You have nothing to worry about," Noah replied. "Truly was completely sober when she did her speech. You didn't even have a sip of wine, did you?" He turned to me and I shook my head. "And she was . . . remarkable. They laughed at her jokes, applauded in all the right places. They loved her."

Abi glanced from Noah to me and back again. "Oh," she said. "Good. Great. So, everything went smoothly?"

I nodded. "It wasn't as good as it would have been if you'd handled it, but it was fine."

"It was a lot better than fine," Noah said. "You were really warm and natural—completely yourself."

My cheeks heated at his words. He sounded so genuine. Not at all as if he were saying it just to make Abi feel better or to boost my confidence.

"Anyway, luckily it's over with now. So, nothing until the lunch with Global Tronics and then the new corporate donor lunch in a couple of weeks. Oh, I have the presentation to Artemis Group." I stopped talking. There was so much happening and if I let myself think about all the things I had to do, it was easy to get overwhelmed. I'd save that for when I wasn't with Abigail. She didn't need to see how much anxiety her absence caused.

"So why did Noah smirk when I asked why I'd not seen any pictures?" Abigail asked. "It's like you two are keeping something from me."

If only she knew. But she couldn't know. She'd think I was an idiot to succumb to advances from such a practiced player.

I shook my head, ready to skirt over it, when Noah said, "We went out for a drink afterward."

Shit.

"You didn't want to get home?" Abi asked. She knew I hated being out late. That for me, the best part of any social function was getting home and back to a good book.

"Just a quick drink," I said, hoping I wasn't blushing. Abigail couldn't know about the way Noah had held my hand, pressed his thigh against mine, kissed me. How he touched me like he couldn't get enough, unzipped my dress this afternoon, and held me until we'd been interrupted.

"Your sister's a lightweight," Noah said.

"Hey," I replied, feigning offence. "I did nearly two shots."

"Two shots of tequila?" Abigail asked.

Noah chuckled. "She drank one and passed out halfway through the second. If I hadn't taken you home, you would have woken up on the curb."

My sister narrowed her eyes as if she was trying to figure out if I'd had highlights or a nose job or something else that made me look different. "Boys, can you go check on dinner? I'm starving."

"Err, okay," Rob said, putting down the wine he was just about to sip. Poor Rob. Abigail wore the trousers in their relationship at the best of times, but now that she was bedbound, Rob couldn't complain about any request Abigail made.

"Take your wine," she said. I got the distinct feeling that hunger was not driving Abigail. She wanted to know something she didn't want to ask about in front of Rob or Noah.

"So," I said, turning to her as they filed out. "You can rest easy, knowing I'm not drinking on the job. I've prepared the slides for the meeting with Artemis next week and I've—"

"Truly," she said, fixing me with her older-sister glare. "What's going on?"

"Nothing. I told you everything's under control and you—"

"Shut up about the foundation. You know that's not what I mean. What's going on with you and Noah?"

Heat crept up my neck, and I willed myself not to

blush. "I don't know what you're talking about. He's helping me fill in for you, which was your husband's suggestion, by the way." She didn't have to know everything about me, right?

"And you're going for drinks with each other, and he's taking you home. And just then? You were so . . . aware of each other. So . . . like you're both only thinking about each other."

There were serious disadvantages in having a twin sister. Why couldn't I have had an oblivious older brother? I took a long glug of wine to avoid answering.

"Truly, I'm not trying to pry." She paused. "Well, I'm totally prying, but I just want you to be careful."

"I don't know what you're talking about. Nothing's going on. Things are . . . professional. . . ." *Ish.*

"Do you like him?"

"Of course I like him. We've always been friends. You know that."

"You know what he's like, Truly. I've never met one of his girlfriends twice. He's not your type of guy."

I rolled my eyes. "I know. Far too good-looking."

"Pft. It's not that. You are totally gorgeous but far too lovely to be used and thrown away by Noah Jensen."

She must be worried if she was throwing compliments around so easily. Gorgeous and lovely were adjectives used about my sister. I got "bookish" and "interesting." "Seriously, Abi. It's not like that. Not even a little bit."

"You're a terrible liar. Tell me what happened, or I'll just call Noah up here and ask him myself."

"Abi, please. Just—" There was no point trying to convince her to drop it. She was like a dog with a bone, and I had no doubt that if I didn't tell her, she'd ask Noah in front of me and I'd likely die of shame on the spot. "Nothing

really. I was on such a high after the speech went well . . .
We went for drinks. And, I don't know. He kissed me. It's
not a big deal. We were both a little drunk—on adrenaline
and tequila." There was nothing more to it than that. "It's
not like we slept together or anything."

She sighed and rubbed her belly. I wasn't sure if she was
soothing her baby or herself. "But today there's so much—I
don't know what—between you. That kiss wasn't nothing.
I'm worried—"

I sat on the edge of the bed, and she shuffled back to
make room for me. "Don't be. It was a one-off. I know that
men like Noah and girls like me don't mix." And I was
telling the truth. The way he looked at me, touched me,
held me today—I *needed* to keep my heart safe.

"You're a beautiful soul who doesn't know how not to
give something or someone everything you have. I'm
worried for you. Men like Noah . . ." She shook her head.

She was worried he'd hurt me. She didn't realize that it
was too late for that. An unrequited crush was the worst
type of heartache. But I was over that. This was different. It
was an alcohol-fueled kiss and it was over. "Don't worry.
My heart is safe."

"Maybe you just need to take positive action to make
sure that remains the case. Call up an ex-boyfriend. Join a
class. Do some online dating. Just don't get caught up
in . . . him."

She'd never known how *caught up* I'd been all those
years ago. But this time was different. I understood the risks.
I knew Noah—what he was capable of, who I was to him.
That knowledge was inoculation. Against falling in love.
But perhaps an insurance policy wasn't such a bad idea.

Maybe Abigail was right, and I needed something else
to spend my time on. I'd kept up with my running, but it

wasn't the distraction I'd hoped for. If anything, it gave me more time to think. I needed something that would *stop* me from thinking about Noah when I wasn't with him. Something that would stop me from looking forward to the next time I saw him.

I needed him in the just-friends box. And then I had to nail the lid shut, just to make sure that's where he stayed.

SIXTEEN

Noah

I needed a drink. I knocked on Rob and Abigail's front door and saw Rob's silhouette through the glass before he opened the door.

"Hey, you know I'm not cooking, right?" He shoved a beer into my hand and headed back toward the kitchen. "You're far too used to my culinary skills. When's the last time you cooked dinner?"

"What a welcome." I chuckled. "I'm here for a drink, anyhow." I took a long swig.

Rob collapsed onto the sofa in their family room, and I took a seat next to him. "We can order Chinese."

"Sounds good." I didn't care about food. I'd been in meetings all day, and I was exhausted. Rob hadn't been my first choice of company, but Truly hadn't returned my call or answered my text. It had been days since I'd seen her and nearly a week since I'd last touched her.

"So, why are you in such bad need of alcohol?" he asked.

I frowned at the footsteps on the stairs. "Is Abigail allowed up?" I lifted my chin toward the sound.

"That's Truly. She wanted Abigail's opinion on shoes or makeup or—how the fuck do I know? She's freaking out over some date."

My body went icy cold, and I took another swig of beer, trying to hide my shock. A date? A fucking date?

Perhaps Rob had it wrong and it was dinner with a donor. Or a friend or—a fucking date? Seriously?

"I'm off," Truly said, appearing in the doorway and almost gasping when she saw me, as if she'd been caught doing something she shouldn't.

I got a weird sense of satisfaction from the fact that seeing me was so unexpected.

She looked incredible. She wore her long black hair in loose, glossy waves over a fitted blue dress that was cut low enough to tease but not low enough to look easy. Where had that come from? She hadn't bought it from the stylist. Her lips were a blush pink, and I'd never seen her in such high heels.

"Hi," she said, smiling at me.

"I called you," I said, and regretted it. I sounded like her dad, chastising her for not checking in.

"You did?" She pulled out her phone. "Sorry, I—"

"Doesn't matter. You look nice."

She glanced down at herself and then looked up with a grin. "Really? Thanks."

Why wasn't she saying anything about the fact she was going on a date? Was this a regular thing? Had she dated since our kiss? Kissed someone else since me? Was she fucking someone?

Jesus, I needed to snap out of it.

"Did you need to speak to me about something?" she asked.

I shook my head and took a swig of beer. What was I going to say? *I wanted to know if you wanted to hang out, have a beer. I wanted to know if I could kiss you again.* "Nothing. I had a suggestion for one of the new donor presentations, but I'll email you."

"Okay, well I'm off." Her gaze bore into me, but I had to keep focused on my beer or I was going to do something I'd regret.

"Make sure you message Abigail before the night is out, or she'll keep me awake all night speculating about how it went," Rob said.

Fuck. Who the bloody hell was she going out with?

Truly rolled her eyes. "Whatever. Bye."

"Have a good time," Rob called.

Have a good time? Whose fucking side was he on? Wait, was I a side to be on? Was I competing for Truly?

Truly headed out with a wave, and I finished off my beer.

"Jesus, you drank that fast," Rob said as I stood and headed over to the fridge for another.

"Thirsty I guess." I knocked the fridge door shut with my elbow and skulked back to the sofa. "So, who's Truly going out with tonight?"

I looked up when he didn't answer.

"No idea," Rob replied. "Why do you care?"

I sighed and tilted my head back against the cushion. "Just curious, I guess." The thought of her being with someone else tonight, letting someone else touch her, churned in my stomach.

"So she's not dating someone regularly?" I asked.

"Is this you being *just curious*?"

"Fuck off, Rob."

Rob sighed and put down his beer. "Look, I don't think she's dating anyone regularly. I know Abi bugs her about it, so I think I'd know if she was seeing anyone seriously. I do know tonight is a first date."

A sense of relief settled in my gut. A new guy. No one who knew her like I did. Someone who'd never kissed her. But that might change tonight. If she liked the guy.

"You can't say you're not bothered and then ask me a thousand questions. Be straight with me—do you like her?"

I took the first sip of my new beer and tried to figure out how I felt. "I've always liked her."

"But as friends, right?"

"I've always thought she was hot. And . . ." We'd had some kind of connection, hadn't we? That's why we'd *become* friends. Closer than I was with most people. She made me laugh, stood up to me, listened to me. She was so fucking fascinating I could listen to everything she had to say on a loop.

Rob flipped the channels, pausing at women's hockey. "Right." He was clearly expecting a better response, but I wasn't sure I had one.

"I don't know. I didn't want her to be one of those women I used to fuck, you know?"

"One of your three-month cycle women. Abigail would have your bollocks."

Perhaps it was because women got more serious around two to three months, and after that something shifted. Maybe I got bored. Or everything became a bit too comfortable. I had no idea, but no one ever made it past three months, and I didn't want to ruin my friendship with Truly and then not have her in my life.

"Truly's great," Rob said, eyes pinned to the television.

I knew that. There was nothing I didn't like about her. "She is."

"If you decide to go there, you'd have to turn into a hardcore relationship guy. You wouldn't be able to fuck it up, or I swear, Abi will ban you from this house. We'd have to break up, too."

I chuckled, but I got it. Truly and I had kissed, shared moments, but it was nothing we couldn't row back from. If things were to go any further, Rob was right, losing Truly wasn't worth a three-month fling.

It was good that Truly was on a date. It just didn't feel all that good right at this moment.

SEVENTEEN

Truly

It was the first time I'd prepared for a presentation and didn't have a bin by my side in case I got the urge to throw up. I paged through the Artemis presentation again. It was good, even if I did say so myself. It sounded less factual than I would ordinarily approach something—more emotional. It just felt right. But I wouldn't be comfortable with it until I found out what idea Noah had wanted to talk to me about. If he'd just sent me the email he'd promised, I could have incorporated it and practiced the changes. I was giving the presentation this afternoon. That wasn't enough time.

I swiped the screen on my mobile. Still no response to my message asking him what the suggestion was.

"Ready?"

I jumped when Noah strode in. He'd offered to come in to do a final run-through before I went to Artemis's offices.

"Well, I would be if you'd sent me the idea you had. It's freaking me out that this thing isn't finalized with only hours left."

He frowned before taking a seat, but didn't respond.

"Noah!"

"What?" he asked as if he hadn't heard a word I'd said.

"When I saw you at Abigail and Rob's on Saturday, you said you had an idea for the Artemis presentation that you wanted to talk to me about."

He nodded. "Yeah. Saturday. How was your date?"

"It was fine. What was your idea? You said you'd email it to me." Noah was always on his phone. I didn't understand why he hadn't replied to my messages.

"Fine? What does that mean? On a scale of one to ten where was it?"

Why was he talking about Saturday night when he was supposed to be helping me prepare for the presentation?

I wanted to forget about Saturday night. Seeing him just before I was going off to have dinner with another guy had been weird. It wasn't as if anything was happening with Noah. Sure, there'd been the kiss. And the . . . situation in the changing room. But nothing since. It wasn't as if he'd suddenly decided I was the woman for him and declared his love for me. In fact it had irritated me more than it should that he'd had almost no reaction to me going on a date at all.

So why was he so interested now?

"It was a solid seven. Now, please, can you tell me what's wrong with this presentation?" I wasn't sure seven was an accurate number. More like a five point two, but I figured a higher number would discourage questions.

"Seven. Okay." He slid forward and took the presentation from me. He rested his ankle on his leg and flicked through the pages, scanning each one from top to bottom. "So seven must mean there's going to be a second date."

"Are you playing the big-brother card?"

He looked up at me from under his brow. "I think you

know that we'd both be in jail if I was your brother. So that's a yes to a second date?"

"Why do you care?" I asked. Part of me, a big part of me, was hoping he'd ask me not to go out on any more dates.

"That's what I'm trying to figure out," he muttered and leaned forward, smacking the presentation down in front of me and pointing to page three. "There. A missing full stop."

"Are you kidding me? A bloody full stop? That's what you had me panicking about?"

"Grammar is important, Truly. And I always had you down as a perfectionist."

"You're an arsehole." I'd already spotted the missing full stop and asked my assistant to make the changes to the copies I'd take with me. Noah needed a new job if this was the kind of thing that was making him call and message me on a Saturday.

He chuckled. "Your mouth has gotten dirtier." He pulsed his eyebrows up, and I ignored the somersault my stomach did.

I shook my head. "Shall we do a run-through in the boardroom?" I rounded my desk.

He stood and took a step toward me, standing a little too close. "You look pretty today." He lifted my hair behind my shoulders, exposing my neck.

"Noah?" I stepped back, and his hands fell away. He'd kissed me. That was it. It had been a moment of madness, which was over.

Abigail had been right. I needed to date instead of spending all my time thinking about Noah. I'd been there before.

"Let's go through the presentation. I can't afford to mess this up."

"You know you're going to be fine," Noah said as he

followed me out. "You're getting so good at this stuff, you're not going to need me soon."

I came to an abrupt halt at the door to the boardroom. "Are you saying you don't want to do this anymore?"

He stood so near that I could feel his breath on my cheek, and his body heat at my side. "I'm here for as long as you want me." His voice was low and serious, and a tiny part of me I kept hidden from daylight wanted to believe he meant in my life and not just to help me with the foundation while Abigail was away.

I took a breath and opened the door. "I'm not ready for you to leave. Not yet."

The problem was, the longer he stayed, the less likely it was that I'd ever want him to go.

Maybe it was time to admit defeat. Or at least come up with a new strategy.

EIGHTEEN

Noah

I liked making decisions, felt comfortable when I was in charge. So it felt good to be back in a suit and behind a desk.

"Is the meeting with the healthcare guys set up?" I asked my assistant. In my head I called him Earnest George, as he had a habit of nodding so hard it made me wince on behalf of his neck.

"Yes, and you have various potential investee meetings." He pulled out a sheet of paper from his file and placed it in front of me. "In fact, I've printed off your calendar for next week and synched it to your phone."

I nodded, scanning the next week of appointments. Walking away from New York and my company with nothing but fifteen million dollars hadn't been difficult. There were fifteen million reasons that made it easier. My challenge now was to figure out what I wanted to do next, but I was finding my feet.

"Are any of the Harbury Foundation appointments

cancelable?" George asked. "It's been difficult to fit in your flying lessons and your skydiving course."

"No. None of them are cancelable. In fact, I'd like to set up a meeting with the clinical head at the rehab center. He or she is bound to have contacts and know a lot about what's going on in the industry." George nodded vigorously and noted down what I'd said. "Did you research epidural stimulation and other treatments?"

Since my accident and recovery, I'd built a wall around what had happened, relegating the memories to the depths of my mind. I hadn't wanted to lurk down there, feeling sorry for myself. I'd wanted to move on, get the most out of life—relish the things that I'd nearly lost. But after visiting the rehab center with Abigail, seeing the state of the facilities and hearing about their fundraising goals, I found myself willing to go there again. Perhaps knowing I could help other people get through the suffering I'd endured made the experience more bearable.

George set three memos in front of me. "I've emailed this to you as well. The first one is just on the epidural stimulation. There's background research, how it was developed, and the outcomes data you requested. I also included information on when and why it's used, as well as when it's not used."

I flicked through the pages.

"The second report is on other cutting-edge treatments —and the third is about alternative, non-medical therapies."

"Great," I said flipping open the page. I'd been fascinated by the use of kung fu I'd seen at the center and wanted to see if there'd been studies about it.

George winced. "There's actually not much scientific data in terms of outcomes and results . . . but there's a lot of anecdotal data from people who've had great experiences.

And it's not just the kung fu. It's mindfulness, visualization. Even some stuff in there about essential oils."

"Research just hasn't been done?"

"There's no material benefit if the results turn out to be good. Big pharma or even medical device companies aren't going to increase profits by figuring out martial arts help with spinal injuries. And like it or not, those are the people who have money to fund the research—or employ lobbyists to ensure government money goes into researching treatments they can make a profit on."

I leaned back in my chair. "Yeah, that makes sense. Perhaps that's something we can work on. I'm not sure if we can run a study on alternative treatments or fund kung fu classes more widely for these types of injuries."

"Are you thinking you'll set up a charity?"

I blew out a breath. That wasn't the direction I'd thought I'd be heading, but I was keeping my options open. "Maybe. I want to look at what the impact might be of all these options."

My phone buzzed on my desk beside me.

I have a proposition for you, Truly messaged.

I grinned. She couldn't know the dirty things that ran through my head at that suggestion. Every time I thought about her, I tasted tequila on my tongue and felt her heat under my fingers. But we hadn't kissed again. We hadn't talked about it. Really, we'd barely talked about anything but the foundation. I knew I wanted more of her time, attention, and touch. But Rob was right, there were serious consequences if anything more happened between us. She wasn't a girl that would float out of my life when I moved on after a few months. She was in my world and I liked her there. I liked being able to talk to her about anything. Enjoyed the way she would put me straight if I got things wrong. I liked that she seemed completely unselfconscious around me. I didn't want to lose any of it. But where did that leave me? Did we change gears and go back to strictly friends, and was that even possible?

"Excuse me," I said, my eyes locked on the screen of my phone as I typed back.

Sounds intriguing.

"I'll come up with some ways in which you might be able to look at the impact of these other therapies."

"Sounds good." My phone pinged again, drawing my attention away from George.

Be at my place at eight.

No invitation to the Harbury Foundation's offices or Rob and Abigail's. I'd not been into her flat since I'd left for New York. My jaw tightened. Was I about to walk into questions I couldn't answer? Was this about our kiss . . . and would it lead to another? Perhaps she'd made a decision about what she wanted. Maybe I'd walk in there and she'd say how she regretted kissing me. I swallowed at the thought of not touching her again.

"Anything else?" George asked.

I shook my head, distracted. If she said she wanted more from me, would I be able to resist, or would I give in to her shy smile and captivating honesty?

I blew out a breath. Truly was probably just freaking out about a meeting she thought she fucked up or wanted some advice on what to wear for her next lunch. I'd just take the evening as it came, pick up a bottle of wine on my way around, and fucking relax. We were friends, right? Friends spent time together over a bottle of wine. We might be teetering on the brink of something else, but right now I was looking forward to seeing her, whatever we were to each other.

NINETEEN

Truly

My tiny living room wasn't designed for pacing. I could only manage two and a half steps before I had to turn around. But that hadn't put me off. Propositioning Noah had seemed like a good idea when I'd weighed up the pros and cons instead of sleeping, then an even better idea when I'd messaged him. But right now, with three minutes until his arrival, it seemed like the worst idea in the world.

I needed stationery.

Pens, paper—not pink. Not bone ivory. White would be more . . . professional. Less emotional. Black pens. White paper. Because that was what my proposition was—black and white. Take it or leave it. Head not heart. I pulled out two fresh pens and ten sheets of paper and was just about to close the door to my home-stationery cabinet when the Post-its caught my eye. Yes. We might need Post-its. Again, yellow. No fancy colors.

This was the perfect solution—a way of getting him out of my system, stopping me from wondering if there was more to his touch or whether he meant what he said, that I was beautiful. This was my opportunity to take back control. I just needed to get through the actual proposition and then I could relax.

I'd not changed out of my office wear. I couldn't negotiate an agreement for casual sex in a comic-book t-shirt. I needed to be businesslike about this, although I'd taken off my shoes and opened a bottle of wine. I'd only had half a glass but my muscles were looser, and my brain a little fuzzy. I'd hoped it would take away my urge to pace but, no, not even pinot noir was that powerful.

I jumped at the sound of the buzzer as if I were guilty of a crime and about to be arrested. If Abigail knew what I was up to, she'd definitely tell me I should be locked up for criminal stupidity.

I reached the intercom just after the buzzer sounded for the second time. I didn't speak, just released the door and began to count my breaths—in, two, three, out, two, three.

In, two, three. Out, two, three.

Yeah, I definitely needed liquid courage.

I scooped up my glass from the table where it sat with the bottle of wine, stationery, and an empty glass for Noah. No one could accuse me of not being prepared.

I opened the door to find Noah waiting.

"Hey," he said, his smile curling around the word like it was a secret between us.

I held up my glass. "Hey," I said.

He frowned suspiciously, and before he could ask me how long I'd been drinking, I headed back to my living room, hoping he'd follow.

"Wine?" I asked, looking up at him as I perched on the edge of my sofa, topping up my glass.

His gaze tracked my movements. "Are you okay, Truly?"

"Of course," I snapped. "Why wouldn't I be?"

He smirked as he raked his fingers through that beautiful blond hair. "No reason. You don't normally drink on a weeknight, that's all."

"Well, things change," I said, pouring the already open wine into his glass. "You're in a suit." I avoided looking at him, scared that the sight of him in all that cool, navy wool would have me pawing at him, given the wine I'd now drunk.

He sighed and shrugged off his jacket, placing it over the back of the chair that no one ever sat on.

I held out his glass, and he took it with one hand, loosening his tie with the other. I pulled my eyes away from his long fingers and the way he always seemed so confident everywhere he went.

"How was your day?" he asked as he sat on the other end of the sofa, one long arm stretched across the back of the cushions, almost touching me like he'd done the night we'd kissed at the tequila bar.

"Good," I said, nodding furiously.

He chuckled. "What's going on, Truly? Do you have bad news you need me to help you deliver to Abigail? An issue with the foundation?"

"Not exactly," I replied, tipping back some more wine. "Not at all, in fact." I had to tell him what I was thinking, but it seemed so stupid now that he was here, all perfect and gorgeous. Why on earth would he want me?

"I just thought we could have some wine and talk. You know."

His smile faltered. "Okay." He took a sip of wine. "You said you had a proposition."

"Yeah, but I'm not drunk enough yet," I replied. I wasn't sure I would ever be drunk enough. "And neither are you."

"I have to be drunk to hear whatever you have to say?" He glanced around my book-lined room. "Are you going to tell me you're MI6 and that you want to recruit me? Because I'm in. I always thought I'd enjoy a life as a spy. It just doesn't pay enough. But I could do it part-time."

I fixed him with a glare. "I'm not trying to recruit you into MI6, Noah." I rolled my eyes. Men. Why did they always think they were a step away from being the next James freaking Bond?

He grinned. "Yeah, I didn't think so. You'd make a terrible spy."

I leaned back into the sofa. "There's no way I could do that job."

"For one thing, they look for people who don't stand out —you're way too beautiful for people not to notice you." He twisted my hair in his fingers, and I closed my eyes, forgetting for a few seconds how that wasn't normal behavior between us.

My eyes flew open. "That's a perfect example." I shifted to look at him properly. "Things like that. The fingers. The telling me I'm beautiful. I need you out of my system. And Jesus God and a banana, I need some sex."

He chuckled and grabbed the bottle, topping himself up. "I'm cutting you off until you tell me what this is all about," he said.

"I just told you. I need to get laid, and you, with all your tequila kisses and unzipping dresses and that thing you do with my neck—you're the man for the job."

"The job?" he asked, his eyebrows retreating into his hairline. "The job of getting you laid?"

Oh my God, it sounded like a disaster when he said it

like that. "Not that it's a job. Just that you're single—" I paused. "Are you single?"

"Yes, Truly, I'm single. Remember the tequila kisses? They wouldn't have happened if I wasn't."

I nodded. Good. So, he was single. That was a start. "And I'm single. Hence, me tequila kissing you back. So, we should just have some casual sex." There, I'd said it. Put it on a platter for him and stuck an apple in its mouth.

I stared at my wine, waiting for a response.

"Truly," he said, his voice gravelly and so delicious that if I could eat it, I'd lick it so slowly it would last an entire year.

I peeked at him, shifting my head as little as possible.

"Is that why I'm here? Your proposition is . . . casual sex?"

Oh God, did he have to say it out loud like that? "But we can't tell Abigail and Rob. Way too messy. That is a hard rule." I eyed the paper and pen, ready to get down to business if he said yes.

He chuckled again, and I winced.

"You're laughing at me?"

He paused. "No, not at you—I . . . This is unexpected."

I blew out a breath. "Unexpected." This was a terrible idea. I sat forward, leaning my elbows on my knees, my head in my hands. Even though I'd been casual about people I'd had sex with, I'd never done casual sex. But with Noah? I just wanted him out of my system. I'd been kidding myself pretending my crush wasn't back with a vengeance. I was so aware of him whenever he was around, so ready to sink into his smallest touch. I wanted to reframe what I felt and move on to a different stage. Travel from love to convenient sex.

"But not unwelcome," he said. "I just don't think I've

ever had a woman call me over to her flat to suggest . . . whatever you're suggesting."

He slid his hand over my back, and my body and mind began to dissolve. That was exactly what I was talking about. I wanted to thicken my skin. Realize it was no big deal when he touched me.

"We won't tell Abigail or Rob," he said. "What else?"

I turned my head to find him staring straight at me. Was he saying yes?

"What else, Truly? I can tell you've thought about this."

"I thought we could write it down so nothing gets forgotten or misinterpreted," I mumbled in a small voice.

He tried his hardest to stifle the grin that burst from his face. "Hence the stationery."

I shrugged.

He cleared his throat and picked up a pad of Post-its, frowned and then tossed them back on the table. Maybe the Post-its had been a step too far.

Over on my side table, he grabbed my beaten-up copy of *The Fellowship of the Ring*, folded his paper in half, and pulled the cap off his pen. "I won't mark it," he said.

"I know." He knew how much I loved that book. I had a couple of hard-backed versions, too, but the book he had was the one I read to preserve the others.

"So," he said, nodding toward the stack of paper. "Are you going to make your list?"

I rolled my eyes as if it had been his idea all along and I was just going along with it. "If you insist."

"We're writing down rules," he said, as if to confirm we were on the same page.

"And what we don't want to happen."

He fixed me with a stare. "And what we *do*."

I began my list, and tried to ignore him, tried to forget

that Noah was sitting on my sofa, inches away from me. That we were talking about having sex. I squeezed my eyes shut, trying to erase the images of my sister yelling at me, telling me I was an idiot.

Noah was right. I had thought about this list. I figured six rules were appropriate. And then if he added six, twelve would be an acceptable number.

"So," I said, shifting back into the cushions and bringing my feet up so I could rest my papers against my legs. "Who's going first?"

"Well, given this is your idea, I think it should be you."

I'd been hoping he'd say that. "Okay," I said, putting a black circle around the number one. "The first one is no telling anyone—especially not Rob and Abigail."

I looked up at him from under my lashes, and he nodded. "The second one is condoms at all times."

"At all times?"

"Like, when we're doing it. Not, you know, when we're not."

He chuckled. "Okay, good. Number three?"

"I don't want to hear about any other women you're dating."

His eyes narrowed slightly. "So, no monogamy on either side?"

"I don't expect that, no. And I won't tell you about my dates, either."

"I thought the whole point of this was that *Jesus God and a banana* you needed some sex? If you're fucking other people—"

"I'm not. But, you know . . ." I lifted a shoulder. Why should it be a one-way rule? "If it did happen with someone else, I wouldn't tell you."

"Good to know," he responded sarcastically.

"Four, we get tested regularly for STDs."

He rolled his eyes like a bored teenager at the back of the class.

"Five, all meetings are arranged in advance. No just turning up." This one was more for me since I didn't want to run into some six-foot, rail-thin model coming out of his penthouse.

"Okay, so we schedule the sex." His grin replaced the sarcasm.

"Six, the sex has got to be good."

He grabbed my ankles and pulled me toward him, then crawled over me. "You think it would be any other way?" he growled.

His hard body, over me, blocked out everything but him. The same way he was all I saw whenever he was around. He dipped his head, pressing his lips into the skin just above my collarbone. But we hadn't finished. I pushed at his chest. "No, Noah."

He pulled away, his gaze dipping from my eyes to my lips and back up. "No? Do I need to sign something first?"

I poked his hard abs. "I haven't heard your rules yet."

"I don't have any. We're going to have hot, uncomplicated sex. Perfect. I'll sign whatever you want me to."

He went to kiss me, and I pressed my fingers against his lips. "I'm serious. We need to be clear about each other's expectations before we start this thing."

"I'm serious, too. I've heard your expectations. I agree with them. I don't have any others."

"So, just like that, you're ready?"

He lowered his body against mine, his erection pressing against my thigh. "I'm more than ready. I've been imagining this for a very long time."

And I was done. There was no more fight left in me.

TWENTY

Noah

The fresh coconut scent of her was enough to get me hard. But sitting there with her carefully arranged stationery as she proposed we have a casual sexual relationship? Fuck, my erection pressed against my zip so painfully my eyes watered. She didn't have to ask twice. I'd have agreed to pretty much anything to kiss her again. I didn't quite understand the pull I had toward her, and I still didn't know how this was going to turn out. Yet even though I was risking something important to me for sex, it was a gamble I had to take. There had always been something about her that was different and totally confounding, and I wanted to explore that.

I groaned into her neck, breathing her in. I just couldn't get enough. Her fingertips crept over the top of my shirt and pressed into my neck in the most perfect way. I wanted to savor this, draw it out, to kiss for hours, but I was too impatient to get more of her, to have all of her.

I popped open the buttons of her blouse. Jesus, the silk

and skin and her perfect scent—I was in sensory overload. I buried my head between her breasts, trying to drown in her. I couldn't remember struggling to hold back with anyone before. It was as if Truly ripped sounds from my throat like some kind of witch. She stole my control—made me dizzy with need for her.

I reached for the hem of her skirt. What the hell were all these clothes still doing on? There were too many barriers between us. I pulled back and removed my shirt. Her gaze dipped to my torso and suddenly all those hours in the gym had been for her.

She pressed her thumb against my nipple, and the sensation was as potent as if her mouth was around my cock. Sweat gathered at my brow as I stopped myself from just pulling out my dick and shoving it in right there. I *needed* more than that. And I knew she *deserved* more.

As I stood to pull off my trousers, she lifted her hips and rucked up her skirt, displaying her black lace knickers. I fought between the urge to kick off my trousers and get a closer look at her pussy. I freed myself of my clothes and sank to my knees.

"Oh yes, you're already so wet for me." I examined the patch of darkened material, then yanked the lace to the side.

She sighed and parted her legs, and my blood pumped louder in my veins.

This. *This* was what I wanted.

Going down on her was *necessary*. It wasn't some favor, or some way of warming her up. I needed it. I'd make sure she enjoyed it, just as I knew I would.

As if we knew that the next step would be crossing some kind of boundary, we locked eyes. She smiled softly and dug her fingers through my hair.

I bowed my head and slid my tongue between her folds,

reveling in her heat, her wetness, the way her hips slowly lifted beneath me. She was so sweet, so fucking drenched. I gripped the top of her thighs, digging my thumb into the crevice where her leg met her body. I wanted to pin her down and make her take everything I had to give her.

I'd never been friends with a lover before. Friendly but not close. Truly was the only woman I'd ever told about my accident, the only one I thought looked cute eating noodles, yet nothing about this moment was anything but perfect. This was exactly how it was meant to be.

I groaned into her sex, wanting more of her.

"Please don't stop." She squeezed out the words as if they wouldn't quite fit, but she had to try.

But there was no chance I was stopping. I couldn't. I licked up one side of her pussy and then the other, pressing and sucking and covering her clit. Going one way and then the other, I was determined to make her feel good, to charge over the line of friendship into something more. Her legs tightened and her fingers clenched my hair.

She was so close, so quickly. Fuck, I loved that she was reacting to me like that—not as friends but as lovers. She wanted me and I couldn't get enough of her desire. She bucked beneath me, so I pressed a hand low on her abdomen, right over her g-spot, and slipped two fingers into her. I grinned against her wetness as she moaned, her breaths coming faster and tighter as my tongue and my fingers continued to lick and pump.

With a final scream, she exploded, her skin flushing, heat radiating from her body.

I was lost.

"Oh God, Noah," she said, guiding my face up. "I . . . I . . ."

Her unspoken words hung in the air—she'd not

expected it to be this good. "I know," I whispered and dipped to kiss her.

Any concerns we had about crossing this line fell away, and it felt entirely natural. Honest and intimate. "I want you inside me," she said.

"Me too," I said.

"Condoms are in my bedroom."

I wasn't wasting time going and coming back. I'd take her with me. I lifted her up and carried her into her bedroom, her mouth on my jaw and my hard-on throbbing between us.

I was pretty sure if I'd timed myself, I'd have a claim to the world record for putting on a condom.

"Come here," I said, gripping her ankles and pulling her arse to the edge of the bed. "I'm going in deep and fast and . . ." I couldn't think. My head was foggy, and all I could focus on was being inside her. I pressed my tip through her sex, rounded her clit and then back to her entrance.

"Yes," she moaned. "Do it."

"What do you say?" I teased her.

"Please. Noah, please, please. I need your cock."

"Good girl." Jesus fucking Christ. This was a side of Truly I'd never seen before—passionate and needy. She was perfect. It was as if someone had just cut the cord of my self-control. My vision tunneled, my muscles bunched, and I slammed into her, hard and so, so deep.

Again.

And again.

I couldn't stop. I couldn't slow down. I needed to get as close as it was possible to be to this woman.

Her knees tightened around my hips, and she arched off the bed. I leaned over her, gripping her shoulders, keeping her in place, because I needed to fuck and fuck and fuck.

She trembled beneath me, bucking as if someone else was in control of her body. She gasped and screamed silently. Fuck, yeah. That was what I did to her. "All your orgasms are mine," I hissed through clenched teeth.

She gazed up at me, her body boneless against the mattress, and grinned. She reached and wiped away a trickle of sweat working its way down my temple. "All yours."

Those two words ended me, and my body spasmed as I emptied myself deep inside her, pushing in as far as I could go.

I dealt with the condom and rolled onto my back, trying to catch my breath as if I were at the end of a competitive sprint. I'd never been that consumed before, never lacked so much self-control. It was as if I'd been chasing after something I wanted to save.

Reaching for her, my hand landed on her stomach. "Hey." I pulled her toward me, needing her close.

"You're a cuddler?" she asked.

I wasn't normally, but I wanted to touch her, wanted her touching me. "Maybe," I replied.

"Well that's another thing I learned about you tonight." She slid her hand down my cock and grasped it at the base.

I groaned.

When I'd first seen her in the church, Truly hadn't been any different from any other woman I'd met. I'd imagined her naked and fucking her. But since she'd blown me off and we'd become friends, thoughts like that had been saved for others. But now she blocked out everything else. Everyone else. It was shocking how fucking warm and open and unselfconscious she was in bed. How was it not more awkward, and why hadn't we done this before?

She squeezed her fist then dragged it up. We both watched as I twitched in her hands.

"So quick to recover."

The only time I thought about fucking a woman twice was before I'd fucked her the first time. Right now that pattern was history. "Not normally, but you're always an exception."

Tucked into my side, she glanced up at me, and I kissed her. We'd morphed from platonic friends to lovers so easily, but looking back, this had been brewing far longer than I'd realized. Way before the tequila kissing. Even before I'd left for New York.

Truly pushed herself up, and I rested my hands on her hips as she straddled me.

"I'm usually asleep by now." I chuckled. I'd never normally reference a past sexual experience, but with Truly, everything was different.

She stroked her hands over my chest as she settled her pussy against my straining cock, content for the moment to slide her soft, wet folds against me. If she wasn't careful, she'd make me come again.

She groaned and tipped her head back, her hair spilling over her shoulders, the dark silky strands a mezmerizing contrast against her smooth skin as she rocked back and forth.

I sighed, mesmerized by the beauty in front of me.

Reaching back to the bedside table, I grabbed a fresh condom. "Truly, I swear, you look so fucking perfect, I'm going to come and I'm not even inside you."

She grinned and tucked her hair behind her ears before taking the condom from me and covering me from tip to base.

She raised herself up on her knees and positioned

herself over me, sliding down so very slowly. I wasn't sure if it was her expression of ecstasy or the sensation of her squeezing my cock as tightly as she was that had me closing my eyes and reciting the alphabet like a teenager trying not to blow his load at his first look at a naked girl.

I gulped down a breath and opened my eyes to find her staring right back at me.

"I don't know if I can do this," she said, panic flitting across her face.

I tightened my grip on her hips. There was no fucking way I was going to let her regret what we'd done. It was too fucking perfect and tonight wouldn't be enough. I knew that already. "Shhh," I said. "Relax."

"It's so good. I can't take it." Relief shivered up my body that she wasn't having a change of heart. I slipped my hands around to her back and coaxed her to lean forward. I tried to ignore the sensation of her body covering mine, her hard nipples pressing against me. I held her and began to move beneath her, pulling out and pressing in while she knelt over me. She whimpered into my chest as I slid in as deep as I could go. Her cries turned to moans.

Fuck, why had we waited so long? All that wasted time we'd spent talking when we could have been naked and fucking. My fingers dug into her arse cheeks, and she began to match my movements. She was so fucking perfect. She knew exactly what made me feel good, what worked for her.

Her body swayed and she collapsed against me, her muscles weakening as her moans grew stronger. But I couldn't stop, so I rolled over and pushed in again, earning a fresh cry of pleasure from Truly as she wrapped her legs around me.

"I fucking love your sounds," I spat through gritted teeth. "Like you can't get enough." I slammed into her again, and she arched her back, her nails biting into my shoulders as her orgasm claimed her. I didn't stop. Couldn't. I kept fucking and fucking, the orgasm that I'd been holding off since ten seconds after my last one building and building.

Truly opened her sleepy eyes and it was her small grin that did it. That secret look she gave me, like I was the best man to ever know her, pushed me over the edge. I thrust once more, pushing into her, closing any gaps between us.

TWENTY-ONE

Truly

I put on the hand brake and checked my hair in the rearview mirror, twisting it up into a clip. I tilted my head, taking in the bruise just below my ear. Shit. I pulled out the clip and let my hair fall loose.

I closed my eyes, remembered the way Noah's teeth felt. I'd bet those half-moon bruises covered my entire body. He'd been rougher, needier than I'd expected last night, as if he'd been storing up all his sexual energy and had unleashed it on me in several hours of casual sex that had felt anything but casual.

I hadn't expected it to be so good, so intense, and passionate. I just hoped I'd survive whatever we'd agreed to last night. I needed to focus on the physical. Put him in a box along with other men who couldn't hurt me because I didn't care enough.

I'd kicked him out after my third orgasm. It'd been late, I'd been exhausted, and I hadn't wanted him to tell me he was leaving.

He'd not argued, probably thankful that I had no expectation he'd stay.

No sleepovers should be rule number seven.

This morning I'd woken, my head fuzzy from lack of sleep but my thoughts full of him. What I needed was distraction. Since Abigail had been put on bedrest, I'd not visited the spinal injuries center. So here I was, ready to have my focus pulled away from what didn't matter to what did—these kids, the foundation, my work.

I opened the car door and headed to the sliding doors of the entrance. The office would wait. I didn't have any Abi-related tasks until a lunch on Wednesday. My number two had stepped up and exceeded my expectations, and for the first time in months, I was confident that the foundation could survive without me for a couple of hours.

"Hey, Maggie," I called as one of the nurses passed me in the corridor.

"Good to see you, Truly. Theo's been asking after you."

"I'll make him my first stop." I was going to go straight to the activities center, but the thought of Theo had me headed right to the ward.

I squeezed the sanitizing gel from its holder at the entrance at the exact moment my phone began to buzz from the depths of my bag. I balanced the gel in one hand while fishing for my phone with the other. Finally, I found it.

Noah. What could he want? "Hey," I answered, tucking the handset under my chin and rubbing the sanitizer between my hands.

"How are you this morning?"

Did he feel obligated to check up on me and my feelings? "Fine. Just about to go into the center," I said.

"Right," he said. "That's actually what I'm calling about. I was wondering if you'd mind if I connected with the medical head there. I've been looking into the epidural stimulation thing Abigail mentioned, and I wanted to ask them some questions about their current solutions and what's on their horizon."

So, he hadn't been calling to check on me at all. He was all business. Which was good, obviously, because I didn't need my hand held. "Why would I mind? I can introduce you if you'd like."

"That would be great." His grin echoed down the phone. "If you're there already, I could come now."

I sighed. "If you can be here soon, sure." I'd come for a little space, a little distance, and to refocus after last night. But Noah sounded like he always did when he was talking about business—passionate, focused, and determined. And that was nothing I could say no to.

"I'll be there in twenty minutes."

I stopped by Dr. Edwards' secretary, arranged a meeting for Noah, then headed back to the ward.

Time for me to see Theo.

"Hey, Douglas," I greeted the boy in the bed next to Theo. "How's it going?" He'd been here since before Theo. His operation had gone well, and I'd heard from the head physio that he was doing better than expected. Apparently as long as he did the rehab, he was on his way to walking normally again.

He shrugged.

"I hear you stood on your own a few weeks ago."

"You have spies in here or something? I've not seen you in the ward or in the activities center for . . ."

It had been weeks, but I hadn't expected the kids to notice. "Of course I have spies." I glanced around the room. "Everywhere, so be warned."

He grinned. "I knew we were being watched."

"It's only me. I wouldn't let anyone else." I plonked myself in a chair between the beds. "Where's Theo?" I asked.

"They've just taken him to watch the kung fu. I think it cheers him up to think that will be him one day."

"And you too," I said.

He shrugged.

"Hey, what's with the attitude?"

"It's just taking such a long time."

I couldn't imagine what it was like to be his age and have spent such a huge proportion of my time unable to simply be a kid. "I have a friend—he's coming here, any minute—and he was just like you. In fact, way worse. Was told he'd never walk again. You know what he likes to do for fun now?"

Douglas's mouth twitched. "What?"

"He *skydives*, that's what."

"What, you can do that if you can't walk?"

"He can walk, run, jump out of planes—everything. He proved them all wrong. You'd never know he was ever in an accident."

"How long did it take him?"

I glanced up to see Noah standing at the entrance of the ward, scanning the beds. I reached up, trying to catch his attention. "You can ask him yourself. He just arrived."

"This guy?" Douglas asked. "No way. He doesn't even walk with a limp," he said as we both watched Noah stroll toward us, spinning his car keys on his index finger.

"Swear to God." It had only been hours since I'd seen him, but my heart thudded against my ribcage as if it had been years. He grinned at me as if we were the only two people in the room, as if we shared a secret that we'd tell no one. Maybe we did.

TWENTY-TWO

Noah

My mouth went dry, and if I didn't know myself better, I'd say I fucking blushed at the sight of Truly. That warm smile of hers undid me. The way it had been last night between us had been nothing short of phenomenal, and this morning any doubts I had about crossing that line with her had completely disappeared. She knew me better than anyone and had a body that was made for me.

"Hey, Noah," Truly said. "This is my friend Douglas. Douglas, this is Noah. Skydiver, pilot, bungee jumper. You name the extreme sport, he's done it."

"Pilot?" Douglas asked, pulling my attention away from Truly. She'd worn her hair loose, and I wanted to bury my face in it and breathe in the scent of coconut.

"No, not yet. I'm having lessons."

"Douglas and I were just talking about you. He's frustrated because of how long it's taking him to recover. But the doctors and physios are telling me he's doing really well and as long as he keeps up with the rehab, he'll be walking in no time."

I nodded, not knowing quite how to respond. The kid seemed to be in such a similar situation to me. "Right."

Truly was one of the few people I'd talked about my accident with. It wasn't that I had anything to hide. I didn't talk about it because I'd moved on. I'd been able to lead a very different life than expected, so why waste time talking about something that could have been so much worse. With Truly, we'd talked about everything and it had just come up one evening when she'd asked about a scar on my arm. The few people I'd told up until that point had felt bad for me— I'd seen it in their eyes. Truly just listened with rapt interest; there was no pity in her eyes. She'd wanted to know the details, how I'd felt, if it had changed me psychologically. It was the first time I'd ever told anyone who wasn't around at the time, and I hadn't regretted it. She'd been so matter-of-fact about it.

"Did they really say you'd never walk again and then you ended up like—just being normal?" Douglas asked.

I paused, never having spoken to anyone in the position Douglas was in and wondering how to approach it. I wanted to provide hope to this kid but at the same time, my situation wasn't everyone's. A lot of people had left this unit in wheelchairs they'd be in forever. But I could give him the facts of my situation, couldn't I?

"Yup," I said. "Told me I'd be in a wheelchair the rest of my life."

"Did you just have crap doctors?"

"Hey, D. I'll get banned from this place if they hear you talking like that with me," Truly said.

Douglas groaned. "Crappy isn't that bad a word."

Truly fixed him with an adorable glare and I wanted to kiss her. "Would your mum agree?" she asked.

Douglas rolled his eyes. "Okay, did you have doctors who didn't know what they were talking about?"

I tapped my finger against the metal footboard that was just the same as the one I'd had on my bed. I'd been in the same position as this kid. Feeling shitty and hopeless. Wondering if I'd ever get to play football or if I'd have any friends when I finally got out of hospital. He deserved to hear a success story. "I think my doctors were pretty clever —they just didn't know my superpower."

"Riiight," Douglas said. "I'm fifteen. Not five. I don't believe in Father Christmas either."

"Whatever. Doesn't bother me if you don't believe it. Fact is I *wanted* to get better. More than anything. And that will is the most important thing you have."

Douglas folded his arms and scowled. Perhaps I shouldn't have been so challenging, but I knew from experience that he'd have to win the mental game if he was going to win the physical one. "I want to get better," he said, his voice softer than the expression on his face, almost as if he was afraid to believe it.

"Maybe," I said, shrugging.

"You think I want to sit around in bed all day with a bunch of babies?"

"I don't know, Douglas. I can't tell what goes on inside your brain. I do know that there's a difference between wanting to walk again and being determined that you *will* walk again."

Douglas didn't say anything. I wasn't sure if he felt chastised or if he just wanted me to say more without him asking.

"Truly," another kid's enthusiastic call echoed out

across the room. She stood and held out her arms, mirroring the kid being pushed toward us in a wheelchair. "Did you come to visit me?"

She reached down to hug him. "Theo! Of course. And guess what I brought?"

She dipped into her bag and pulled out a book. "*Fantastic Mr. Fox.*"

Theo made a fist and pulled back his arm at the fact Truly'd brought the book. She giggled at his enthusiasm.

Jesus, this woman was a fucking angel. She knew these kids. They loved her. She didn't have to be here, spending time with them, brightening their day. It was more evidence that she underestimated herself. She thought she was all back office and numbers when it came to the foundation. That she wasn't good with people. She was so wrong.

"Douglas, did you hear? Truly's going to read us *Fantastic Mr. Fox.*"

I caught Truly's eye. She winked at me and a rush of warmth crashed over me. This woman would be my downfall.

"I'm too old for that book," Douglas said.

"Hey, I'm not too old for that book," I said. "It's one of my favorites."

"It's the best," Theo said, his voice straining as his nurse helped him into bed.

Douglas shrugged. "You're staying?" He glanced at me.

"I have a meeting with one of the doctors, but I'll come back afterward." I wanted Douglas to know he could walk, and if I could help guide him into that way of thinking, wasn't it my responsibility to do that? "Is that okay?" I asked Truly.

She nodded, beaming up at me. "Sure. Dr. Edwards is

expecting you . . ." She glanced at her phone. "Right about now. I'll be here for an hour or so."

"You really should stay the rest of the day," Theo said. "At least until dinnertime because you haven't been for sooo long."

"I won't stay away so long next time." She ruffled the top of his hair. This boy needed to lead negotiations at the UN. He had a bright future ahead of him.

She glanced up to find me watching her. I just couldn't not. She was so fucking beautiful. So fucking good.

TWENTY-THREE

Noah

"Are you around later?" I asked Truly over the whoosh of the sliding doors as we left the center. Her rules hadn't said anything about how often we'd see each other. But after today I wanted to hang out, hear more about her time at the center. How she'd been with Douglas and the way Theo clearly adored her had me wondering if there was more I didn't know about her. Her eyes had lit up around those kids, and she'd looked positively giddy about reading Roald Dahl to a five-year-old. She was adorable. And even though I'd come to the center to see the clinical head, what I'd really wanted to do was stay and listen to Truly read.

I didn't want to miss out.

On her.

"I've had a pretty late start this morning, so I think I'll work late." She fumbled in her bag, looking for something.

I nodded. Sounded like a brush-off, which was fair enough. Two nights in a row didn't really scream casual, and I could hardly suggest that we didn't have to fuck, we could just eat and go to bed. That was what couples did.

And we weren't a couple. She'd been clear about that.

Although we were friends.

I wasn't sure where the line was.

"Tomorrow night would work," she said, and my heart lifted in my chest. She growled as she pulled her car keys from her bag. "No, I've said I'll go and see Abigail tomorrow. Give her a rundown of what's happening at the foundation. Obviously, I only tell her the fun stuff. Otherwise she worries. Maybe after?"

"Sounds good." She didn't need to know that I might just drop around for a beer at Rob and Abigail's before as well.

"How was your meeting?" she asked, scanning the car park as if she'd forgotten where she'd parked.

"Interesting." I pointed out her car and she grinned.

"Are you thinking of founding some kind of healthcare business?"

"Maybe. I haven't quite figured it out yet. There are new treatments available that the center doesn't have because of funding and then the ones that aren't available yet but will be soon—more people should have access to this stuff. I need to figure out if I can make that happen."

"Not even all your money can solve the problem," she said. "You can't give everyone the ability to walk, Noah."

I chuckled. "Right? I thought I was rich but this . . ." We reached her car and I paused.

"Being rich is about more than having money. The fact that you're interested and . . . It's nice. That's all." She stared at her feet.

"Back at you," I said, enjoying the blush my compliment elicited.

"It's my job."

We both knew that wasn't the whole truth. Truly had said herself that she liked to be excellent at what she did, so no job would ever be *just* a job for her. And I could imagine that this kind of work was as heartbreaking as it was rewarding. No amount of money would ever be enough.

She lifted her eyebrows. "So, I'll see you tomorrow night?"

I nodded. I wanted to kiss her, and not just on the cheek to say goodbye. I wanted to be closer to her. I wanted to take her face in my hands, and press my lips, my tongue, my body to hers.

I wanted to communicate without words.

She turned and pulled open her car door.

"See you tomorrow," I said, then stood and watched her pull away instead of moving along to my car.

This wasn't me. I wasn't the guy who lusted after some girl and sat back while she dictated what kind of relationship we were going to have. I was the one who set the boundaries. I said when we were done. I wasn't sure if it was the fact I could still feel her smooth skin under my fingers, or that I could still remember the way my body tightened as I came inside her that made her different.

Maybe it was the way that she looked sexiest in a worn t-shirt despite looking incredible in a ball gown.

Or was it the way I'd found her diving into *Fantastic Mr. Fox* when I'd expected her to be sweating over spreadsheets and pouring over PowerPoint presentations.

I'd abide by her rules for now, but I wasn't sure how long they'd last.

TWENTY-FOUR

Truly

"B-r-u-n-c-h," Noah spelled out as he sat on the edge of the bed and put on his socks, which were always the first thing to come off and the first thing to go on.

And he thought I was a geek?

I watched him in the reflection of my dressing table mirror as I smoothed moisturizer over my neck. "Thanks. Now I know how to spell brunch, I just don't know why."

"So, we don't starve. It's not like you have any food in this place. Were you planning on being somewhere?"

Instead of answering, I focused on making a perfect circle of tinted moisturizer in the palm of my hand. "Maybe," I said. He shouldn't even be here, staying the night should have gone down as one of the things we agreed not to do. But last night, my body had been so wrung out that every muscle had melted into the mattress—I hadn't had the energy to kick him out, and apparently he hadn't had the inclination to move.

He caught my eye in the mirror. "If you have plans

then . . . do whatever, I guess. But if you don't, let's have brunch."

"You want to ask Rob?" I asked. If Rob was there it was just a group of friends having a meal. If it was just Noah and me that was . . . different, wasn't it? I wanted to keep our relationship simple, not pretend to myself that it could be something else.

"Nope," he said, pulling on his jeans. "I want to have brunch with you, and I don't want to listen to plans for when the baby's born or how Arsenal are going to do this season. I just want to hang out. Take the piss out of the way you order. Relax together."

His bronzed torso stretched wide as he slid his arms into a blue t-shirt that slowly covered the line of blond hair that created a trail down to my favorite part of him. I definitely should have sent him home last night.

"So basically, you want me to entertain you." I pulled my mascara wand out of its case with a pop as he held my gaze in the mirror.

"You can see it like that," he said, stalking toward me. "Or you can see it as hanging out with a friend and having fun."

Before Noah had gone to New York, we would have gone to brunch without me second-guessing it. But at that time neither of us had seen the other naked. Could hanging out be a part of a casual sexual relationship? I was pretty sure spending time with a non-boyfriend who was the best sex that you'd ever had, and who was still the only man who could turn your legs to jelly with a single glance wasn't a healthy idea. But if he was just a friend?

All these lines around me were becoming blurred. The only thing that was clear was that I *wanted* to hang out with him. When he teased me, there was always an undertone of affection in the way he did it. And when I did it back, he seemed to revel in it. He made me laugh, and I enjoyed the way I could elicit a chuckle from him. So maybe one brunch would be okay.

"Okay, brunch—but I have two conditions."

His gaze flitted through the room.

"What are you looking for?"

"Paperwork. I'll have to sign something, right? It is brunch, after all. And we might have to refer to said conditions during the course of the next couple of hours."

"You're an arse."

He dipped his head to the curve between my neck and my shoulder and placed a kiss. "Maybe. Tell me your two conditions," he mumbled against my skin.

"Well, first, you have to make a donation to the center. We're a little off our target for this month."

He flopped back onto my bed. "You want me to pay you to hang out with me?"

"I don't see you asking anyone else to brunch. And you want free rein to make fun of me."

"And number two?"

"You'll have to tell me what to wear."

He raked his fingers through his hair. "I'm not bothered by what you wear."

"But you know how clueless I am about these things, and how little I care."

He headed into my wardrobe. "You have a *Stranger Things* t-shirt. That's so . . ."

"Geeky, I know."

He poked his head around the door. "I was going to say cool. It's a great show."

"*Such* a great show."

"So wear this and some jeans."

"Noah! I can't go out in that. That's stuff I wear at home. You see? This is what I mean. I have the stuff I hang around the house in, and stuff I go to work in. But there's nothing in between."

"Why wouldn't you go out in a t-shirt and jeans? You look phenomenal in jeans. That arse was made for tight denim."

"Pervert."

"And a cool t-shirt gives me a reason to stare at your chest, so from my perspective it's a winning outfit."

I growled at him. "You're not being very helpful."

Despite my semi-protestation, I pulled on the clothes he'd picked out and we headed to brunch.

"You let your driver have the weekends off after you've worked him twenty-four hours a day during the week?" I asked as I climbed into the passenger seat of his black Range Rover. "Very generous."

"Is me having a driver weird to you?" he asked, slamming the door shut and pressing the ignition.

"What do you mean, weird?"

"Do you see me differently? You know . . . because of the money."

I shrugged. "It's not like you're wearing thick gold chains and refusing to drink anything but Cristal."

He winced as he concentrated on the road. "That tequila I bought was a little showy."

Showy? Who had he been showing off for? The bar staff? Me? "It tasted good, but I'm not the best judge. It could have been a tenner a bottle for all I know. Your suits are a little nicer, and I haven't seen your new place, but you seem the same." As I tried to reassure him, it occurred to me that he *was exactly* the same guy. The guy who seemed to go through women like they were disposable adjuncts to his life. The one I'd had a crush on so deep I was clambering for ways to stop it developing again. Why was I on my way to brunch with him after a night of a thousand orgasms? I'd told myself casual sex was the way I'd inoculate myself against him, get over him. I had a feeling I'd been kidding myself. He hadn't changed and neither had I. So why were we here? It was like I was inviting trouble.

"No, you haven't," he said. "We should change that. What are you doing tonight?"

"Change what?"

"The fact that you've never seen my place. I always come to yours. So, come over. Tonight."

He wanted to hang out again tonight? I should be flattered, but I knew I needed to push those feelings away. I couldn't trick myself into thinking this was developing into something more than it was. It wasn't as if Noah was going to wake up one day and decide I was the woman he'd been waiting for.

"I think brunch is enough for one day."

He chuckled as he pulled into a parking space. "I'll convince you by the time you've ordered." Noah had never lacked confidence. And why would he? He'd probably never had a woman knock him back. I'd only said no at the wedding because I could spot danger a mile away.

"This okay?" he asked as I glanced up at the building we were about to enter.

"Sure," I said. I freaking knew I shouldn't have worn this t-shirt. London wasn't the sort of city that everyone had to dress up in, but if we were going to a fancy five-star hotel, I could have at least managed a blouse or something.

"You're gorgeous. Stop stressing." He grabbed my hand and pulled me inside. Before I knew it, I was sitting at a linen-covered table, three wine glasses and seventeen sets of cutlery presented in front of me.

"I thought brunch was meant to be casual," I hissed at him as our impossibly beautiful waitress gave us oversized menus.

"There's an option for unlimited champagne. How formal can it be? Anyway, the food's good and so is the view."

Through the huge windows, the Thames stretched out, a silvery pond between the buildings, and the millennium wheel sat stark against the bright blue sky. "Do you miss New York?" I asked. I wanted to know more about what had happened there. Had brunch become part of his routine while he was over there? How many women had he sat across from on a Sunday morning after ravaging their bodies the night before?

"Urm . . ." He glanced down at the menu and then set it down. "No. It was time to move on. I did what I set out to do and I was ready to leave."

No, Noah hadn't changed at all. He'd always liked a challenge. A project. An end date. It seemed to be the same in his relationships. "And you're happy to be back in London?"

He stretched out his legs, his denim sliding against mine. "London is home. But it's an adjustment, especially as I don't know exactly what's next."

"Oh, how did your meeting go at the center? Do you think you'll end up doing something charitable?"

He grinned, his smile taking over his face. "You know, I'm not sure, but I think I want to combine business with philanthropy. As you know, my money won't make a difference on its own. Healthcare requires billions."

"And all you've got is a measly fifteen million."

"Noah?"

I snapped my head around as a blonde woman approached our table.

"I thought it was you," she said, her American accent as strong as the expensive perfume she wore. She, at least, was dressed appropriately for this place. Her skin-tight black trousers showed off a model-thin figure. Her shoes, although flat, were Chanel, as was the handbag slung across her body.

Noah stood and greeted her with a hug. "Ginny, good to see you. What are you doing in London?"

"If I said I was following you, would you take out a restraining order?" She laughed a little too loudly. "Just kidding."

I glanced between them. If I didn't know him as well as I did, I wouldn't have noticed the unease that settled in his eyebrows, jaw, and forehead.

"I'm just over for work and having brunch with a few girlfriends. I'd invite you over, but no doubt you'd end up taking one of them home. Oh! Actually, Lydia is here and you know her very well." She paused and turned to me. "Sorry."

Was she trying to upset me? Get me jealous? Apparently, in this restaurant alone, there were three of us who Noah had seduced, seen naked, and shared orgasms with.

My stomach churned, and all I could focus on was the fact there was a list of women Noah had been with, and at some point he'd be done with me and discard me too. I didn't want to be a name on a list. Someone Noah used to bang.

I should never have come here today. It wasn't the kind of thing that kept things casual between us. I only had myself to blame.

"This is my good friend, Truly," Noah said.

I smiled from where I sat. "Hi."

"Well, it's great to see you, Noah. I won't interrupt. Ciao, for now." She gave me a little wave and twirled off toward a table of six women, all of them ten times more beautiful and glamorous than me.

I stared at my menu as Noah took his seat.

"I met her in New York," he said.

"I gathered," I replied, not looking up. I'd lost my appetite.

"Have you decided what you're going to order?" he asked.

I placed my menu down. "Yeah, nothing. I'm not hungry. I'm going to go."

"Hey, you promised me brunch."

"Yeah, sorry, I forgot I have to catch up on something in the office. Stay and have lunch with Ginny." I nodded toward the table where she sat. "I need to go." I grabbed my bag from the back of my chair and stood.

"What? I don't want to have brunch with Ginny or Rob or whoever else you suggest. I want brunch with you."

Oh God, what he was saying was exactly what I wanted and everything that was bad for me. "I'm sorry. I can't."

"What's the matter?" He followed me as I headed to the exit.

"Nothing. I just remembered I had something to do."

"Did Ginny upset you?"

I shook my head as we stepped out onto the street. "No, of course not. Why would she have?" I reached out to hail a cab.

"For God's sake, I'll take you to the office if that's where you're headed. But please stay. Tell me what's wrong."

"Nothing." In an effort to be convincing, I forced a smile. "I'll see you around," I said as a cab pulled up.

I shouldn't have been upset. We all had a past, and Noah had never lied about his. I knew who he was and what he was capable of when it came to relationships and how he saw me. I was angry at myself that I was so uneasy at being in a restaurant with at least two of Noah's ex-lovers. This was meant to be casual, but what I felt for Noah wasn't, despite me trying to convince myself otherwise. I'd been an idiot, and I needed some space away from him so I could organize my thoughts, breathe, decide what I was going to do. Already I was in too deep. And if I wasn't careful, I was going to drown.

TWENTY-FIVE

Noah

I pulled a beer out of the fridge and took a seat next to Rob on the sofa with a sigh. I'd hoped Truly would be at Abigail and Rob's when I dropped around.

I still wasn't sure what had happened to make her ditch me at brunch. I'd tried to call her, but she hadn't picked up. And the few messages that I'd sent had been met with a combination of silence and one-word responses.

"What does it mean if a woman goes cold on you?" I asked aloud, then wished I hadn't as Rob shifted, a smile curling his lips.

"Who's gone cold on you? I didn't think that was possible."

"I'm talking hypothetically."

"Yeah, of course you are. Tell Uncle Rob all your worries." He shuffled in his seat to face me.

"I don't have worries. Not with women. Not with anything."

Rob took a sip of his beer, content with my response. He

knew it was true. Except while it wasn't exactly a worry, I struggled to understand what had happened with Truly.

"So if I take a woman to brunch. We're there, everything's perfectly fine until . . . another woman approaches."

"Did she throw a drink at you?"

"Who? The woman I was at brunch with?"

"No, the one who approached your table. She was an ex, I assume."

"Yeah. We weren't serious. Only lasted a couple of weeks. But no, no drinks were thrown. We exchanged a few words, it was all perfectly amicable and then all of a sudden T—the woman I was with decided she had to leave."

"Did she say why?"

"She'd forgotten she had to do something at work, which was clearly bullshit because it was Sunday, right?"

Rob nodded. "Yeah. Unless . . . did she get a phone call or message or anything?"

"Nope. Everything was fine. One minute we were flirting. The next minute—boom she'd left."

"Was this other woman who approached you flirting? Were you flirting back?"

I grimaced. "No!" The idea that I would flirt with Ginny was crazy. I'd never embarrass Truly like that.

"Maybe she thought you were."

Truly was no idiot. Could she have been jealous of some woman who meant nothing to me? I didn't pretend to be celibate, and I'd told her that Ginny was from New York. Even if I was dating Ginny, it had been Truly's idea not to have monogamy as part of our arrangement anyway. Jealousy didn't make sense. Ginny was firmly in my past. I was at brunch with Truly because she was who I wanted to be with. There was no one else I'd rather spend time with.

Shit. I'd not thought about it like that before. Truly was

the person I wanted to spend my Sunday with. Wanted to spend every night with. I wasn't sure I'd ever felt like that about any woman. But then I'd never fucked a friend before.

A knock at the door and my heart began to pound. It had to be Truly. Who else called around on a Monday night? I could ask her face-to-face if it was her, clear this up between us.

"That's Lev," he said, getting up.

"Your brother?"

"Yeah. He's passing through on his way to . . ." He paused and narrowed his eyes. "No idea."

I'd met Levison a couple of times. Once at university when he'd come to visit, and another time at Rob and Abigail's wedding. My main impression was that he was a cocky little shit who acted as if he was Rob's older brother rather than five years younger.

"Hey," I said, getting up as he came into the room. He was taller than I remembered, dressed in an expensive suit which he filled out well—he'd been quite lanky back when I'd last seen him.

"Noah, I wasn't expecting to see you. Congratulations on the float of Concordance Tech." We shook hands, his grip firmer than I expected, an expensive watch on his wrist. "You bumming around for a bit?"

"Working on a few things. What are you up to?"

"Private equity. Set up my own fund."

That was impressive at any age, but before thirty? "Going well?"

"Harder you work, the bigger the reward, right?" he said. "We should talk. Have a meeting. See what we can do together."

Rob pushed a beer into his brother's hand. "Enough of

e talk, Lev. I want to relax, not watch a pissing
"

ev was no competition as far as I was concerned.

"We were talking about women," Rob said as Lev
shrugged off his jacket.

"Well, if we're not going to talk about work—and there's
no way Arsenal are going to be the topic of conversation—
then women it is. Speaking of, where's that delicious Truly?
I've not seen her in over a year."

The hairs on the back of my neck rose. Of course, he'd
know Truly. I guessed they were family and saw each other
regularly. When I'd approached her at the wedding recep-
tion, she'd been talking to Lev, who'd clearly been hitting on
her despite the fact he'd been seventeen.

"Is she seeing anyone?" Lev asked.

I not only wanted to confirm that she was, I wanted to
shout that I was the lucky bastard who got to see her naked.
But as Truly had clearly set out in neat, black handwriting
on crisp, white paper—rule one of our relationship was that
Rob and Abigail didn't find out about us.

"You know what she's like," said Rob. "Married to
the job."

"Like her sister," Lev said and despite my irritation, I
couldn't help but chuckle at him baiting Rob.

"Abigail isn't married to work. She's not been in the
office for weeks."

"Whatever. We all know what her priorities are. I'm not
sure you're even top five."

Rob went to protest but Lev held up his beer bottle.
"But, to be fair, you're still punching above your weight
with her, so good on you." Lev was the better looking of the
two brothers and clearly had no difficulty with women.
Truly's smile flashed in my head, and my pulse began to

throb in my neck. Was Lev going to make a play for Truly? He wasn't clever enough for her, wouldn't appreciate how beautiful she was. I bet he was the type of guy just to concentrate on what was on the outside. But as beautiful as Truly was, her personality and character were what made her special. He'd never get it.

"You're a dick," Rob said. "I don't see you married to someone more beautiful."

"You're right," Lev said. "I'm not. You did well there." He grinned.

He could have dug the knife in deeper. I'd expected him to say something about not buying the cow while he was getting milk for free, but maybe he wasn't as much of a dickhead as I remembered. "I should go upstairs and say hello. I bought her this, actually." He pulled out a paperback from his jacket pocket and held up a copy of *Less than Zero* by Brett Easton Ellis.

"She'll love it," Rob said.

"I know Truly's the reader, but I thought this would suit Abigail. She could have been one of these kids." He slid it onto the coffee table.

Christ, that was nice. Thoughtful. Perhaps he wasn't the cocky little shit that I remembered. And he'd clearly made a bit of money since I'd last seen him. And he knew Truly was a reader. How well did he know her exactly?

There was another knock at the door, but this time I knew it was Truly. Somehow, I could just tell. I could feel her nearby.

Rob scowled, but got up to get the door.

I smelled coconut as soon as the door opened. Maybe the sound of her voice triggered some kind of Pavlovian response in me.

"Noah and Lev are here." Rob's faint voice tripped

down the corridor followed by the unmistakable sound of silence.

"Truly?" Lev jumped to his feet. "Is that you?"

She appeared at the doorway, taking a breath as if preparing for something. "Hey," she said with a grin I hoped she was having to work at.

Lev scooped her up in a hug, lifting her off her feet, and I wanted to peel him off her and shove him back onto the sofa while I took my time, lifted her hair, and pressed my lips to that curve between her neck and shoulder that felt so much like home.

But of course, I didn't. I sat, gripping my beer bottle, wondering how much pressure it would take before it shattered.

"God, you look more perfect every time I see you," Lev said, setting her down but keeping a hold of her hand. "Are you seeing anyone? Let me take you to dinner."

Jesus Christ, who was this guy? He didn't get to date Truly.

She answered with a grin. "You just get more charming every time I see you."

Truly's gaze slid to mine, tentative and unsure as though she didn't want to look directly at me. "Hi," she said, her voice breathy and her gaze hitting me in my solar plexus. Whatever had got under her skin on Sunday was still clearly there. She took a tentative half step toward me and I closed the gap, sliding my hand around to her lower back and placing a peck on her cheek.

As she tilted her head to accept my kiss, her fingers scraped against my abs as if touching me was her right. It inflated my heart so much it knocked against my ribs.

Yeah, Lev. She's mine. Claimed.

I wanted to stay there with her, holding her close and

out of the reach of anyone else, but she extracted herself and headed to the fridge.

"Anyone want a beer?" She pulled out a bottle of wine and a glass from the cabinet.

The three of us sat, Lev and I watching Truly as if she might disappear if we took our eyes off her. As she knocked the fridge door shut with her hip, Lev sprung to his feet. "Sit here," he said.

"Actually, I'm going to see Abigail and leave you boys to whatever it was you were talking about before I arrived."

"Noah was asking for advice about women," Rob said, clearly proud that anyone would ask his advice about anything.

Truly almost choked as she took a sip of her wine.

Yeah, I wanted to say. *I was asking about you.*

"And you went to Rob?" Lev said. "Maybe choose your guru better next time."

Truly smiled and slipped out of the room as I imagined she'd done plenty of times before without my noticing. Except this time, Lev and I watched her leave.

Should I follow her? Catch her before she got to Abigail? I wanted to talk, tell her how much I liked being with her. I'd wanted her to come back to my place. To see that side of me, to see how she looked in my bed. I'd hoped she'd stay and we'd cook and hang out, and I'd get the chance to give her a foot rub that might turn into something else.

I groaned. What was wrong with me?

"You okay?" Rob asked. "You're acting really weird."

"Yeah, I just finished my beer," I said getting to my feet. Now that I was here, there was no way I was leaving before Truly.

Not while Lev was still here, drool dripping from his chin.

But much as I hated to admit it, Lev was just one man in a city of millions. I couldn't stand between Truly and all of them. I'd not heard any more about her dating, and I'd assumed I was the only man in her life. Maybe I was wrong.

TWENTY-SIX

Truly

I caught my reflection in the hallway mirror and relaxed my face, trying to become expressionless before Abigail saw me and pounced on my dark mood. I padded up the stairs toward my sister's bedroom. I wanted comfort, reassurance of some kind. I missed my mother most when dark clouds gathered above me. Instead of comfort and understanding, now she only elicited worry and sadness as she slipped further and further away from us into the arms of dementia. Abigail was my only family now.

If I'd known Noah would be here, I wouldn't have come. Seeing him was always my weakness, and I needed some space and distance. Casual meant uncomplicated sex and him leaving afterward. It didn't mean seeing each other every night or texts throughout the day. And it definitely didn't mean brunch. If I'd just followed my instincts and stayed home on Sunday, I wouldn't have these shadows of disappointment hovering over me.

"Truly," Abigail said as I put my head around the door.

"Time for a hug?" I asked.

She coaxed me forward with a flap of her hand. "Always. What's up?"

I crawled onto the bed next to her. "I hope you're washing these sheets regularly. I never see you out of them."

"Every other day. I'm driving Rob bananas making him change the bedding so much."

I tucked into the crook of her arm. "I'm sure he's only pretending you drive him nuts. He loves looking after you."

"Oh, there's no doubt he adores me. Doesn't mean I don't irritate the shit out of him."

I giggled. "You might irritate each other, but you both like being married, right?"

My head rose and fell as she took in a deep breath. "Yes of course. We were so young when we met, but I still really fancy him. Part of it is that I know he'd do anything for me. That loyalty is . . ."

"Unusual," I finished for her.

"Yeah. He puts me first, you know?"

"Because you're so special."

She tightened her grip. "Anyway, why are you asking questions about me and Rob? What's up with you? You seem a bit down."

"I don't know. I've been thinking about what you were saying about my life being one-dimensional. I'm usually so focused on the foundation because what we do is important, but maybe you're right. Maybe there's more out there for me." What I left out was that during the few weeks Noah and I had been sleeping together, something had changed in me. Given me permission to want more. Instead of being focused on today and what was right in front of me, I'd kinda looked up and around and wondered what was down the road. I knew it could never be Noah, but for the first time in a long time, I wanted something more than the foundation. "But I'm not sure how to do that," I continued. "How to make room."

"You make room for me and Rob, so you know how to do it when you want to."

Somehow I'd found time to spend with Noah, even if it was around the edges of the rest of my life. "That's true. It's easy not to think about it though because . . . it's scary, you know?"

"What is?"

"Spending your time on things, not knowing whether or not it's worth it. Or if you'll be good at something." It wasn't just speeches that were out of my comfort zone. Relationships were too.

"Sometimes you can just have fun, you know. You don't have to make every minute count."

"I'm not sure I'm good at doing things just for fun."

"Not even sex?"

"Does that count? It's a really good calorie burner—and exercise is important!"

Abigail laughed and then whispered, "Not the way I'm doing it at the moment. I just lie here like a sack of potatoes."

"Poor Rob."

"What I'm saying is that not everything in life has to have meaning—it's not like that. Nobody lives like that. Most of the time Rob and I are dealing with domestic, boring stuff."

"But you're each other's family. It's different."

"But how do you find someone who might become your family without trying different people out and just doing the fun bits together?"

"So, you're saying you're in favor of what? Drugs?

Casual sex?" I was pretty sure she wouldn't approve of me having casual sex with Noah.

Abigail giggled. "Yes, casual sex is fun. I'm totally on board with that. But I'm also in favor of you dating someone who might become part of our family one day. Someone who will worship you like Rob does me. Someone who thinks you're the most beautiful woman he's ever seen and can't wait to get home to see you every night. But you have to meet men to see if any of them measure up."

I grumbled into the pillow. The problem was I wanted someone who wasn't Noah to be Noah. Someone who could make me feel the way he did. Wanted. Desired. Despite being a geek and not knowing what to wear or how to act in front of strangers. Noah seemed to like me despite all that stuff. Maybe even because of it.

"Lev just asked me to dinner. Again."

Abigail groaned. "He's relentless."

"You don't approve?"

"For fun? Maybe, but the guy is a player. And I swear most men below thirty have an emotional age of fifteen. Anyway, are you even attracted to him?"

I thought about it. He was attractive, there was no doubt about it. The last few years he'd discovered the gym and his success had brought confidence. And underneath it, he seemed to be a nice guy. "He brought you a gift. A book."

"He's a sweetie. Underneath. But is there chemistry?"

The only man I'd ever felt real chemistry with was Noah. "No, not really."

"If you'd just met him, I'd say you'd need to go out a few times to see if any developed. I'm not one of these who believes it has to happen the second you meet, but you've known Lev a long time."

"Yeah. I agree. I don't want to date Lev."

"And Noah?"

I tried not to tense in her arms. "What about him?"

"Has anything happened since the kiss? Is it just a coincidence that we're having this conversation now, despite me nagging you for years about finding new interests and a boyfriend?"

I sighed and pulled away, then reached for my wine. "There'll never be anything between Noah and me. I know he's no good for me. I totally get it." I turned the glass in my hand. "But I wonder if I'll ever find anyone who is . . ."

Noah was always going to be a player, and he never hid his past. Brunch had only been upsetting because I'd been pretending to myself that I could handle casual when what I wanted us to be was special. "I think I've been spending too much time with him." I glanced up before correcting myself. "You know, because of all of his help."

"He's quite flirty with you."

I shrugged. "Maybe a little. But that's his nature, right?" I just wanted to come out and confess everything—tell Abigail about the way I dissolved under his touch, how I liked that he listened to what I said, even when I got passionate about the craziest of things. And although I didn't want to hear my sister's judgment and scorn, what I was really afraid of was if she knew that we were having sex, she'd tell me I shouldn't see him anymore. My head understood that already. It was just my heart pulling me to him. Even now. Even after brunch and me realizing how I was in deeper than I'd ever wanted to go.

"Maybe what you need to do is water down the effect of having him around. If he's the only guy you spend time with, that could be dangerous, but if you were to get out and date more, perhaps your feelings for Noah would get weaker."

That made sense, didn't it? Because I wanted my feelings for Noah to lessen. That was why I'd agreed to casual sex. I wanted to overwrite what he'd meant to me with something less important. I wanted to be over him. "I went on that date with that guy you set me up with, but he wasn't for me, and it's not like I meet many new people at the office. What do I do, sign up with an agency? Or create a profile on Grindr?"

Abigail winced. "Well unless you have a pretty huge confession to make then I'm not sure Grindr is the right website, but online dating sounds like a good idea."

"Why don't I qualify for Grindr?"

"Urm, because you're not gay and looking for a hot hookup."

My cheeks burned in embarrassment. "Oh. You see? This is why I can't date. There's so much I just don't know. I'd make a complete fool of myself."

"You're completely adorable. You need a man who will fall in love with you because you don't understand what Grindr is, and one who'll appreciate the fact that you know how many light years we are away from Mars."

Now she was just being ridiculous. "On average, Mars is only one hundred and forty million miles away. It's not measured in light years."

"See? Adorable," Abigail said. "I can see you with some professor type. Always carrying around books. Patches on his jacket elbows. You'll have super-smart babies who you have to have by C-section because their heads will be so big."

"Jesus. The way your mind works is crazy. You act as if you're the dumb twin, but we both know that's not true. You just got a lot of other stuff I didn't."

"We're just different, Truly. And I love that you care

about Mars and Keynes and Faraday and whatever else. It's what makes you so special. We just need to find you someone who sees it, too."

Someone like Noah who wasn't Noah. Except I wasn't sure I was completely ready to give Noah up yet.

"So online dating?"

She nodded. "Grab my laptop and we'll take a look at what's out there."

Right now, as stupid as it was, I knew I couldn't say no to Noah. Despite knowing he was bad for me, despite being disappointed in myself for feeling too much. Dating someone else might provide me with the strength to turn him away at some point.

Online dating would be a good first defense, but I needed a double layer of protection from Noah. I also needed walls—more rules if I was going to continue seeing him. And although the best defense would be to put a stop to things between us, I wasn't ready. Yet.

TWENTY-SEVEN

Noah

I pressed my palms flat on the brickwork and tried to steady my breathing before I pressed the buzzer for Truly's flat.

She'd left Rob and Abigail's with a small wave in my direction, and before I'd had a chance, Lev had offered to show her out. I'd nearly busted the beer bottle I was holding as I'd listened to her giggle as she chatted with Lev at the door. He'd come back with a smug, satisfied look on his face. I'd given it twenty minutes before I'd made my excuses and left.

I had to see her. I wanted to know what was wrong—and I wanted her to tell me she wasn't going to go to dinner with Lev or anyone else.

I pressed the buzzer again and this time the answer was immediate. "Noah? What are you doing here?"

"Can I come up?"

She released the door. What was I going to say to her? I could hardly charge in and demand she not have dinner with anyone I didn't approve of.

"Hey," she said, waiting in her doorway as I stepped out of the lift. She had her hair piled on top of her head and her yoga pants on—the gray ones that made her arse look particularly great.

"Hey," I said, raking my hand through my hair.

"I saw you like half an hour ago." She frowned as I stalked toward her.

"I know. But I couldn't do this to you then." I snaked my arms around her.

She pushed against my biceps as if she were trying to hold me back. "Noah. What are you doing here?"

I released her a little, and she stumbled back, then turned and headed inside.

"What happened at brunch? You just ran off and things have been off and today—"

"Nothing. Would you like to sit down?"

"I want you to tell me why things have been weird between us." I wasn't going to accuse her of being jealous, I'd sound like a dickhead, but if she was, I wanted to reassure her.

I followed her through to the living room where her laptop lay open on the table, the screensaver on. She was always working. "You deserve the night off," I said, nodding at the computer.

She flipped down the lid and we both sat on her couch.

"I've not seen Lev in a while," I said.

She didn't respond.

"I guess you see him a lot," I continued.

She shrugged. "Here and there. I'm not sure he and Rob are that close."

"He has a thing for you," I said, wanting to see her reaction.

She tilted her head sideways as if I were being ridiculous. "He has a thing for women."

It was clearly more than that. I imagined Lev wasn't short of female company, but I could tell by the attention he paid her that he was definitely into Truly.

"You've never been tempted? Or succumbed?"

"Succumbed? He's not ice cream."

Was she being deliberately evasive? She was usually so honest about everything.

She went to speak, then stopped. My pulse throbbed in my neck. Did she have something to confess? "Go on," I said. "You were about to tell me something."

She shook her head. "I was going to ask a question."

"More deflection."

"Are you jealous?" she asked, her eyes sweeping over my face as if looking for clues.

"I don't get jealous. Just interested, I guess. Didn't think he was your type."

She raised her eyebrows and turned so she wasn't facing me on the sofa. "My type? What does that mean?"

Her voice sounded a little clipped. I pulled her closer and despite her resistance, I slid her toward me so her thighs brushed mine. "It wasn't an insult. He just seems a little . . . smooth. All about money. You know?"

She turned to me, raising an eyebrow. "This coming from the multimillionaire player who ran into two ex-girlfriends at brunch."

So, this was about brunch. Well, I wasn't about to let it drop. "So running in to Ginny did bother you."

"It did not. Why would it? We're just casual. And no, I've never *succumbed* to Lev."

I mentally high-fived myself. I hated the idea of him

being around her so much, of having some sort of claim to her. "And you're not going to dinner with him, are you?"

"Our arrangement . . ." She paused. "When I wrote out the rules, there was nothing that said anything about going to dinner with people. You're free to have lunch with—"

I cupped her face and rested my forehead against hers. "I don't want to have lunch with anyone."

I wanted her to return the sentiment but she just stayed silent. "You're here. Let's just . . ."

What? I thought to myself.

Talk? There was no one else I wanted to speak to.

Enjoy each other? There was no one else I'd have more fun with.

Fuck all night into the early morning? There was no one better. No one I wanted to take to bed more.

I stroked my thumb over her cheek and she began to pull away.

Spotting something out of the corner of my eye, I released her and stalked behind the sofa. She still had it. The turntable I'd bought her. I peered behind it. And the record. "Shit, Truly."

She looked away. "What?"

"You still have this?" Every memory I had of the accident came swooshing back at once. I pulled out the white sleeve from the cover and peered at the transparent, circular window. *The Unforgettable Fire.* The last time I'd heard this, I'd been here. With Truly. Tipping the black vinyl from the sleeve, I lifted the lid of the turntable and placed it on the metal spike with a satisfying squeak.

"Noah," Truly whispered. "Don't."

Ignoring her, I clicked and pressed until the record spun. I nudged the arm onto the first track. Crackles and hisses rang out, followed by tinny, rapid drumbeats.

"My dad loved U2."

"I remember," she replied.

I'd forgotten. As a kid, I'd listened to this album over and over in hospital. Played it nonstop for days on my headphones after I'd been told I'd never walk again.

At first it had covered my misery, wrapped around me like a warm blanket until it had morphed and changed and became the fire underneath me—a soundtrack to my motivation to prove everyone wrong, to have a different kind of life than the one I'd been told was my fate. I'd left it behind with the therapy. Until I'd found it in that secondhand store and bought it as well as a turntable and brought it back to Truly's.

We'd listened to it together silently, side by side.

Something had shifted that night. I'd wordlessly shared something with her that I'd buried deep down inside me. Fear. Sadness. A determination to fight for what I wanted.

She was the only person I'd ever shared this music with. And she was now entwined with all those bad memories, pulling them into the light. Instead of fear and sadness, all I felt now was hope and happiness.

She'd seen every part of me and she was still here.

She knew everything there was to know about me, and I couldn't think of anything better than that.

She knew my past, and I knew I wanted her to be part of my future. But was that as a lover or a friend?

The first track faded away into the next. She topped up our wine, and I pulled her closer. Our breathing synchronized and then the gritty, sexy pulse of the bass and the crash of the drums in "Bad" trickled through the speakers.

"I love this one," she whispered.

"Me too," I replied.

"I play it on a loop sometimes."

She still listened to this? Even all these years later? Did she think about me when she did? "You do?" I asked, gently crawling over her so she lay flat on the sofa. Was this record and our history as important to her as I was beginning to realize it was for me? It was just a record, but it was also far more than that. It was about something painful for me that she'd made better by sharing it with me. And now it felt as if our memories and our past were inextricably mixed together. Perhaps our future was too.

"When I don't want to feel alone," she replied, dusting my jawline with her fingertips.

"You're not alone," I whispered and buried my head in her neck, tasting my favorite part of her. I never wanted her to be anywhere I wasn't.

I settled between her legs as she brought her knees up to either side of my hips. We fit perfectly like this.

"Casual," she whispered as if half asleep, her hands sliding my shirt up my stomach.

"So beautiful," I said, unable to take my eyes off her as she undid the buttons of my jeans and wrapped her hand around the base of my cock. I closed my eyes in a long blink. All these thoughts and feelings, about her, the accident, what was next for me. Everything was colliding all at once and yet it all made sense when I was with Truly. My past, my future, my fears, my hopes—everything seemed to be culminating, and at the center was the woman who knew me best, looking back at me with her amber eyes and well-worn yoga pants.

She pressed her fingertips into the flesh just above my hips, and I kicked off my jeans, getting rid of any barrier between me and her touch. She got to touch me anywhere, and I wanted her touch everywhere.

She made everything better. She made *me* better.

Part of me seemed to belong to her. Did she know? Did she feel the same?

I pulled back and looked her in the eye, trying to communicate how much she meant to me but unable to find the words.

She unfurled a sexy, secret smile and I growled. I wanted to devour her.

I pulled at her top and she pushed away my hands. "This is new. And I like it." She lifted her t-shirt over her head and dropped it beside the sofa. I'd never seen the black lace bra underneath but it was perfect and showed off her smooth skin, tempting me with what it hid.

I yanked down one cup and took a nipple in my mouth as Truly threaded her hands into my hair. She arched against me, making my heart race and my cock throb. I wanted to feel all of her all at once. Slipping my hand underneath her, I unclasped her bra and pulled it off, her heavy, delicious breasts spilling out from under the lace.

Shit, this girl.

I filled my hands with her, rubbing my thumbs over her nipples, relishing the softness in my palms, enjoying her.

She wriggled, trying to free herself of her yoga pants and underwear, which were the only things that remained between us. It was too much. I was so desperate, so needy for her that I didn't want to waste time with all these clothes. We should just stay naked forever. The desire to have her soft flesh pressed against mine without interruption took over, and I pulled back and tore off the rest of my clothes. "You're so fucking beautiful I don't know if I should just stare at you or fuck you."

"I choose the second option."

"You wanna get fucked?" I crawled over her, my dick jerking over her stomach.

Her mouth parted and her tongue dipped out to wet her lips as she nodded.

So sexy.

I reached between her legs, checking for the slippery, wet skin, and gasping as my fingers pressed through her folds, and she moaned.

"What is it with you?" She shook her head. "I just . . ." She frowned as if she was confused. "It's like I lose all my self-discipline. Like my head turns to mush and all I see is you. I can't get enough."

I grinned. I liked the thought of being the man who made this cerebral, always thoughtful woman lose her mind.

Sex wasn't just sex with Truly. Maybe it was because we were friends. Because I knew the way her brain worked. Understanding her heightened everything. It was ridiculous but sex had never been a shared experience before. It had been about lust and getting off—mutual but separate. With Truly it was all so connected—I knew what she was thinking, what she liked, why on some days it took her longer to come. And I enjoyed working out all those little details. It was as if my vision was sharper when I was with her.

She fisted my cock, pulled her hand up and released me. It was her sign that she was impatient. She didn't want to waste time with my mouth on her. She wanted me to fuck her. To fill her up. To make her come.

And it would be my pleasure.

I pulled a condom from my wallet, and Truly sighed.

"Be quick," she said.

Her nipples pebbled and her skin flushed.

"Be careful or I might make you wait." I rolled on the condom. "I might take you right to the edge over and over and not let you come."

Her eyes widened in shock, and her breaths came a little shorter.

"Later, Truly." I was far too hard and far too ready to be able to follow through on my threat. "Just now, I'm going to give you exactly what you're desperate for." I pressed my tip against her hot sex, my jaw tightening as I tried to keep from shoving straight into her.

She pawed at me, pulling at my shoulders, needing more.

The feeling was mutual.

"Like this?" I inched my way deeper into her.

She nodded, grabbing at my hips.

I took her hands from me, clasping them in mine and pushing them over her head and thrusting into her.

She was tight and perfect and all mine.

"Oh God," she moaned around me and surrendered, as her thoughts focused on this moment rather than whatever she'd been doing today or had planned for tomorrow. The moment became about pleasure. About us. And there was nothing better.

The heat and the drag of her was so perfect that I couldn't imagine I'd ever want anything else. Not in thirty minutes, not tomorrow. Not ever. I'd always want to feel exactly like this.

She twisted underneath me and widened her legs, trying to get me deeper, closer. I glanced down at where we were joined.

The drumbeat coming from the record player, her moans, the sound of my flesh against hers, built and built and built until it all merged into one perfect moment.

I couldn't hold back. Not for a moment longer.

"Truly," I called out.

"Yes, yes, yes," she panted, and I covered my mouth

with hers, hot and wet and honest as she tensed underneath me. My release ran through my veins as we came together, our pulses connected and sharing the same beat as the music.

"Shit, Truly," I said when my mouth reconnected to my brain. It was as if I'd just come round after being knocked unconscious.

She pressed her fingers against the pulse in my neck. "That was . . ."

I was collapsed over her, but I wasn't sure if I could move. "It certainly was." I shifted off then scooped her up, my weak limbs somehow finding the strength.

I wasn't done, but I needed to lay her out and take my time with her.

I headed to the bedroom and put her down on the bed, but when I moved away to get some water, she clung to my arm. "You need to rehydrate."

"Don't be long." She scowled but loosened her grip.

I grinned and darted into the kitchen to collect glasses and a bottle of water. I liked that she didn't want me gone for even a few seconds. I understood it. There was some tie between us that I'd never felt with anyone before.

"You see? Five seconds. Ten max." I stopped in the doorway. Truly was gone. "Hey, where did you go?" I set the water on the bedside table.

She wandered back into the bedroom. "I had to pee." The girl was far less self-conscious naked than she was in a ball gown.

"Come here." I grabbed her ass and pulled her against me, pressing soft kisses down her neck and along her shoulder as my cock jerked between us. How was I ready for her again? She had some kind of override switch on my libido that I never knew existed.

"Your kisses," she said with a sigh.

I pulled back, waiting for her to finish her sentence.

She curled her fingers around my neck. "They're just perfect." She shook her head as if she'd just told me it was set to rain for the next ten days straight or that *Stranger Things* had been cancelled.

"You're perfect."

"Don't say that." She stood on tiptoes and pulled me closer, pressing her lips to mine, her tongue trailing against my lips.

I groaned and tipped us both onto the bed. I tangled my limbs with hers as I skirted my hands up and down her body, touching every inch, exploring every dip and curve.

As I slid my palms up her inner thigh, Truly shifted and reached for my cock. "Having you in my mouth gets me hot," she whispered, her heavy breath coating my cock. "Do you think that's weird?" she asked, then licked up the length of my dick.

I groaned, straining to keep my hips on the bed.

"I think it's a little odd that getting you hard gets me so wet," she said.

"Jesus, Truly." Her words were as much of a turn-on as her mouth—it was almost too much.

She rearranged herself so she straddled me, and I could see exactly what her filthy mouth was doing.

Her fist at my base, she circled my crown with her tongue then paused. "I think it's because it's so perfectly straight and thick. Like velvet and steel mixed together," she said as if she was trying to figure out the formula.

I was way past *why* and had raced forward to *I want your mouth on me*. I was done with analysis, and I just wanted to feel. To enjoy her wet, hot lips.

She swept her free hand up my chest then slowly began to take me deep, deep, deep.

Shit. I gripped the sheets and closed my eyes, fighting the urge to push up into her throat, wanting to feel her gag and watch her eyes water. She pulled back, the scrape of her teeth dampening down my climax.

"I love feeling you like this," she said, her head bobbing back down as she took me deep.

She continued to lick and suck, setting off sparks along my skin, heating my blood and driving me wild. I just couldn't get enough. But I wanted to see exactly how turned on she was, sucking me off like it was her job. I sat up, and she pulled back before I caught her and dragged her back to the mattress, capturing her legs in mine and sweeping my hand between them.

She was as wet as the fucking ocean, her clit swollen and hard. I grunted as I circled her nub with the pad of my thumb.

"You didn't believe me?" she whispered. "You must know what you do to me." Her eyebrows pinched together as I trailed wet fingers over her nipples, pushed her to her back, and sucked them clean.

She sighed, pulling her legs wide as I dipped down to my favorite spot at the bottom of her neck. Flinging her arm out, she lazily tried to wrestle the bedside-table drawer open. I pressed another kiss to the inside of her elbow, then took over finding a condom.

As soon as I was covered, I thrust into her as deep as I could go, and she screamed so loud she could drown out Big Ben.

"You like that?" I asked, pulling out and ramming into her again. We'd played around enough. I needed to get to the top of that mountain. I had to fuck, and I knew this is what she wanted, too.

"Don't stop."

"Never," I snapped. "I'm *never* going to stop fucking you." Already she'd stolen my breath, my thoughts, my mind, and I was totally focused on getting us both to the top.

She trembled underneath me, her loud moans turning to dull whimpers as if she'd given in. Her fingernails dug into the tops of my shoulders, and her knees clenched against my hips as sweat trickled down my spine. Waiting for that moment where bliss crashed over her face, I wanted this buildup to last forever, and I wanted to make her come right this second. With Truly, I wanted everything.

She choked out my name, and her body tensed and shuddered as I cried out and thrust in one more time, giving in to the fucking perfection that was Truly Harbury.

TWENTY-EIGHT

Truly

I might not want to be here, but I knew dating was the right thing to do. The night Noah came round and we'd listened to U2, sex wasn't the right description for what happened. It was more than that. An intimacy had ballooned between us that night.

And it scared the shit out of me.

I'd left Rob and Abigail's determined to build some walls, retain some distance, but as soon as I'd seen Noah, I'd been unable to do anything but put down my tools and surrender completely.

But I wasn't a quitter. I just needed to get back on track. Which was why I was in the bathroom at an expensive Thai restaurant in Mayfair. If I couldn't build walls, maybe I could water down the concentrate of Noah's attention. Like Abigail had said, I just needed to see what was out there, spread my focus.

I checked the time on my phone. Okay, so now I was on time instead of my usual ten minutes early. I could leave the bathroom and meet my date for the evening. I didn't believe being late was fashionable. Just rude. And if James was late, then I'd leave. I couldn't be with a man who wasn't on time; it would drive me crazy. No, wait. I was trying to give people a chance. I'd wait ten minutes and *then* leave.

I wiped under my eyes, removing any stray eyeliner, then slipped my phone into my bag and headed back to the hostess table.

"Miss Harbury," she said, "the other party has arrived. Let me show you to your table."

Oh, so he was here. Stupidly, part of me was disappointed. If he'd been late I'd have had the perfect excuse to go home and finish the book I was currently reading. I should be pleased. This could be the start of something.

James and I caught each other's eye across the restaurant, and I smiled despite myself. He was just as handsome as he'd looked in his profile pictures. And he hadn't lied about his height. At five ten, he was shorter than Noah, but not short.

He swept his hand through his hair as the hostess showed me to the table, then pushed his thick-framed glasses back on his nose before greeting me. His glasses were cute on him. Noah didn't wear glasses but that didn't mean they couldn't be cute, right?

"Truly," he said, awkwardly greeting me with a kiss. "You're . . . I mean. I like . . ." He cleared his throat. "You look very pretty."

A blush crept over his cheeks, and he took half a step toward me as if he was going to help me sit.

"Thank you," I replied, quickly taking a seat so we didn't have to do the awkward chair thing.

He nodded and took a seat opposite me. "I ordered two glasses of champagne. I hope that's okay." He had full lips, and his hair was longer than I'd seen in the photographs, but it didn't look like a style he'd chosen, more that he hadn't gotten around to having it cut. He had nice white teeth and kind eyes.

I smiled and began to relax, silently congratulating myself for not deciding he wasn't right for me in the first ten seconds. I was officially dating. "That sounds wonderful. Have you come straight from work?"

"Well, sort of. I work from home. So yes and no. You?" We'd had a few emails and I remembered he was in IT, but I couldn't recall him saying exactly what he did.

"Yes. From the office."

"You said you worked for a charity. That must be rewarding."

The waitress delivered our menus and talked us through the specials. Throughout, she had James's full attention. He focused on what she was saying as if he were going to be tested afterward and losing would see him a contestant in the Hunger Games. It was kinda adorable, and I didn't think about Noah at all for at least a full two minutes.

"That was a lot of information," he whispered, leaning across the table. "Did you decide? We could do that sharing platter she suggested?"

I shrugged. I hadn't really been focusing on what she was saying. I was more taking in how James reacted to her. "Sounds great."

He was considerate and thoughtful and not too passive. So far so good.

He beckoned the waitress back over, ordered for us, then turned his attention back to me. "Sorry, we were talking about your work."

He seemed genuinely interested, and given the foundation was such a huge part of my life, it was reassuring. Noah had always understood the importance of my work, probably because his own goals and achievements were such a big part of his life.

"It's rewarding. Tiring sometimes. There's always more to do, but yes, I get real satisfaction from what I do. What about you? Do you love your job?"

A grin spread across his face. "I really do. Cyber security. It sounds like a nothing job, right? But I do a lot of bespoke systems for high net worth individuals and companies. It means I do a lot of testing and that's the fun bit. It's like being a cybercriminal without doing anything wrong. I'm constantly trying to break into my own clients' networks." His voice dropped as if he were trying to conceal what he was saying. He was clearly passionate about what he did. That was attractive, I told myself. Something I also found attractive about Noah.

"Sounds like something from a spy film," I said.

"You know, I shouldn't say it, but I swear watching those films gave me career advice. It looked so cool when I was twelve or thirteen—outsmarting the CIA or stealing people's identities. That's when I found what I wanted to do."

I laughed. "Are you working for the CIA?"

He grinned. "I wouldn't tell you if I was, would I?" He glanced up as our drinks were delivered. "But seriously, I do some government work. The pay is terrible and their systems . . ." He shook his head. "I do it because I don't want national security compromised. Not for the money. Or the challenge."

"So you're like a nerdy James Bond."

"I like that idea," he said, his smile widening.

I liked a man who owned his geekdom. Noah wasn't a

geek but he didn't seem to mind my geek-like tendencies. Someone like James, who no doubt had his own stash of comic-book t-shirts, was probably far more suited to me.

"And how are you finding internet dating? Have you been doing it long?" he asked.

I shook my head as our food arrived and the waiter explained what everything was. "No, actually this is my first date."

"Interesting. I imagine men are hitting on you night and day."

I grinned. "Not even a little bit. But you've been doing the online thing for a while?"

"On and off, you know? Up until last year, I was in a five-year relationship."

"Five years is a long time." I was pretty sure that previous relationship talk wasn't first date conversation material, but five years was more than many marriages.

"It is. And no one believes me but there was no big argument. No major stumbling blocks. Just two people who decided they wanted different things and fell out of love. She gave up her job in HR and is a ski instructor in Verbier now. I went over with a group of friends over New Year. We're still friends." He grinned.

"Wow. That seems unnervingly healthy."

"I know, right? And now I'm sitting here with you."

I giggled. He was cute. More confident than I'd first thought and although he started off handsome, he seemed to get better looking as the evening went on, despite me only drinking half a glass of champagne.

We disagreed over books. He liked Hunter S. Thompson while I preferred something a little more real like Jane Austen or Charlotte Bronte.

We agreed on *The Last Jedi*—we settled on a score of seven out of ten.

After we both decided that neither of us wanted pudding, we wandered out onto the pavement, and I was a little unsure about what was next.

"I had a really good time tonight," he said.

It felt good to hear that from someone who seemed like such a great guy. A great guy who wasn't Noah. "Me too," I replied.

"I think you're beautiful and interesting and I want to do this again."

My stomach didn't quite do a somersault, but there was definitely movement. "That would be really nice," I said.

He caught my hand as I tucked my hair behind my ear, and skimmed his thumb over my knuckles before placing a kiss on my cheek. "I'll try to hold off on calling you until tomorrow, but I'm going to hold you to a second date." He held his arm out to flag down a passing cab.

As I climbed into the cab, I couldn't fight the surprising sense of relief that swept through me that he'd kissed my cheek and hadn't tried anything else. I liked him. He was sweet and good-looking. We had things in common, and I'd enjoyed my evening with him. He was thoughtful and charming enough without it being cheesy. In any number of ways he was far more suitable for me than Noah would ever be.

But he still wasn't Noah.

I wasn't blanketed in goosebumps when he smiled. I didn't melt when he touched me. I didn't *want* him like I longed for Noah.

I turned to face the back window as the cab pulled away, and I waved at James, who was standing in the street waving back at me.

And at that moment, I knew that kissing someone who wasn't Noah wasn't an option. Which only told me that kissing someone who wasn't Noah was *exactly* what I should be doing. Despite knowing it was what was best, it still felt wrong. Nothing but being with Noah felt right.

TWENTY-NINE

Noah

While falling solo from twelve thousand feet, I should have been concentrating on something other than Truly Harbury. But she was all I could think about. I took a seat on the changing-room bench, trying to figure out what this girl had done to me.

"You okay?" Michael, my instructor, came into the room, unzipping his overalls.

"Yeah, sure."

"Was it anti-climactic? You handled that like a pro." This last jump that I'd just completed was the end of the Free Fall course, and I was now qualified to skydive on my own.

"Are you going to join the club?" he asked.

I shook my head. It had never been my intention to take skydiving up as a hobby. I wanted to complete the course, get certified. That's all I'd focused on. "No, I don't think so."

"What made you take the course?"

"The challenge," I said.

"So you didn't enjoy it?" Michael asked.

I pulled on my trainers and began to lace them up. "Yeah. The peace up there? The views. It's incredible."

"Exactly. That's why we all do it. The feeling of freedom. The private views. So, why not join the club?"

I had loved it. But I saw no point in continuing it. I'd experienced it. I knew I could do it. Why keep doing it? "I think I like the sense of accomplishment. And if I joined the club I'd risk getting bored. Walking away now means the memories will always stay fresh."

"Wow," Michael said, pulling on his jeans. "That's brutal, mate. So you never keep doing anything you like to do too much in case you stop liking it? Shit, when did you give up sex?" He laughed.

He'd got it wrong. It wasn't that I stopped doing things I liked doing in case I lost interest. More that my interest was getting good at things—the fight, the challenge. The enjoyment for me was in the journey. Once I knew I could do something, I didn't see the point anymore. I never got bored with sex, although I was never with a woman for long enough . . . *Shit*. Did I apply this philosophy to my sex life too? Was that the reason things with women never lasted long? And how did Truly fit into all this?

I pulled on my t-shirt and grabbed my phone from my jeans pocket. "I've gotta go. Thanks for getting me down in one piece. My mother's grateful."

I shook Michael's hand and headed out to the car, dialing Rob as I went. "I've just come up with a crazy theory that I need you to talk me out of," I said as he answered.

"Has anyone successfully talked you out of anything in your life?"

"Probably not, so I need you to up your game. Are you around tonight?" I asked. "I thought I'd come over."

"Let's go out. Abigail and I just had a row. We need a night off from each other. I'll get Truly to come around to be with Abigail, and I can be your wingman for the evening."

I wasn't interested in going out but being somewhere where Truly and her sister weren't when I floated my theory to Rob was for the best. I'd known for a while that my feelings for Truly were different to what I normally felt, that she was special. But something was holding me back from telling her, saying that I wanted more than casual sex.

Maybe today I'd found the reason. Perhaps subconsciously, I'd always felt that women were just another challenge, but I didn't want her to be just a higher mountain to climb, simply a more-compelling challenge that I'd move on from when I conquered it. I wanted to be better than that. She deserved more than that. And my friendships with her, Rob, and Abigail would never recover if that's where I ended up.

I didn't want to be right but if I was, I should put a stop to sex with Truly. Steer our relationship onto more solid ground where I wouldn't be tempted to see her as something to be conquered.

THIRTY

Noah

We walked through the door of the Crown and Horses just before eight and grabbed a table by the fire. I knew Rob hadn't been here since Abigail's collapse. "How's Abi?" I asked.

"She said she was sick of my face. Of course, that may have been a result of my pointing out that her feet appeared to have doubled in size."

I tried to contain my grin. Now it made sense why he'd suggested coming out tonight.

"In other words, everything's fine." Rob shrugged.

The waitress came over. "Can we get a bottle of the pinot noir?" I said. "And a couple of menus."

The fact that Abigail and Rob weren't divorced by now showed how perfect they were for each other. "Being in bed all this time . . ." I paused. My accident wasn't the same, but I could relate in some ways. "It's tough on her."

"On both of us." Rob chuckled.

"Excuse me," a pretty, petite blonde approached our

table. "My friends and I"—she looked over her shoulder at a group of girls by the bar who were staring back at us—"were wondering if you'd like to join us. You're looking a little lonely."

"Thanks for the offer, but we're good at the moment," I said.

She pouted, looking at me from under her very long lashes. "Well, that's a shame. But if you want to hang out later, you know, one-on-one, give me a call." She slipped a piece of paper into my hand.

I took it because I didn't want to be rude, but there was no way I was calling her. Why would I bother when the alternative was guaranteed great sex with a woman who was one of my best friends? The same woman who'd been taking up more of my thoughts, more of my brain, than any woman ever had. I wasn't sure how I was going to walk away if Rob confirmed this theory of mine.

"Hey, what's up with you? That girl was gorgeous and offering it up on a plate. You should go over. Someone should be having some fun around here."

I shrugged. No woman in here could make me laugh the way Truly did. Certainly no one could make a *Stranger Things* t-shirt look as good. "I have plenty of fun."

"You do? What happened to that girl who went cold on you? All I've heard about lately is epidural stimulation, kung fu, and the foundation."

"She warmed up," I said.

"So you decided not to make a move on Truly, then?"

I took a swig out of my beer and avoided eye contact with Rob. "I don't want to fuck up our friendship or things with you and Abigail."

"Yeah, sex makes things complicated."

Sex with Truly hadn't made things that complicated at

all. There'd been the brunch issue, but that had passed. No, sex had made things better. Going back to things being platonic between us didn't seem possible. But at the same time, there wouldn't be any choice if Rob confirmed my theory. It was just difficult for me to imagine a time when I would want to stop getting naked with her.

"Condoms stop it from getting too complicated," I replied.

Rob groaned. "Don't remind me. Complicated and boring. You realize that all I'm going to be able to talk about from now on is my kid? Plus I'm going to smell of vomit."

"All you talk about now is Arsenal and Abigail, so you actually might be more interesting."

"I doubt it." He sighed and knocked his beer against mine. "Anyway, we're here to talk about you, and I can't help thinking this theory that you want talking out of is connected to why you're turning down pretty blondes. Am I right?"

I blew out a breath. Now that I was here, I wasn't sure I wanted to hear what he had to say. If he confirmed my suspicion, I'd have to take action—I'd have to end things with Truly.

"Come on, spit it out."

The thing was, Truly deserved to be let go if I was right. "I'm not just some guy who sees women as a challenge, am I?"

He didn't answer straightaway. "Rob, did you hear what I said?" My jaw tensed as I waited for him to respond.

"Jesus, yes. Keep your knickers on. I'm thinking."

"What do you need to think about? It's a simple question."

"I don't think you're the guy who sees the most gorgeous girl in the room and goes after her and doesn't stop until he fucks her. No. We've just seen that," he said, nodding his head at the girl who'd given me her number.

Good, he disagreed. I'd put my new theory about myself down to lack of oxygen after the jump. "Exactly. Bernard was like that at uni."

"Yeah, that guy was a dickhead. But . . ." Rob continued.

"I don't think there's any need for a but. I rarely chase after a woman. I'm not out just to get laid."

"I think there's a *but*. If you look at what drives you, it's all about the challenge. You liked to be told you can't do something and yet find a way to get it done. I mean, Christ, weren't you dropping to near-certain death earlier today with just some shards of silk attached to your back?"

"It's called skydiving, and I'm not the first guy to like extreme sports, so shoot me." I knew I shouldn't have asked him. If I'd kept my theory to myself, I'd have been able to keep sleeping with Truly.

"But you like the challenge. You get off on the high of having conquered something. In business as well as sport."

"Agreed. But if that applied to my sex life, wouldn't I be out fucking every woman that moved? Conquering as many as I could?" My heart sank into my stomach. He was about to put the final nail in Truly's and my coffin.

"I don't think you conquer women. I think the women you're with fit with you. They're just convenient sex. They don't seem to matter to you."

I liked that he wasn't confirming my theory, but I wasn't sure I particularly enjoyed the alternative he presented. "I'm not a dickhead. I don't pretend that it's serious with them or anything, or that I have feelings for them that I don't."

"That's not what I mean. I'm just saying, they're not integral to your life. Like you don't seem to share stuff with them or really befriend them, if you know what I mean. The ones I've met don't seem to know you that well."

That was definitely the difference between all the other women and Truly. Truly knew me. I knew her. We shared stuff. But of course we did, we were friends. Good friends. "Yeah, I think you're probably right. I always have so much going on that whoever I'm with only has a small part to fill."

"Honestly, I think you just haven't met the right girl yet."

I rolled my eyes. "Thanks, Dr. Freud. Insightful."

"I know it sounds clichéd but that doesn't mean it's not true. I think when you're with the right woman, it will be different. You'll start organizing your life so she's at the center rather than slotting her in for a quick shag here and there. You'll want to see her. Want to spend non-naked time with her. She'll be your best friend."

Like Truly.

"If friendship is the only criteria, you and I should have started fucking a long time ago."

"As handsome as you are, my friend, I just don't have the urge to see you naked. It's not just friendship. It's chemistry. When you know, you know. It's tough for Abigail and me at the moment but it's just a rough patch. Generally, marriage is pretty great. Getting to hang out with your best friend all the time—I mean, she's a hormonal mess at the moment, but I love her. I still want to tell her every thought in my head and wake up to her stuffy nose every morning."

Was that what love was? Wanting to tell someone everything? I felt that way about Truly but that didn't mean a full-blown relationship with her would be successful. "Yeah, you and Abigail are great together but not everyone gets to have what you have."

"You just need to be open to finding someone who's

going to be more than convenient sex," Rob said. "The marriage thing isn't important—you don't need a piece of paper. But don't you want to find someone to build a future with? Share everything with? Don't you want more than your usual three-month cycle?"

The ground underneath me was shifting, and I wasn't sure what I wanted. Every time I left Truly, I couldn't wait to see her again, and I'd never felt like that about anyone. She was the only one I wanted to share the ins and outs of my day with. She was beautiful, funny, insightful, and challenging. There was nothing like the feeling when I made her laugh or captured her rapt attention with whatever I was saying. She was my favorite person.

I checked the time on my phone. It would be too late to go over to Truly's this evening smelling of booze, but I couldn't help but grin at the thought of her bedhead and rumpled t-shirt, the way she'd be warm and heavy with sleep, and how she fit so perfectly against my body. How we'd have slow, intensely perfect sex and then we'd talk about everything and nothing before she fell asleep mid-sentence. I couldn't think of anything better, and I couldn't imagine a time I'd want anyone else but her.

Maybe Rob was right. Perhaps I'd just found the right woman in Truly, but how the fuck did I know for sure? How in the hell did I test Rob's theory without either being told by Truly that she didn't want anything more than casual sex with me or fucking up with her, getting it wrong, and blowing apart years' worth of friendships?

THIRTY-ONE

Noah

"I'm downstairs," Truly said from the other end of the phone. "I just need you to hear me out because I've made quite a few changes. It will take twenty minutes, maximum, I promise. And I'll owe you." She'd been freaking out about an upcoming presentation for a week, so even though she didn't give me an explanation, I'd bet money that's what she was here to talk about.

I glanced up at Edward, who I'd just hired as my head of development. At twenty-six, he was young, but had a solid background in healthcare, and the more I looked into it, thought about it, talked about it, the more that was the direction I was headed.

"It's fine. Come on up. We're on the eighth floor."

She canceled the call without saying goodbye the way she did when she was in a hurry, and I grinned, pleased that filling in for Abigail hadn't turned her into a different version of herself when she was around me.

"I have to take this meeting, but if you can find a way

through to the CEO of Wayford Pharmaceuticals, then the next step is to set up a meeting."

"Sure, and in the meantime, I can work with the lawyers to find out the best way to structure a partnership." Edward gathered his papers and stood.

There wasn't any gap between her knock at the door and Truly bursting into my office. "Oh God," she said, looking at Edward. "The girl back there said to come right in. I didn't realize you were in the middle—"

"It's totally fine. Edward and I were just finishing up." I glanced at him and found his cheeks flushed and his gaze pinned on Truly.

Yeah, I knew that feeling.

"Hi," Truly said, holding out her hand. "I'm Truly. Noah's helping me out with a presentation."

Her explanation irked me. That was how she chose to introduce herself to a third party? As someone who needed my help? Not a friend, at least?

"Hi," Edward said, shaking her hand a little too vigorously. "I'm the new head of development," he muttered.

"Excellent. Developing what, exactly?" Truly asked.

Edward shot me a glance.

"We're looking at some healthcare stuff, maybe spinal injuries," I said. She turned to me, her expression a sucker punch to my chest. She was excited, happy.

For me.

"That's awesome." She stepped toward me as if she were going to give me a hug, then stopped herself. "It sounds like you're at an exciting stage."

Edward was still blushing and couldn't take his eyes off Truly even for a second. He needed to leave.

"Edward, I'll catch up with you later," I said. Truly was

beautiful, there was no doubt about it, but he would trip over his own tongue if he wasn't careful.

As if he'd woken up from a Truly-induced trance, Edward flinched. "Yes, okay. See you later. It was very nice to meet you, Truly."

She glanced over her shoulder at him as she unpacked her bag. "You too. Good luck." She had no clue that he was completely captivated by her, which was one of the reasons she was so completely captivating in the first place.

"Hey," I said, taking a seat.

She glanced up as if she'd misheard me. "Hi?" she asked.

"I've not seen you for a few days."

She paused and pressed her lips together. "You don't mind me dropping in like this, do you? It's just that the meeting is this afternoon, and I can use our original new donor presentation, but this donor could be huge. I mean—" She held her arms out wide in front of her. "A really big fish. I've done some research, and it turns out he's a real numbers man, so I changed up the presentation to reflect that."

I leaned back in my chair, taking in her passion and confidence.

"What?" she asked, grinning at me.

"You look beautiful. It's weird not having seen you for a few days."

She rolled her eyes. "I'm sure you had plenty to keep you busy. There's a busty blonde sitting right outside your office."

Did she think I was dating other people when I wasn't with her? She'd said she didn't want to hear about it if I did date, but I'd thought it was sort of obvious I wasn't seeing anyone else.

"Come to mine tonight," I said, ignoring her comment.

She held up her presentation. "I need you to go through this with me."

"I know. But come round tonight."

"What if I have plans?" she asked.

Normally, to anyone else, I would have said, *No problem, if you have plans, we'll do it another night.* Because I wouldn't care enough. "Change them," I said.

Her eyes widened, then her face softened into a smile as she shook her head. "Maybe. Let's go through this, okay?"

"I'm taking that as a yes." I tucked my chair under my desk and leaned forward, giving her my full attention. "Show me what you've changed."

She handed me a presentation pack, and we got down to business. She'd changed up a big chunk of the middle in favor of going into much more detail about how the foundation spent its money and measured success. The way she'd presented it was smart and clear. Someone without financial experience could understand it, and someone with financial experience would get more detail and depth.

"And if he wants the underlying numbers for these figures?" I skimmed my fingers down the far right-hand column on the table.

She handed me a printout. "I can go as technical as he wants. I'm just worried because Abigail always told me I was way too detail oriented and didn't focus enough on the big picture."

"But from what you said this guy likes detail."

"Right. And they are *very* choosy about where they donate their money."

"Probably because so many of these nonprofits are flaky on detail."

She grinned. "Exactly what I'm hoping."

"Truly, do you realize how far you've come in just a few short months? You're doing an amazing job. Two people's jobs, in fact."

She nodded, closing the presentation and tapping her fingers against the paper. "Yeah. I didn't make these changes to make myself comfortable. It's what I think the donor will want to see."

"Exactly. You're killing it. Shall I cook tonight to celebrate?"

"I don't want to celebrate until it's a done deal. I'm doing okay, but I'm still no Abi."

"No. You're right, she wouldn't have changed the presentation," I said, standing and moving round the desk, needing her physical reassurance. "You've made it better. You have to see that."

A blush dusted her cheeks as she stood and began packing up her bag. I wasn't trying to hurry her off. I just wanted to be closer to her. I leaned against the mahogany and circled my arms around her waist, wanting her close. She twisted away from me.

"Hey, stop that."

"Why? I've not seen you for days." This woman. So soft, warm, and serious. Why was she blowing me off?

"Yeah, but this isn't what we do." She took half a step away from me as she zipped her bag and slung it over her shoulder. "I'll see you later." She paused, her eyelids flickering like she was thinking through the pros and cons of something. "Yours sounds like a good idea, actually. And don't cook. We can get food delivered."

I shoved my hands in my pockets, ensuring I kept them to myself. "You don't want me to cook?"

"I might eat before, actually. Cook for yourself if you like. I'll head over around nine."

Jesus. Nine? Did she want me naked and ready to perform as soon as she rang the buzzer? We'd agreed on casual, but we were friends as well as lovers, weren't we? I wanted to hang out with her. Hear about how the presentation went, laugh over Edward's obvious crush on her. "I have a drink with a contact at five thirty and then I'll head home. I should be there around seven, so come over earlier if you like."

"I don't think so," she said, fiddling with the clasp on her bag.

Jesus, was she being deliberately annoying? "Are you doing something earlier? I'd like to cook for you," I admitted.

She blew out a breath. "I just think it's easier if we don't act like we're dating when we're not dating."

"But we'd have dinner before I went to New York. We're friends, Truly."

She blushed. "I know. But . . ." She fixated on the collar of my shirt, clearly not wanting to meet my eyes. "You know, we're having sex now. And things can get a whole lot blurry."

I knew that feeling. But I was intrigued by the blur, didn't quite know what to do about it. Had Truly decided that blurry wasn't what she wanted? Was I not what Truly wanted? I could just ask her, but that wasn't fair because I had no clear answer if she asked me the same question in return.

I stepped toward her and this time she didn't move away as I pressed my body against hers and brought my lips to her forehead. "Knock them dead this afternoon."

For a second she melted against me and then, as if she'd fallen asleep on the Tube and was worried she'd missed her stop, she jolted and headed to the door. "See you around nine," she said without looking back. I watched her walk away, a niggling, empty feeling in the pit of my stomach.

I wanted to cook for her.

I wanted her to come over at seven.

And I wanted her to stay the night.

THIRTY-TWO

Truly

I put on my earrings and slid my new gold cuff onto my wrist. I'd found the bracelet online, picked it out myself without any help from Noah. It was the first piece of jewelry I'd ever bought. I usually did with hand-me-down jewelry from my mother or my sister. I twisted my wrist, admiring it against the navy of my dress—it went perfectly. I was getting better at not feeling like a fraud when I put on an evening dress, which was ironic since I was about to attend the winter ball, the last event that required a ball gown before Abigail came back. The jitters in my stomach that I felt before a presentation or speech were shadows of what they had been, and I was almost excited.

I turned sideways to check myself in the mirror. I shivered as I remembered Noah's arms around me, his gaze staring back at me in the dressing room when I'd tried this dress on. His hands always felt as if they were made for me. I pushed the thought aside. Building walls between Noah and me hadn't been easy, but I knew I had to keep them up if I was going to protect my heart.

It would have been so easy to give in to his dinner-date invitations, either out or at his place, but after brunch I knew I needed to keep Noah in a box marked dangerous and only bring him out when I was in a casual mindset. It was easier to spend time at his place rather than mine. That way I could turn up late and leave early. Whenever we agreed to meet at my place, Noah would turn up with takeout hours early, and I'd have to literally kick him out of bed in the middle of the night.

It was easy for a man like Noah to do casual without getting feelings involved. He'd had plenty of practice. I'd decided that we could be friends or we could be lovers but being both was too close to perfect to be healthy for me. So the boundaries were in place despite Noah continually testing them.

My door buzzed. Shit, who could that be? I needed to leave. "Noah?" I asked, peering at the screen. We'd agreed to meet at the venue. "What are you doing here?"

"I was running early. Thought I'd pick you up."

"You didn't need to. It's not like we're going on a date. But come on up." Noah wasn't to know that every time he stepped over a boundary, he made my life a little more difficult.

I buzzed him in and started dropping lipstick and money into my evening bag, so I'd be ready when Noah arrived. If he was like this with girlfriends, I didn't understand why his relationships only lasted a few months. He was always so thoughtful and considerate, open and giving.

A bang at the door caught my attention. How did he always get up here so fast?

I opened the door and stepped back as he held out a

bunch of flowers. Red roses? That was so nice—romantic, even. I began to grin and stopped myself. He made it so difficult to keep him in my casual box. Everything got more and more blurry around him, however hard I fought to keep things clear.

"You look completely beautiful," he said.

"Why?" I asked, still distracted by the wall-crushing flowers.

"Well, it's difficult for you not to be beautiful, I suppose. It's just who you are."

"Thank you," I replied. "I meant the flowers. How come?"

He paused as if he were about to say something, and I turned and headed back to my bedroom.

Noah followed. "I thought we should mark tonight. It's the final hurdle. You did this. You thought you would drown and tonight you collect your gold medal for the one hundred meters freestyle."

I pressed my lips together to stop my grin from taking over my face. "Yeah. It feels good." Noah was right. I'd never thought I'd get to this point. It had been such a huge mountain to climb, and with his help, I'd done it. I'd conquered a thousand new things each entirely out of my comfort zone.

"It should. You've done fantastically."

Noah had been so encouraging. When I'd had no confidence in myself, he'd had enough in me to make me believe I could take the next step. Without him, I wouldn't be standing here, looking forward to this evening. I owed him so much. "I couldn't have done it without you."

"That's not true. I'm pretty sure you could do anything you set your mind to."

More compliments. *This man.*

I pulled out the blue-and-black evening sandals that I'd bought for this dress. "We only need to make a third of what we did last year for us to hit our fundraising target."

Noah sank to his knees and guided my foot into the shoe. *Boundaries*. He was always crossing them.

"I can do that," I said, unwilling to accept his help.

He smoothed his hand down my shin and circled my ankle with his fingers. "I know, but I'm here and it's easier this way."

Not in the long run, I wanted to say. Instead I watched as he guided my hand to his shoulder to ensure I was steady, then expertly fastened each strap.

If only being with Noah wasn't so easy. Wasn't so enjoyable. If only I didn't feel exactly like the best version of myself when I was with him.

"So after tonight, your job will be done," I said. "All your good deeds for a lifetime wrapped up into five months."

"You're saying you won't need me?" he asked as he stood so close his suit skimmed against my body.

"You're not to be needed." I looked away before he overwhelmed my focus. We needed to get going.

He slid his hand around my back. "Hey, what does that mean?"

"Have you seen my keys?" I asked, glancing around. There was no point in having this conversation. I didn't want to insult him and ruin the evening.

"Truly," he growled. "What did you mean?"

I stepped out of his arms. "There they are." I spotted my keys on my dressing table and dropped them into my bag. "Are you ready?"

He frowned but nodded. "Yeah, the car's downstairs."

I rolled my eyes, teasing him, despite being delighted I didn't have to stand outside and hail a cab in the cold.

"Seriously, does the money thing bother you?" he asked as we rode downstairs in the lift.

"Does it bother me that you have money?" I asked as I stepped into the lobby. "No," I said as he shook his head. "Should it?"

"But you make comments. Tease me."

I shrugged. "All in fun. You're the same guy either way as far as I can see."

"Most women would be impressed and enjoy it."

"Well, first off, I'm not most women."

A sexy smile curled his lips. "That's the truth."

"And second of all, it doesn't affect me. We're not dating. You're not husband material." His stare bore into my cheek, and I turned to him. Did he care what I thought? "It's handy. You know. To have a driver. But really, it's nothing to do with me."

He held the car door open and helped me inside before braving the traffic to get in the other side. "If we were dating. If you *did* see me as husband material—would the money be a good thing or a bad thing?"

Was he wondering if women were going to use him for his money? "Are you asking if the money makes you more attractive?" Could *anything* make him more attractive?

"Yeah. I guess."

"For me, it's more that you're passionate. I like that you set your sights on something and then go out and achieve it. Although that side of you is . . ." It was all these parts of Noah that made him so special, that I found so attractive—exactly the parts of Noah that made it necessary for me to set boundaries. "But no, the money isn't the thing that's attractive about you."

I glanced across at him to find him grinning at me. "What?" I asked.

He shrugged. "Inside and out, I find everything about you attractive."

Boundaries, I told myself as my stomach swooped. High, high walls. Electric fences. Barbed wire.

PERHAPS IT WAS the light that sparkled from the huge chandeliers above us, maybe it was Noah in black-tie attire, sitting beside me, or maybe my dress was just too tight. Whatever it was, I couldn't remember the last time I'd felt so happy. I'd nailed the speech, announced the spinal injuries unit as the main recipient of this year's donations, and to top it all off, the auction was only halfway through and had already raised what it had last year. I couldn't believe I was here at the end of the year, past target, and all of it achieved without Abigail.

I turned to Noah and grinned. "Thank you. I meant it earlier when I said I couldn't have done it without you."

He brushed his thumb over my cheek as if I belonged to him. "As I said, you're wrong, but I'm happy to share the glory."

"Next lot up for auction is a weekend in Paris," announced the portly auctioneer who did this event each year. "You'll be staying at the re-opened Hotel de Crillon in Paris. Who'll start the bidding at a thousand pounds?"

"Ten thousand," Noah bellowed beside me.

The ballroom filled with gasps and a thousand eyes turned in our direction. "You don't need to do this," I whispered, trying to keep the smile on my face. He'd done so much for the foundation already. I didn't want him to think he had to donate.

"But I want to," he said. "You deserve to get away."

What? "No," I said, grabbing his wrist. "You can't bid on this for me."

"For both of us," he said.

Christ, I wanted to climb into his lap, wrap my arms around his neck, and *love* this man. That feeling was always just a couple of seconds away. Being with him hadn't cured me of him. I hadn't grown bored or disinterested or disenchanted. I hadn't rewritten our relationship into something that meant less to me. My walls were close to crumbling. Things needed to change, or I was going to end up with a broken heart.

Now the fundraising year was over, I had a wardrobe of acceptable office-wear and I'd gotten used to being the face of the foundation, I'd have less reason to see Noah. That would be a start.

The only person who was going to get hurt in this situation was me. But what could I do? Walk away when I was so happy? It was a lose-lose situation because either way I ended up without him. My head told me it would be easier to rip the plaster off now. Escape while there was still hope I wasn't irrevocably in love with him.

No one countered Noah's outrageous bid of ten thousand pounds for two nights in Paris. And while he was giving his details to a foundation staff member, I watched as someone made a beeline for our table from across the room.

"Noah?" A man came up from behind us just as Noah had finished making his payment. Noah pushed back his chair and stood.

"Morgan?"

"I thought that was you! We finally meet."

"Truly, you know Morgan Davis from Pickwick Health-care," Noah said.

I stood and shook the stranger's hand. Although I'd never met him, his reputation preceded him. "You must be talking to Noah about epidural stimulation. Your company has done amazing work. Delighted to meet you."

"You're Truly Harbury? How wonderful to meet you. I've known your sister for years, of course. It's such a shame she couldn't be here tonight."

"I'm taking lots of pictures for her. And of course, I feel like I know you because of all the wonderful support you and your company have given the foundation over the years. We really appreciate it."

"Well, we believe in the work you do. It's very comple-mentary to our business."

I grinned. "Your product is going to change lives," I said.

"We really hope so. Even more if Noah accepts my offer."

I kept my smile in place as I glanced at Noah, inviting him to explain.

"Morgan wants someone to be a European ambassador for the project," Noah said, grinning.

"And the Middle East," Morgan corrected. "Noah would be perfect, wouldn't he? With his background, he can speak with real experience. And with his thirst for adventure, the travel is bound to appeal to him." Morgan clasped Noah's shoulder. "You'll help me convince him, won't you, Truly?"

"I said I needed time to think about it. You only mentioned it yesterday," Noah replied, glancing at me.

"I know," Morgan said. "I'm just impatient. Our product could do so much and partnering with you is the perfect combination."

The auctioneer interrupted us and introduced the next lot, so we said our goodbyes and took our seats again.

"This is what I wanted to talk to you about when I called you yesterday," Noah said as the auction rattled on around us. "But you didn't pick up. Again. Remember?"

I'd been making myself ignore some of Noah's calls, trying to keep some space between us. "Oh yes, sorry. I was in a meeting."

"I wanted to get your view on Morgan's offer. It would mean a lot of travelling. Perhaps we can go back to yours and have a drink. I really want to get your perspective."

"Sure, later maybe." Was this why they said to be careful what you wish for? I'd wanted a little distance from Noah, and it looked like that's exactly what this Morgan guy was offering. If Noah was travelling a lot, he wouldn't be able to drop by to watch Netflix or join Abigail, Rob, and me for lunch. I'd be forced to see him less. No doubt, sex with me would be less convenient, and he'd start seeing someone new. Perhaps someone he'd meet during his new role. She'd be far more suited to him—sophisticated, gorgeous, and able to accompany him to functions without him having to fear she'd say or wear the wrong thing.

This was how it was meant to be. Things between us were drawing to a natural conclusion.

I should be thrilled. Or relieved or thankful. This way I'd avoid getting in any deeper with Noah. But the way my eyes stung and my insides ached at the thought of Noah leaving—of things changing between us—made me think I was in too deep already.

"Excuse me. I need to go to the ladies' room." I stood and grabbed my clutch.

I kept my head down, avoiding eye contact with anyone, and headed toward the exit. I pushed at the heavy gold door of the ballroom and burst into the bright lights of the lobby and toward the loo.

I slumped on one of the buttoned, pink-velvet stools set in front of a mirror in the powder room and stared at my reflection. In a few months, I'd be one of the women Noah used to sleep with. He would have moved on to someone else, his past firmly in the past as it always was.

Where did that leave me?

In the same place that I'd been when he'd left for New York all those years ago. Except this time was worse because I'd seen it coming and still couldn't stop it.

But at least I'd held part of myself back. I could have given in to *all* his requests for dinner and late-night phone calls. My boundaries and barbed wire fences could have been long abandoned. Noah and I stopping whatever it was we were doing now was a good thing. I'd see it clearly in a few weeks or months. I was so close to falling for him, but this new job was my chance to save myself from certain ruination.

After touching up my makeup and going to the loo, I made my way back out to the lobby.

"Truly?"

I glanced up and found Noah coming toward me.

"I thought maybe you were sick or something. You've been gone ages. You okay?"

"Yes, totally fine. Just got chatting with someone."

"You want to leave?" he asked. "Let's go back to yours. Relax. I really want to know what you think about me doing this ambassador thing."

"It sounds amazing. You should definitely do it." I tried to be decisive in my tone. This was my get-out-of-jail-free card—a positive thing. If things ended between us now, I got to walk away with my heart still intact and hopefully we'd still be friends.

He smiled but it wasn't convincing. "You think? I don't know." He shoved his hands in his pockets. "It's a lot of travelling. Of course I'll be back a lot. Weekends and stuff. And you'll have to come out and visit. We can still . . ."

"Be friends," I said, hoping he'd take the hint.

"Well, yes, of course. We've always been friends, but I'm saying, nothing needs to change between us."

He was oh-so-wrong. "I think it's the right time to go back to being *just* friends, though."

He frowned at me, searching my face as if he didn't fully understand what I was saying. "What are you talking about? Did I upset you?"

I wasn't sure if he was capable of doing anything that didn't make me like him a little bit more. "Not at all. But this Europe thing—you should concentrate on that. Your next challenge. And like I said, I'm so grateful for all the help you've given me—"

He caught my arms as I went to move away. "Wait, so now you've met your fundraising targets, things are over between us?"

"Things?" What was it he thought we were doing? "What things? We agreed on casual. And casual ends sooner or later."

Noah released my arms and stepped back. "You want to end things. Why? Because of the offer from Morgan? I haven't even said yes yet."

"But you should. It sounds like exactly the sort of challenge you relish. And I'm not asking for anything from you," I replied. "Like you said, we'll be friends."

"But I want more than that. I want to be friends with

you, but I like the sex too. And you can't tell me the sex isn't good because we both know it's fucking fantastic."

I fought back a grin. There was no doubt about that on my side, but it was good to hear that he felt the same way about the physical relationship between us. "So what is it you're picturing for us?"

I wanted to smooth out the ridge between his eyebrows. He seldom looked so serious. "Well, I like the sex stuff. And lately, we've had fewer dinners together, but I like spending time with you. I want to be your friend, hang out, eat Chinese, and argue about string theory and whether Lucas should have kept Han shooting Greedo first in the special editions."

God, I'd missed all that stuff the last few weeks when I'd been trying so desperately to keep him at arm's length. "We both know that it's who Han is at that point in the film. Of course he should have still fired the first shot in the 1997 version."

"Right," he replied. "So why stop all that?"

"Because I can't do it anymore, Noah," I said, honesty bursting from me as if someone had popped a water balloon of emotions inside me. "It's too difficult. I'm not that girl. You know me—I'm all in with whatever I do, and I've tried with this casual thing but—"

"Hey, casual was your idea. I didn't put rules in place."

"I know. I did. I thought it would help."

"I just don't get it. What are you saying? You don't want the sex or you don't want the *Star Wars* stuff?"

I folded my arms. "Tell me what is it you really want? You want the *Star Wars* marathons and the sex but looking ahead, what do you want with me?"

He grinned. "Well, *Star Wars* marathons and sex sound good to me. Why would anyone want anything else?"

"But I will, Noah. My feelings for you grow every time I see you, and if I were to let you in—stop dodging your calls and ditching dinner with you—"

"I bloody knew you were avoiding me."

"And I'm telling you why. I can't do casual sex with my best friend. Not anymore."

"I don't understand why you're having this sudden change of heart. We like each other. You're one of the few people in the world who doesn't bore me, and I never know what you're going to say next. I want to see how this goes."

"You say you like this now, but what about tomorrow? What happens to us next month? After the Europe job there will be another opportunity. Another mountain to climb and you'll move on. In New York or freaking Beijing or wherever. There will be a different challenge. And when you leave, I'll be left in ruins, Noah. I have to protect myself."

"So you don't want casual. Fine. Let's officially date. Let's see how things develop."

He really wasn't making this easy for me. "We can't, Noah."

"I don't fucking understand, Truly. What have I done wrong? What is it that you want from me?"

"I'm not asking for anything. But . . ." I'd never expected anything from Noah. And our time was up. "I need more."

"I'm saying, let's date. Isn't that more?" His gaze was focused on me, intense and almost irresistible.

Why didn't I just say yes to him? It wasn't as if anything he was saying was untrue. It would be so easy. I wanted him to stay in London, call me up in the middle of the day, slide his arms around me and pull me toward him, all heat and sunshine. But I'd need that forever. How long would Noah want it for?

"Noah . . ." I said. Should I tell him every single thought in my head? Did I have anything to lose?

"Is this because you're dating? Have you met someone?"

I sighed in exasperation. "Don't you get it?" I asked. "It's exactly the opposite. I can't hold myself back from you. When we're together, it's so easy for me to imagine a future together, to think about being a couple, having kids who grow up with Rob and Abigail's and hate us because we make them learn the periodic table rather than let them play Fortnite. I can imagine growing old together and fighting over Scrabble in a nursing home." I took a deep breath. "I'm a step away from being so in love with you that I can't function. And I know if I let myself take the next step, if I let you in even a little bit more, I'll love you for the rest of my life."

Noah's eyes widened, shock covered his face, and he stepped back. "I had no idea."

I looked away, my gut churning in horror over what I'd said, even though it was all true. I wanted the sex and discussions about string theory, but I also wanted more than that. "You've not done anything wrong, Noah." I shrugged, my voice wobbling. "But you need to let me go or I'm going to drown in you."

He pushed his hands into his pockets, his head bowing. "I don't know what to say. I don't want to hurt you but . . . This is . . ."

He didn't finish his sentence. But I did in my head.

It wasn't how he felt, what he wanted, or how he saw us together.

It wasn't who he was.

And that's why I had to leave.

"I know," I said. "I never wanted it to get to this point. I thought I had it under control. I thought with the rules and everything—this is my fault." I swallowed and took a deep breath. "And I'll fix it and everything will be fine. You'll go to Europe. You'll meet someone. I'll throw myself into work and everything will get back to normal. When I next see you—we'll be . . . friends."

"Wait," he said. "I've been thinking about this." He paused and blew out a breath. "I know you're different. You're special. I want you more than I've ever wanted anyone."

My heart clanged against my ribcage. I'd never thought I'd hear this from him.

"But, there are no guarantees in life. I can't tell you how I'm going to feel in a few months or years. Whether or not I want kids or whether I'll want to be playing Scrabble in my old age. I just never look that far ahead." He shook his head, his mouth tight as he struggled to find the words.

I nodded. I knew who this man was, and I couldn't blame him for being himself. "I get it. We're different. We want different things." I needed more. I needed certainty.

Silence stretched between us before he stepped forward and cupped my face. "I'm sorry," he said, as he placed a kiss on the top of my head. "I'm so sorry, I just . . ."

"I know," I replied and stepped back, letting the truth of how incompatible we were solidify between us. And then I turned away, into the cold London night. This time I knew for certain he wouldn't be following me.

THIRTY-THREE

Noah

In New York all the views were skyward. And that's what I needed: a fresh perspective. I stepped out of the car and glanced up. New York felt so much smaller than London—more compact. Less sprawling. New York was decisive and sharp against London's worn softness. I breathed in the contrast, the sounds of the taxi horns and the yelling of the hot dog sellers. The tightness around my ribcage that I'd had since my conversation with Truly just a few days ago loosened, and I knew I was in the right place.

Refusing the offer of a porter's help, I took my carry-on from the driver and headed through the lobby of the Time Warner building toward the lift to the Mandarin Oriental hotel lobby located on the thirty-fifth floor.

"Noah," a female voice said from behind me. I turned to find Francesca Sanderson smiling at me. "I'd recognize the back of that head anywhere. Good to see you."

The lift pinged open and I stepped aside to let Francesca through. "It's days like today when Manhattan els small. How are you?" I asked. I'd known Francesca two or three years ago. For about three months of one particularly sidewalk-melting summer.

"Perfect." She beamed. "Just down for the night from the Hamptons. I've given up my place in the city, so this hotel is like a home away from home. What about you?"

"I'm here from London for a board meeting." I'd been due to fly out on Monday but decided to come early after my conversation with Truly at the winter ball. Part of the reason I liked Truly was that she was always surprising me. But the last thing I'd been expecting was her to end things between us. On the surface, we'd left things amicably, but I was pissed off and I wasn't sure why or what to do about it. I just knew that I didn't want to see Truly. I wanted to stop thinking about her. I needed a break from London.

"Oh, you went back. I heard about the float. Congratulations." She smiled at me, her auburn hair looking like she'd just been to the salon and her makeup emphasizing her dazzling green eyes. She'd always been gorgeous.

"Thanks. I'm still on the board but . . ." I felt a disconnection to the business now that it was owned by someone else.

"It's not yours anymore? I guess it feels weird."

I chuckled. "Yeah. A little. What are you up to now?"

"Oh, you know. Still consulting."

"Still working too hard?" Francesca was one of the most disciplined women I'd ever met. She got up at five to work out, something her inside thigh muscle grip could vouch for. She was in the office by seven, and even when we'd gone for brunch at the weekends, she looked like she'd just stepped out of a magazine shoot—glossy and glamorous. She was Truly Harbury's exact opposite.

"Always." The doors slid open at the lobby level of the

hotel, and I held the doors as Francesca stepped out. "We should grab a drink," she said as she glanced at her expensive watch. "Unless you have plans?"

"Sure," I said. It was nice to see Francesca. She was always sweet and uncomplicated, and from what I remembered, decent in bed. Spending the evening with a friendly face felt like a good distraction from what I'd left behind in London.

"The lobby bar is open already, unless you want to change?" she asked.

"No, I'm good. Let's check in and I'll meet you over there."

She smiled, and we split off toward separate check-in desks.

I was done first, and I made my way over to the bar and grabbed a seat by one of the floor-length windows overlooking the park. It was a picture-postcard view—the green parkland sunk into the middle of the towering skyscrapers. I hadn't even thought about the four years I'd spent here since I'd been in London. Seeing Francesca brought a little bit of my history into my present. I couldn't remember giving her a second thought after we split, either. I was good at moving on, leaving my past in the past. My relationship with Francesca had been simple. There had been a lot of sex and some dinner dates. I didn't remember us talking or sharing things. I certainly never had to escape to a different continent in an attempt to stop thinking about her.

London was different. Truly was different.

When I'd seen Truly after being away from New York, I'd wondered why we hadn't been better at keeping in touch. I wanted to hear about her work, wondered if her hair still smelled of coconut. I'd been *excited* to see her.

Seeing Francesca after so long was . . . fine. Perfectly pleasant. A distraction from another woman.

"Hey, did you order?" Francesca asked as she took a seat opposite me.

"No, not yet."

She beckoned over a waiter in a way that only women in New York could. She crossed her legs, her shiny, strappy heels knocking the table. I was pretty sure Francesca wouldn't own a *Star Wars* t-shirt let alone a *Stranger Things* one. Fuck, Truly looked good in that t-shirt. Looked good in everything.

"Whiskey?" she asked.

"A Manhattan," I told the waiter. I never drank cocktails in London. Whiskey straight, beer, or wine, but cocktails weren't pivotal to London culture in the way they were in New York. We might speak the same language, but there were so many differences, large and small, between New York and London. The most important one was that Truly wasn't here.

"So, tell me, break any hearts recently? I see you're not married." She glanced at my left hand. I'd forgotten how forward New York women were. It was how Francesca and I had ended up together in the first place. She'd introduced herself to me in a bar like this one, asked me if I was single, and I'd gone home with her. She'd made it easy. Women like her always did.

"Oh, I think you're the heartbreaker here," I replied, sitting back. Francesca's invitation for a drink was an opening line after which we'd both decide whether or not we wanted to go to bed together.

"No heartbreaking here." She drew a square around her heart with her finger. "I love my work. It might not bring me flowers, but the money keeps me warm at night."

I chuckled. "Well, at least you're clear about your goals." We were alike in that way—goal oriented and driven—although money had never been my motivator, just a helpful by-product.

"So, tell me about your work," she said. "What are you up to now that you've made your fortune?"

"I'm dabbling in a few things. I've been helping a friend with charity work and looking at the healthcare industry." We chatted as if we'd just been introduced or were old business colleagues, but it felt as if I were at a networking event, being polite and swapping small talk.

"Charity work? That doesn't sound like you." She smiled around the edge of her glass and took a sip of her drink. "You're a corporate bad boy. A titan of the stock market now."

She didn't know me at all.

"What can I say? I'm complicated."

Francesca was attractive, but I wasn't attracted to her, and I wondered if I ever had been really. There was no chemistry, and I wasn't really interested in anything she had to say. I'd been fighting back the urge to call Truly since boarding to tell her how my airline wasn't using the Airbus 380 and that instead I was on a Boeing 777. I didn't care if Francesca had an alternative theory to Stiglitz on globalization. But if Truly did, I wanted to hear it. I wanted to tell her every *nothing* thought I had along with every important one, and I was pissed off that she didn't get it. To end things because she was worried she'd feel too much? That was bullshit.

I unclenched my fist and tried to concentrate on the woman in front of me rather than one three thousand miles away. "Are you still at the same firm?" I asked to be polite.

"I've moved a couple of times," she said, taking a gulp of

the cocktail that had just arrived. "You have to move on to move up in my business, but I'm hoping I'll get partnership at this firm. If not, I'll leave in a couple of years."

I nodded. "The endgame is important to keep in mind."

"Speaking of—shall we finish our drinks and go up?" she asked.

That's why we were having drinks, wasn't it? It wasn't just to catch up. We weren't friends. But what she was offering didn't hold the appeal that it would have done before I'd gone back to London and started sleeping with Truly. I didn't want just convenient sex or a woman slotting into my life, as Rob had described it. I might want Truly out of my system but going to bed with Francesca wasn't going to make that happen. I couldn't even have a cocktail with a woman without comparing her with Truly and then being filled with regret. That wasn't Francesca's fault.

"Yeah. I actually need to make a few calls, so I should probably go."

She raised her eyebrows. "Oh. Okay. I thought I—"

"I'm seeing someone." On the face of it, I'd lied to her, but it didn't feel dishonest. Running into Francesca brought things into focus for me. For the first time in my life, I'd been left heartbroken, and Francesca wasn't going to put me back together again.

"Oh. Good for you. I'm going to hang out here for a while then," she said, leaning forward as I stood and kissed her on the cheek.

"Enjoy. It's good to see you, Francesca."

It had been enlightening. Knowing Truly was in the world, there was no way I could take Francesca to bed. It wouldn't be cheating. Truly hadn't even demanded monogamy when we were sleeping together, let alone now when she'd ended things. But I didn't *want* anyone else. I wanted the woman who looked sexy as hell when she was hunched over her laptop, cross-legged on the sofa, eating cold Chinese food. The one who could match me question for question in a pub quiz. The person who, despite being a workaholic, still found time to read to sick and injured kids.

I didn't want Francesca or any other woman. I wanted Truly. I wanted her with me every night, by my side, beautiful without realizing it, funny and warm. I wanted her thinking I was the dumbest man on the planet because I hadn't read all of Shakespeare's sonnets. I wanted to peel off her yoga pants and fuck her in her *Star Wars* t-shirt. I wanted to fight with her, love her, live with her, explore the world with her.

And I needed to find a way to address all her fears, prove somehow that I wouldn't ruin her or whatever she was afraid of. I might not be able to produce the empirical evidence I knew would talk her around, but I had to figure out something. I had to convince her that although I couldn't give her any guarantees, I could tell her that there'd never be any other woman for me but her. That the only woman I could picture in my future was her.

THIRTY-FOUR

Truly

As I stood in the doorway to Abigail and Rob's place, a dark cloud of devastation clung to me despite me telling myself over and over that I'd made the right decision. I'd been practical, gotten out before I could get too hurt. I hadn't expected to feel so heavy with regret. I wanted a different ending for Noah and me, and that was ridiculous. I knew better, but for some reason my heart was taking a little longer to see it my way.

I needed my sister.

Noah had gone to New York for a board meeting, so I could be sure to risk lunch at Abigail and Rob's without running into him.

"Truly?"

I jumped as Rob opened the door.

"What are you doing out here? I didn't hear the bell."

"I was about to ring it." I'd been stealing myself, trying to pull my proverbial socks up and push down this misery that rose from my belly.

"Come up immediately and tell me everything," Abigail called from upstairs.

Rob chuckled. "You didn't send her pictures from the other night, and she had to rely on Sarah or Sierra or someone—I don't know. I do know she's fuming."

Sending pictures had been the last thing on my mind the night of the ball, and I couldn't face showing her pictures yesterday, so I'd told her I was too sick to leave the house. I rolled my eyes and handed Rob a pot of single cream and the two leeks he'd asked me to pick up on the way. "I may be gone some time," I said, starting on the stairs.

"As it's just three of us today, I'm not going to bother bringing a table up, if that's okay. Can we make do with trays?" Rob asked.

Three of us. Back to how things were before Noah had come back from New York. "Trays sound good to me. Give me a call when you're ready and I'll come give you a hand."

"Truly!" Abigail shouted.

"I'm coming," I replied, sprinting up the stairs.

"What were you talking to Rob about?" she asked.

"Trays. Why?" I bent and kissed her on the cheek.

"God knows what he's getting up to while I'm stuck up here."

"Well whatever it is, it's not much if he's getting up to it one floor away from you. Anyway, don't think about it. You're nearly cooked. Just a few weeks to go." I flopped into the sofa, my muscles as exhausted as if I'd just been for a run.

"So. I've been waiting. I haven't gotten a voicemail or pictures or anything. How did it go?"

I groaned and pulled my phone from my back pocket.

"You don't seem very enthusiastic about it," Abigail said. "Are you worried about how you looked in the dress because Simone sent me a couple of pictures and you looked amazing. Beautiful. You have nothing to worry about."

"No, it's not like that." Normally I would be worried about what I looked like in the photographs—not through any kind of vanity but because I always felt so out of place and awkward. But I knew I fitted in that night. I didn't have to see the photographs to know I was appropriately dressed and my makeup wasn't over the top.

"Then what?" Abigail patted the bed behind her and shuffled over onto her other side.

I crawled onto the mattress next to her. "Nothing. I'll show you how it went." I didn't want to look at photographs that no doubt included Noah, didn't want to be reminded of that night. But there was no way I would get away with not showing Abigail what she'd been dying to see.

I took a deep breath and opened the correct file on my phone.

She took the handset and began to flip through the pictures. The first one was of me giving the speech. Noah must have taken it. My head was up, and I was grinning at the audience. I'd come a long way in the last five months. I could never have imagined I would feel almost comfortable up there, thanking everyone for their support over the course of the year.

"You look really confident in that first one, right? And that dress is beautiful on you."

"Not bad." I smiled and swiped across the screen. There were lots of photographs of the different speakers, then the auctioneer and the tables. At the very end was a photo of Noah and me. We were looking at each other like we were the only ones in the room. His eyes were soft and fixed on me, and we were sitting far too close to be just friends. My heart squeezed tighter and tighter until I could barely breathe.

"You look good together," she said. "You're both gorgeous."

I rolled my eyes. I may no longer think that Noah needed to be committed to a mental institution to sleep with me, but I'd never accept that I was in his league. He was in a tier all by himself.

"But more than that, I've never seen him look at anyone like that," Abi said, peering closer at the picture. "Not any woman I've ever seen him with. Is there anything you want to tell me?"

"No, like what?" Now things were over, there was no point in confessing to something I knew Abi would scold me for.

"I don't know. I always thought that maybe you had a crush on Noah. And then when you told me you'd kissed, I think part of me hoped something might happen between you, even though I was worried he wasn't right for you."

"Hoped? I wouldn't have expected that." I groaned and lay on my back, facing the ceiling. Maybe a confession would help. "You really want to know?"

She shifted onto her side so she was facing me. "Tell me everything."

Abigail listened without interruption as I started at the beginning, before Noah'd left for New York right up to the night of the winter ball.

I turned my head to find Abigail openmouthed. "So you two have been, like, sleeping together? Since the night of the awards? Call it twinstinct, but I knew something was going on."

"A little after. Don't tell me I'm stupid. I know that already."

"Stupid wasn't what I was thinking," Abigail said. "I'm impressed you're doing something that doesn't relate to spreadsheets. Relieved is more like it."

"Well, it's all a big disaster, because of course my plan backfired and my crush reappeared. And now we're over. Not that we ever really began in the first place." For all I was hurting now, I couldn't regret the last few months with Noah. I'd had fun. Enjoyed his company. My life had been about more than just work for a few months, and I felt more confident than I had in my entire life. Noah had this weird way of making me feel like me but a better, sparklier version.

"Are you sure ending things is the right thing to do? It's not like he's saying he wants everything to stay the same. You said he wanted to date, see how things go. What is it that you want from him?"

"You know what he's like. We might date for a few months and then he'll move on. Look for his next challenge or whatever. And in a few months, I'll be . . . completely lost to him."

"But how do you know? I mean, he's different for you, right? You said it yourself. No other man has ever come close to being what Noah is to you. Maybe it's the same for him." She held up my phone, which still showed the picture of Noah and me at the Ball. "They say a picture paints a thousand words."

"Noah doesn't end up with a girl like me. Be serious."

"What, a woman who he's best friends with? Someone he'll devote his very valuable time to helping for the last five months? Someone he goes to balls with even though you are clearly quite confident and able to go by yourself?"

"He wanted to help the rehab center. And anyway, I never said he wasn't a good guy. That's part of the problem."

"But see it from his perspective. He's been sleeping with you without any kind of commitment or monogamy at your suggestion. You wanted to keep it casual, so you could get over him or whatever. And now you leap from that to wanting, what? A ring and a lifetime commitment?"

"I'm not saying he's got to propose. Just that he sees a future for us, that our feelings for each other aren't so very out of step. I don't want to join that long list of women that Noah has dated."

"You need to have confidence in the way he looks at you. In the way he touches you."

"That I'm different? When there's no evidence or certainty or—"

"There are no guarantees. Not in any relationship. There's no spreadsheet that you can plug in variables and it will churn out a definitive future. That's not the way love works."

Without certainty, I knew I was headed for heartbreak. Why would I put myself through that?

"Maybe you're looking for the wrong kind of evidence," Abigail said. "Sometimes you need to give that big old brain of yours a rest and let your heart take over. Give him a chance to fall in love with you, and maybe he'll see the future together that you can so easily picture."

"You're saying I'm overthinking."

Abigail started to giggle.

"Laughing at me isn't going to help." I released her hand, which I'd been holding.

She clasped her hands over her mouth but her eyes told me she was still laughing. "You're right. I'm sorry." She gasped. "But you overthink *everything*. You know you do. It's your decision but give your heart a vote at least."

We fell silent, as I tried to imagine what it would feel like to have Noah in love with me.

"I just need to get over him, but it's not as simple as it sounds." I'd expected it to feel better the more time passed, and although it hadn't been long, the pain seemed to be getting worse, not better.

"Maybe that should tell you something."

"I know. I should try harder," I said.

"That's not what I meant. Maybe Noah's the guy you don't get over because he's the man you're meant to be with."

Hearing those words was painful, because as much as I tried to fight it, my heart kept telling me the same thing—Noah Jensen was the one for me, but I didn't see how that meant anything but unhappiness for me.

This conversation had gone the exact opposite way to how I'd expected it to go. I'd expected for Abigail to be furious with Noah and me but satisfied that I'd turned him away. I'd expected this pit of regret in my stomach to feel slightly less uncomfortable. Instead it felt worse—bigger—as if it were clawing out more space inside me.

"Have you ever considered that this whole idea of you needing evidence and certainty is just an excuse?"

I knew I hadn't escaped Abigail's tough love. "An excuse for what? I've been totally honest with you."

"It's just that we both know you enjoy what you're good at. You don't like public speaking and you thought you were terrible at it but that's clearly not true. You've handled everything so brilliantly since I've been on bedrest."

"But we're not talking about public speaking."

"No, but it's not like you feel like you're an expert in relationships. None of us are. Maybe you're just applying your normal logic—you're not familiar with it, you assume you're not going to be good at it, so you won't even try."

"You think I'd walk away from Noah and the way I feel about him, just because I don't think I'd be good in a relationship?"

"Maybe that's part of it. And the lack of certainty makes it all the more difficult to take the risk."

I didn't know how to take a chance on someone who had the power to wound me so fundamentally, so completely that I'd never recover. But when I asked myself the question of whether I'd prefer to live with the possibility of losing Noah and the idea of potentially being destroyed if he ever left me, the answer was clear. *I choose Noah. Whatever the cost.* So what else could be holding me back unless it was myself and my fear that *I'd* mess things up, not that he would?

THIRTY-FIVE

Noah

Having clearly defined goals and conquering them was what I did, and I had Truly on lock. I just needed a plan to get her back.

Being back in London, in the confines of the car with the rain beating down on the windows was comforting. I'd told Bruce just to drive around, despite the weather meaning most of the time we were stuck in traffic. I did my best business thinking out of the office, and I was hoping it would translate to the personal. I needed a solution, a winning argument.

"Bruce, can you head to Highgate?" If I couldn't figure it out, there were two people who knew Truly as well if not better than me. Although I had no idea if they'd be willing to help.

I pulled my phone out of my pocket as the car stopped with a jerk as someone pulled out in front of us on the outer circle of Regents Park.

"Rob?" I asked as the phone stopped ringing.

"I told you not to fuck things up," he whispered back. "I'm not quite sure what the bloody hell is going on. I just know that Abigail would be pissed if she knew I was talking to you."

"Who's on the phone?" Abigail's question rang out in the background.

I tipped my head back on the seat. "Look, I didn't end things."

"End what?" Rob asked.

"Who is it?" Abigail called.

"Tell her it's me," I replied. "I'm on my way over. I need your help."

"She's going to kill us both," he replied. "It's Noah," Rob called to Abigail. "He says he's on his way over."

"I'll see you soon." There was no point trying to explain anything now. If Abigail ripped me a new one then so be it. If it helped me get Truly back, I didn't care.

As we continued our journey, I tried to come up with ideas that might convince Truly I was serious about her.

I could put her on the deeds to my flat? I wasn't sure she'd agree to that—it wasn't my money she was after. Perhaps I could suggest we buy a new place together.

I could research the difference between women's and men's brains. Show her that just because I didn't see things in the exact way she did, didn't mean I didn't want her. But I was sure she'd just see that as bullshit and misdirection.

We pulled up in front of the house. Rob must have heard us pull up as he came to the door before I was through the front gate.

"I'm surprised you came here of all places," Rob said, leading me inside.

Where else would I go? "Let's go up," I replied, glancing up the stairs.

"You first," Rob said.

Abigail's expression was neutral as I stepped into her bedroom. "Hey. Thanks for letting me come over. I need some help."

She shook her head. "What am I going to do with you two?"

"I don't know what you know and what you don't, but you need to understand that I want to be with your sister," I blurted. I wasn't a blurter. I was careful and considered in what I said, but Truly changed everything.

"That's a start." Abigail sighed and hauled herself up so she was half sitting, half lying, and I took a seat on the sofa next to Rob.

"You're not going to kill him?" Rob asked. "Or me?"

"Well that depends on how the rest of this conversation goes," she said, flashing her husband a grin.

I was prepared for whatever Abigail was dishing out, as long as it led to the right result.

"I don't know how to convince her to come back to me. How I give her the certainty she needs."

"From what I can make out, she wants to be with you but she's scared she's going to get hurt, and you? Well, I'm not quite sure. What are your reservations?"

"I don't have any. I want Truly. I don't want anyone else. I've just come back from New York and—"

I paused.

"And what?" Abigail asked.

"I missed her." I wasn't sure I'd ever missed anyone in my life before. "It pissed me off that I couldn't call her up and tell her about my day. That I didn't know what she was doing or who she'd been talking with or what she was having for lunch."

I looked up and Abigail was grinning at me. "So what are you going to do about it?"

"You're not going to tell me to leave her alone and that I'm not good enough?" I'd expected a rollicking. I'd thought I'd have to convince Abigail of my feelings for Truly and how hurting her was the last thing I'd ever do.

"You're a clever man. You know you're not good enough for her. So, no, I'm not going to tell you that. I like you, Noah. And I like the way you look at my sister and what you're saying. What you need to know is that I'm not opposed to physical violence when the need arises. Just make sure it doesn't."

I nodded. "Received and understood. But know this, Abigail. I've never been so serious about anything. Comparing her to other women is ludicrous. Of course she means more to me than anyone ever has, but more than that, other than walking, I've never wanted anything in my life more than I want Truly."

Abigail nodded decisively as if I'd passed her test. "So, what's your plan?"

"That's why I'm here. I know I want her, but I just don't know how to convince her of that. I won't lie to her but at the same time, I want to give her what she needs if that's possible. I just don't know what that is."

Abigail sighed. "You're going to have to win over the left side of her brain. She doesn't trust the right. Love isn't logical."

Didn't I know it? "Yeah. She likes facts. Knowledge. Certainty. And what I'm offering her is let's-see-how-it-goes. For me that's more realistic, but not so much for her."

"She wants more than that. She needs evidence you can be relied on," Abigail said.

"Have you told her that shit about you not wanting

anything more than her since you recovered from the accident?" Rob asked. "I mean, that sounds pretty convincing to me."

Had I? The conversation at the ball had been completely unexpected and had caught me off guard. "I can't remember what I said. But I don't think so."

"Then Rob's right. You should definitely tell her that," Abigail said.

"And then, you could marry her. That's certain. Factual. Futureproofed," Rob said.

Abigail cackled. "Don't be ridiculous. Truly's not going to say yes to a marriage proposal." She paused. "Not yet, anyway. She won't believe you're sincere at this point."

"And I wouldn't be. I'm just getting my head around all this stuff. Feeling like this for someone. It's all new to me. I need time to adjust. But I want to do that with her by my side."

"I think you should start by being honest with her," Abigail said. "Tell her what you're like. How you're goal oriented. You find a mountain you want to climb. You plot out how you're going to do it and then you execute. It's not like you have the rest of your life mapped out—just what's right in front of you."

"That's exactly it. She told me how she can see us getting old and arguing over Scrabble but that's not me. I work short term. I've never thought about long term because I know how your life can turn on a dime and change everything."

"Come on, that's not entirely true," Rob said. "Concordance Tech took you two years of preparation and false starts here in London and then four years of working your arse off in New York before you achieved your goal and walked away. Six years is hardly short term."

Rob was right, but the thing with Concordance Tech was I could see the finish line. "But I don't get what I should be aiming for in a relationship. What's the end goal?"

"Wow, you and Truly are like the same person, you just don't know it. You both are so highly structured." Abigail rolled her eyes. "The end goal is happiness. It's connection. It's building a life together, sharing experiences and memories. And along the way you'll have joint goals and go after them together."

It was as if pieces of a jigsaw were rearranging themselves in my brain, finally starting to create a bigger picture. What Abigail said made sense. Completely.

"Truly needs to know she's in your plans, and that the future you see for yourself includes her."

"She is. She really is. I got a business offer a few weeks ago that would involve a lot of travelling, but I couldn't imagine a life where I only saw her a few times a month. I tried to talk to her about it but that's when she ended things."

"So what happened? Did you accept the offer?" Abigail asked.

I shook my head. "I said no yesterday. It's not the life I want. Even though she ended things, I can't picture my future without her. Can't accept that we're over for good. And if we're not over, then I know I'll never be happy travelling when I could be home with her."

Rob cleared his throat and grinned at his wife.

"Sounds to me like you have the evidence you need," Abigail said.

Without knowing it, I was organizing my life around this woman. Rob said it would happen like that. He'd warned me.

"You think me having turned down the job will be enough?"

"I think the reasons you turned down the job should convince her," Abigail said.

And now I saw it. Loving Truly wasn't a goal or a challenge. She was a way of life. She was and would be at the heart of everything, forever.

THIRTY-SIX

Noah

I was probably about to get arrested. The air was still and frigid, and my fingers had become stiff as the minutes ticked by. It was as if the cold and dark added to the pressure on my chest. I was desperate to see her. I'd been watching the entrance to Truly's building for forty minutes. Where the hell was she? There'd been no answer when I'd buzzed up, but I'd been determined to wait for her.

My heart lifted as she appeared on the other side of the road. I took a step toward her before I realized she wasn't on her own. She was with a guy. Who had a dog.

Surely Abigail and Rob would have mentioned if Truly was on a date? But then I knew from experience that Truly didn't tell her sister everything about her love life.

Fuck, what had I expected? That she'd remain celibate? That everyone's lives stopped when I wasn't in them? She had every right to date other men. Sleep with other men. I just didn't know if I could stand here outside her flat while it happened.

I waited as the two of them disappeared inside. The lights went on in her living room window and her silhouette appeared. I imagined her seeing me when she drew the curtains. Fuck, I should never have let her go. I should have said anything it took to keep her from walking away.

My imagination was my own worst enemy. Were they having drinks before doing whatever they were going to do, or had they gone straight to her bedroom? Would she think of me when he touched her?

I began to pace, and on each turn, I inched closer to the front of her building. I wasn't about to stand by and let whatever was going on up there just happen. Not as long as I had breath in my body.

I sped across the street and caught someone coming out of Truly's building, grabbing the door before it slammed shut. Too impatient for the lift, I took the stairs to the fourth floor and arrived winded. I rested my hands on the door frame, trying to catch my breath, then knocked on her door. Would she be shocked when she answered, or would she want to know why I was here?

"Noah? What are you doing here?" She glanced at her watch. "It's late."

"I know. I'm sorry but I have to speak to you about something."

She glanced over her shoulder.

"It's important," I said.

Finally, she opened the door and let me in. She didn't look pleased to see me, but she still looked beautiful. Her hair was up, but some curls had escaped to fall around her face. She'd changed into a *Star Wars Episode V* t-shirt—of course, because it was the best of all the films—and pajama bottoms. She looked incredible. "I wanted to talk to you and—"

"It couldn't wait?"

"I guess I'm impatient. You should go and tell the other guy to leave."

"What are you talking about? You think I've got a man stashed in my bedroom?"

I sucked in a breath. "The guy you came home with."

"Oh my God." She paced into the kitchen and filled two glasses with cold water from the tap, shoving one at me before she headed back into the living room. "He's my neighbor. I met him in the park while I was out. We walked back together."

My neck muscles unbunched, and it took every ounce of my willpower not to grin like the cat who got the fucking cream. *Thank fuck.*

"Now that you have the lowdown on my evening, can you explain to me why you are here?" She took a seat on the sofa.

"What you said at the winter ball caught me off guard. I wasn't expecting to have a conversation about our relationship, our future together in the lobby of a London hotel that night."

She took another sip of water, watching me over the rim of the glass.

"I need you to know that I've never known anyone like you. I've never felt what I feel for you for anyone." I blew out a breath. "Let me start again."

"Noah, I'm not sure this is a good—"

"Just hear me out, Truly. I'm sure you have everything worked out in that head of yours. That you've told yourself to move on, that we weren't right on paper or whatever. But a week ago you were imagining us with gray hair, playing Scrabble, and I don't believe that disappears overnight." I exhaled and she didn't try to interrupt me again.

I took a deep breath. "I love how you like to be excellent at everything. How you think your sister outshines you when the opposite is true."

She looked away. "That's just not true. Abigail is . . ."

I collapsed on the sofa next to her. "Abigail just has a shit ton of confidence and understands her power. She's a total Michael Hutchence."

"You think my sister is like the lead singer of INXS?" She looked at me as if I was in the middle of some kind of mental breakdown, which was quite possibly the case.

"Yeah. Michael Hutchence thought he was the best-looking member of his band, so people went along with it. The rest of the band were happy with him taking the spot-light, but all those guys were good-looking. Hutchence just had the hair and a leather jacket."

"What is it with you and eighties rock?"

"Whatever. If you want to spend your whole life thinking your sister is prettier, more popular, better than you at God knows what, then do it. Just know that I disagree. You are the most beautiful, most special woman I've ever met in my life. No one has ever come close."

She offered me a smile, and it warmed me, encouraged me, like a small beacon of hope.

"You mentioned I like a challenge, that I enjoy conquering things," I said. "You're right. The accident set some kind of pattern in my brain where I liked to set myself a challenge and achieve it."

She nodded and brought her legs up, tucking them underneath her.

"So, that's how I work. I don't look beyond what I'm focused on—what the challenge is. And I think that's partly because I know how futile looking too far into the future can be. I'm better at concentrating on whatever's right in front of me."

"I understand that," she replied. "And what happens if you look up and decide I'm not going to fit into whatever you have on your radar next?"

"I heard what you said at the ball. But, Truly, I've lived like this a long time and it's taken a while to see where you're coming from, but I am trying. I understand that you like certainty and knowing what's next but there are no guarantees in life."

She rolled her eyes. "You sound like my sister."

"But I *can* guarantee you this. I don't look in my future and see anyone but you. I can't imagine tomorrow without knowing what you thought about breakfast. I can't imagine next year without waking up beside you. You are the only woman I want. The only woman who's ever really inter-ested me. I like hanging out with you. I like kissing you. I think you're the smartest woman I've ever met. And I've missed you—even though it's just been a few days."

She uncurled her legs and we sat staring at each other.

"Is this you wanting what you can't have? Because I've now become a challenge?" She pushed her hair over her ears like she meant business, like she wanted to get into the nitty gritty of the situation.

"No." My tone was firm. Definitive. "Women have never been like that to me."

She laughed. "They're a three-month challenge. Once they fall in love with you, you're done. You move on."

I frowned. She wasn't getting it. "You've got that wrong. Women have never been a challenge to me—not until you. That's the whole point."

"If that's true, I don't want to be your first challenge. I'm not wired to handle that. I'm not strong enough to hold a part of myself back out of fear you'll leave me." Her voice faltered, and it was as if each syllable was a spike through my heart.

"I'd never want you to hold back from me. What I've realized this last week is that you're my lifetime's challenge —the girl I never conquer. You're the woman who joins me in the challenges to come. We face them together."

Truly set down her water and looked at me from under her lashes. "I'm scared. Of everything. Of me wanting you more. Of me messing things up."

I shifted to sit on the coffee table opposite her and took her hands. I caught her knees inside mine. "This is worth being afraid for. You and me. You know it."

I circled my thumbs over her wrists, her pulse tripping under her skin. She was always so comfortable without words, with thinking through everything she said before she spoke it out loud.

"I feel as if I belong to you, Noah. And it's the scariest thing I've ever known in my life."

I hadn't thought about it like that before, but when she said it, it made perfect sense. I felt whole when I was with her and like a piece of me was missing when we were apart. "I feel the same way."

She cupped my jaw. Her touch was like going home. "There's no guarantee that this is going to work. But I'd never live with myself if I messed things up."

"We have to trust that when one of us messes up, the other one will get it right. Life doesn't stand still, and anything is possible—we could all be wiped out by asteroids next month—but I do know that we have to try."

She scowled at me, hating that I was getting the science wrong.

"Okay, not next month." I had to fight the urge to

chuckle and pull her into a hug. "I'm trying to make a point. You're the only person who really understands me. The only person I tell every thought in my brain without censorship. I can't let you go." I don't know why it had taken me so long to see what was right in front of me. "It may have taken some time, but I've realized how you're not just some girl I want to date. You're my partner in crime. The love of my life. The person I want to be with forever."

She closed her eyes and took a deep breath. "The love of your life?"

"Of course." I pulled her onto my lap. "I love you, Truly Harbury."

She skimmed my jawline with her fingers. "I think I feel the same way."

"You *think*?" I chuckled. "You're not much good at this romantic stuff, you know."

She grinned. "I'm really not. You're going to have to help me. You know how I don't like to be out of my comfort zone and how much coaching I need when I'm forced to do new stuff."

"We'll figure it out. It can be the first challenge we face together."

She slid her arms around my back and pressed her face against my shoulder. "I accept. And you should know that Abigail and I had a talk—I was going to call you. Tonight."

"You were? What were you going to say?"

"How I wanted to try. That I didn't want to be without you, that I wanted to keep loving you."

"We're going to do more than try, you know," I said. Every moment I was near this woman, I felt more certain that being with her was the most important decision I'd ever make in my life.

"We need to figure out how it's going to work with you

away for the next twelve months. It might be too much of a—"

"I'm not going anywhere without you. I turned down the job."

"Noah, you can't say no to such a wonderful opportunity. I know how passionate you are about it, and I don't want you to wake up and resent me if you don't follow your heart and your passion."

"Don't you get it yet? You're my heart. You're my passion. Anything else is gravy, as long as I have you."

"So, you're staying in London?"

"*We're* staying in London. We'll need to figure out who's moving in with who or whether we look for something new."

"We're moving in together?" She looked slightly panicked.

"Of course. I don't want to waste time not being together."

She shook her head as if she couldn't quite believe it. I'd have to show her in the weeks, months, and years to come. Eventually she'd understand that she was everything I'd never aimed for and yet everything I'd been working my whole life for.

THIRTY-SEVEN

Noah

She stroked her fingers over my cheekbones as if she were checking everything was still just the same. But it wasn't. I'd realized what could be lost now. I knew how high the stakes were. She swept her thumb over my lips, and I grabbed her wrist.

"I'm going to kiss you now," I said.

I pushed my fingers through her hair, then paused to take in her beauty before I pressed my lips lightly to hers.

Just once.

It was as if a dam had burst.

Her fingers fumbled at my buttons, and I reached for the bottom of her t-shirt and pulled it over her head, revealing her high, firm breasts. "Fuck, I've missed you," I said, pushing my hand down her pajama bottoms. I found her hot and wet and my entire body sagged with relief that she was mine again. As she started opening my trousers, I growled and stood, lifting her up with me. I didn't want this to be some fumbling, quick fuck on a couch. I wanted to lay her out, see that smooth expanse of warm skin, that beautiful smile and her incredible curves—absorb it, take it in. "I'm taking you to bed where I'm going to do wicked, wicked things with you."

I pulled out my wallet and tossed it onto the bedside table. Stripped off my trousers and pants while I caught her watching me undress. "How do you feel?" I asked.

She shifted in the dull streetlight that filtered through the curtains. "Relieved. Nervous. Horny."

I chuckled. Always so fucking honest. "Me too."

She slipped off her pajama bottoms and lay back as I crawled on top of her. I stared down at her, taking in her face, her collarbones, her fucking incredible breasts. I wanted to fix this moment in my brain; it was so fucking perfect. I dipped down to kiss her, my tongue flicking across her lips. Having her naked beneath me was almost overwhelming, and I didn't want to fuck this up.

"Hey," she said, stroking her finger over my eyebrow. "You're thinking too much. It's just you and me."

I groaned and rolled to my side, bringing her with me. I'd known from the moment I laid eyes on her that she was dangerous and every second I spent with her proved me right. We entwined our legs, and I brought her mouth to mine.

God, had kissing—just kissing—ever been so good? I wanted to own every inch of her. I worked down her neck and across her collarbone kissing and licking, claiming every square centimeter of her as mine.

"I've missed this," she said, placing her index finger over one spot on my shoulder. "This little mole. And this dip here." She traced her finger down to the valley between my biceps and triceps.

God she was so fucking adorable. "I missed all of you," I confessed.

"You don't have favorite bits?"

I glanced down at breasts that swayed with each tiny movement she made.

She laughed. "Well, that's predictable, I suppose."

"I'm not generally a boob man, but these?" I said, scooping them up and letting them fall. "These are something else." I ran the backs of two fingers down in a straight line from her collarbone to her navel, enjoying the way patches of goosebumps appeared. "And your skin. The feel of it—so soft and smooth and warm." I trailed my hand lower. "And this," I said, dipping one finger between her folds. She sighed, then I brought my finger to my mouth to taste it. "Always so fucking sweet."

My body began to buzz—in expectation or need, I wasn't sure. It was time. I rolled her over, clasping her hands in mine, and slid my erection against her folds as we held each other's gaze.

"Condom," she whispered.

Shit. I always wore a condom but tonight, I didn't want to. I wanted to be as close to her as I could. But I wasn't going to push.

"Or not," she said. "I've not . . . not with anyone since you. And I'm on the pill."

"Me neither," I replied. Maybe we'd been more serious than either of us realized from the outset.

As I positioned myself at her entrance, she smiled and brought her knees up, opening herself to me.

"I like watching you touch yourself," she said.

I groaned. "You know you might kill me if you keep saying stuff like that." I dipped to steal a kiss.

"I want an orgasm before you die, okay?"

I grinned. "I think I can handle that." I pushed in deep as she clawed at my chest and tried to catch her breath. I stilled as I got to the end of her. She was so tight, so fucking perfect, and if I thought about how good it all was I was going to lose it. "You okay?"

"Yeah, it's just always so good."

We always fit together so perfectly. "For me too."

"I want you to let go. Take what's yours," she said.

I tipped my head back. Shit. That was exactly what I needed. To make her mine. I was dizzy at the thought, but I pulled back, and the slide of her thighs against my hips propelled me forward. I began to thrust. Desperate to be closer, I glanced at her, wanting to see how good it was. Her eyes were unfocused and lazily half shut as she tightened her grip on my shoulder. I concentrated on the pinch of her fingers and her sharp exhale. I couldn't remember ever getting this much pleasure from the way I made another person feel before. But being able to make Truly open up was the biggest turn-on.

As I stilled, she twisted beneath me, and I grunted at the drag of her body, then gave her what she wanted, pulling out and sliding back in. She arched beneath me as if she wanted to get closer, and I pulled her leg up, pushing her knee to her shoulder to get deeper. The warm-up was over, and I was ready for the main event. I tensed and thrust into her faster.

"It's so good, so good," she chanted.

God, her feedback was another thing I'd lived too long without. I loved hearing exactly how she felt. How *I* made her feel. Her hips mirrored mine as we moved together, climbing higher and higher, getting faster and less careful. It was as if we were dissolving the last few weeks and wiping the slate clean. It was wild and urgent and somehow completely necessary.

"Truly," I called out, needing to hear her. "Truly."

She thrust her hand in my hair. "I'm so close." She tightened beneath me, squeezing so hard, I thought I might burst. "Just . . ." Her breaths got higher and shallower. She was seconds away, and I wanted to hold back until I got her there. "Just . . . Oh God," she screamed, and I pulsed into her, emptying everything I had as we came together.

My pulse banged in my ears, and my whole body throbbed, but it wasn't enough. I wanted more. "Again," I spat out. "I need you again. Now."

Her eyes widened, and she nodded. I was like a junkie who'd had my first fix in weeks, and now I couldn't get enough.

I turned onto my back and scrubbed my hands over my face, groaning as she fisted my still-hard cock.

Her palm pressed against my abs as she lifted a leg across mine, then leaned forward to kiss me. She pulled back almost too quickly, and I couldn't decide if I wanted more of her kisses or that sweet, tight pussy clamped around me. Flicking her hips back and forward, she swept her heat along the length of me. I had to sit her on my dick right at that moment or I was going to lose it.

She grinned and shook her head. "So impatient." She guided me to her opening, closed her eyes, and let out the most delicious moan as she sank onto me. Jesus, how had I thought I could live without this?

"Fuck, Truly." I couldn't stand it any longer. I needed to fuck her hard and deep. I flipped us over so she was on her back and began to thrust. I just needed to fuck and fuck and fuck until the space between us was entirely gone.

I lay on top of her, our chests pressed together, her heat

and mine, our sweat mixing. I dropped my head to her shoulder as I continued to fuck, kiss, and lick, wanting to consume all of her. And she seemed to feel the same as her fingers dug into my arse, pulling me deeper into her.

This wasn't anything to do with conquering a woman. This was all about connection with the woman I loved. It was about need and desire. And realizing what I'd been so close to losing.

I pushed myself up, desperate to see her need for me in her eyes. Her head was thrown back, her eyes squeezed shut. Her moans got louder, higher, more desperate, but I didn't slow my pace. She ran her nails up my back and tightened around me, her eyes opening into mine as she climaxed. I reached between us, pressing her clitoris, wanting it to last for her, but the slick wetness on my fingers was too much and I pushed her, harder and harder into the mattress, as my own climax overtook me, pleasure flooding every limb, every vein, every fucking thought.

I was exhausted. My legs, my arse, my arms ached with effort. Even my jaw was tight. I collapsed onto my back.

"I just want you with me all the time."

Truly rolled to her side, slid one leg over mine and skirted her fingers up my torso. "I'm here. With you. And I'm happy."

We were forever bound. Connected. And together we were ready to take on the world.

EPILOGUE

Noah

I should have been more nervous but being near Truly always calmed me.

The children were gathered in the activity room, some wheeled in from the ward in chairs, and even a few in beds. Truly had handed over the foundation's check. The center had announced that its twenty-five-million-pound target had been reached and the speeches and thank yous were over. The entire room was full of smiles and excitement—a perfect setting. "We just have a final few words from an old friend of the center." The medical director nodded at me.

I stepped forward and took the microphone with me, trying not to catch Truly's eye and failing.

Her face was a mixture of shock and confusion. I hoped that didn't last.

"Thank you, Dr. Edwards. I won't keep any of you long, I just have a few words." For the fiftieth time that day, I reached into my trouser pocket to ensure the velvet box was still there.

"I have been where you are now. When I was fifteen, I was in a car accident and was told I'd never walk again. I can't say I'm pleased it happened, and I'll carry the scars—inside and out—for as long as I live. But there was an upside. I learned I had the sheer force of will that's required to face down the odds and beat them. That I could be told it's impossible to do something, then do it anyway. That accident and my time spent here taught me what's important in life and what isn't. I learned to squeeze out every drop of life so I could taste exactly how sweet it is.

"Many of you know Truly Harbury and recognize how special she is. How kind and caring, how dedicated and driven." A blush flushed across her cheeks and she still looked utterly confused. I grinned and turned back to the audience. "And just as I knew that I would defy the odds and walk again, I understand how precious Truly is. How important she is. How living my life without her wouldn't be living life to the full."

I pulled out the velvet box from my pocket and turned to her. "Truly, I love you and I want to spend the rest of my life with you, watching as you create happiness as you have done today and with every moment you spend working at the foundation. Hopefully, you'll create some of your own happiness as I work at being a man who deserves you. I love you, Truly Harbury. Will you marry me?"

The pressure of a thousand stares made Truly feel further away and the only one in the room at the same time. Time seemed to slow down. Her expression slid from confused to understanding, and then she took a couple of steps toward me.

Did she want to be my wife as much as I wanted to be her husband?

"Noah," she whispered, ignoring the ring I held out as she smoothed her hand over my cheek.

Mutterings in the crowd might have caught my attention if I hadn't been so mesmerized by the beautiful woman in front of me I'd just asked to be my wife.

"I want to be your husband," I said, desperate for an answer.

She nodded, and a grin tingled at the corners of my mouth.

"Is that a yes?" I asked.

She nodded again. "Yes! That's a yes," she said, and the room erupted.

I circled my arms around her waist and lifted her up. "Really?" I asked. "You're not just saying that so I'm not humiliated in front of a crowd?"

Her giggle reverberated against me. "No, but you almost deserve it. Introverts don't do public proposals. Did no one tell you?"

"We have the rest of our lives to eat Chinese food on the sofa and argue over which *Star Wars* movie is the best. You saying you'll be my wife deserves a more public celebration."

Small hands began tugging at my trousers, and I set Truly down. Children surrounded us to look at the ring and ask us about wedding plans. All I wanted was to have Truly to myself. I'd spent too long without her.

After hundreds of handshakes, high fives, hugs, and kisses, we finally managed to extract ourselves and head back to the car.

"We don't have to get married, you know," she said as I linked my fingers through hers.

"What are you talking about?" I pulled her hand up to my lips and kissed her knuckles next to the diamond.

"I don't know. I just—you don't seem like the guy who does things like get married."

"I'm the guy who marries *you*. Not just anyone."

She bit back a smile.

"I want to be your protector, your provider, your champion, your confidant. I want to be everything that I can for you. And that includes being your husband." The image of Truly in a white dress with flowers in her hair, looking up at me as if I were her world, was burned in my brain.

That was what I wanted.

Her.

Forever.

Truly

"You've really done an amazing job these last few months," I told Frankie, who had been heading up the foundation's finance department since Abigail had gone on leave. "So good that I want to make your position permanent." I wanted to fly across my desk and give her a big hug. She'd earned this opportunity, and I was so pleased to be able to give it to her.

"I don't know what to say," Frankie stuttered as she sat back in the chair opposite my desk.

Abigail and I had agreed this was the best decision all around. Frankie had done a great job, and I didn't want her to take a step backward when she'd proved herself capable of being at the next rung of the ladder. Plus, it freed me up to do other things.

"Say yes." I grinned.

"Well of course, yes. But what does that mean for you? You're not leaving, are you?"

"Never." I would spend the rest of my career at the

foundation, but I was taking on a different role. "Abigail and I are both going to be working on the donor side of things. Turns out that I don't mind the presentations to small groups of donors and some of the new reporting we produce on measurability is getting a great response from people, and I'm better at talking about that than Abigail."

"I don't know of any other charitable foundation that has such robust quantitative data."

"And we want to make sure we stay ahead. So we'll be working together on that. And then I'll present it to donors new and old. Abigail will still do the big speeches, some of the presentations, along with a lot of the general schmoozing. She's so good at it. But dividing it up between us will mean that we'll be able to do more amazing things. Two of us working with donors should bring in a lot more money."

"This is exciting," Frankie said. "We're growing."

"Professionally, financially, and maybe even emotionally." I laughed as I opened my desk drawer and put away my notebook.

"I'm so thrilled you asked me. I wondered how I'd feel going back to my old role after filling in for you these last few months."

"It's good to move forward, but sometimes it takes something drastic to make us see that." Abigail's bedrest had been worrying, but in the end it had brought nothing but good things. Abigail had been fine, baby Olivia the most beautiful baby ever born, and managing Abigail's role while she'd been gone had even forced Noah and I together.

"You don't need to ask me twice. And if it's okay with you, I'd like to get started straightaway." She bounced up from her seat and headed toward the door.

I knew I'd made the right decision. "I wouldn't expect anything less. But don't stay too late."

"I won't, and have a good time tonight," Frankie called from halfway down the corridor.

I glanced at the clock. I didn't have long before Noah and Rob would be here, and I needed to change and refresh my makeup.

"Did you tell her?" Abigail appeared at the door. "I thought I heard someone say something."

"Come in and close the door. I need to change before Rob and Noah get here." I pulled out the outfit I'd chosen for our engagement dinner from the suit carrier hanging on the coat stand behind my desk. "And yes, she was delighted."

"I'm so happy we're doing this. It really takes the pressure off."

"Me too. We have so much going on in our lives that it's the perfect solution." I stripped out of my blouse and skirt and unzipped the black jumpsuit so I could step into it.

"And fun, too. I'll have a partner in crime at these functions now."

"Some of them," I said. "Not all."

"Hey, I've not seen that outfit before. It's great. And it's one shouldered?" Abigail asked as I hooked one arm into the sleeve.

"Yeah, Noah bought it for me."

"Excuse me? Your fiancé went out and bought you clothes? I hate you."

I laughed as I zipped myself up. "Not exactly. That stylist that I told you about had me try it on, but I'd decided against it as it was so much money. Noah got it without telling me."

"But that was before anything had happened, wasn't it?"

On several occasions Abigail had made me recall almost

every detail of my relationship with Noah. She'd said she hoped it would teach me not to keep things from her in future. "After tequila kissing but, yes, before anything else."

"He was smitten practically as soon as he got back from New York," she said.

"I hadn't really thought about the timing." Maybe there'd been more between us sooner than I'd realized. I bent and did up my strappy heels. Noah liked to do it for me when we were at home—I swear that man had a shoe fetish. But as he wasn't here, I'd do them myself. He could take them off later.

Abigail launched forward as someone tried to open the door.

"I think it's your husband," I said.

Abigail flung open the door. "Don't you knock?" she asked Rob. "Truly was getting changed."

"Sorry. We can come back."

Seeing I was dressed, Abigail coaxed them in and Rob pressed a kiss on his wife's cheek and Noah and Lev followed.

"Hello, sexy." Lev grinned at me.

"Hey, that's my fiancée you're talking to," Noah said as he knocked Lev out of the way before he could do anything other than give me a very chaste kiss on the cheek. "Although she is very sexy." Noah looked me up and down, paying particular attention to my bottom before hooking his arm around my waist and pressing his lips against mine.

"You don't look so bad yourself," I said, pushing against his chest to keep him from turning a hello kiss into something more. Noah in a navy suit couldn't get hotter.

"So are we all ready?" I wasn't quite sure why Lev was here. I'd thought it was just the four of us having a quiet dinner to celebrate the engagement, but I didn't really mind.

"Oh, I just want Noah to sign some documents and I'll be on my way," Lev said, pulling out a file from his briefcase. "I know you guys have dinner and actually, I have a date."

"Who's the lucky girl?" I asked.

Lev shrugged. "I'm trying internet dating now that you've broken my heart by getting engaged, Truly. I've got to see what's out there."

I rolled my eyes. I was more than sure that Lev had never had a broken heart in his life. "So are these the documents for the new company?"

Noah nodded. "Yeah. Lev set us up with a co-investor so we can grow the tech business." Noah turned the papers and set about putting his signature on the back pages of the bundle Lev had handed him.

"And you said you might never set up a company again. I knew the money would be too much to ignore," Rob said.

"It's not about the money." Noah shook his head. "Developing this software was something I wanted to do at Concordance Tech, but it didn't make sense when we had our focus on the float. With private money, we can really spend some time getting it right without having to worry about how it will be perceived by shareholders."

"And knowing you, you'll end up a billionaire," Rob said.

Noah finished signing, closed the papers, and stood. "Not going to say no to that possibility. It would mean more money for research. More help we can give to kids who need it." Noah had decided that half his profits from his future business ventures would go into a foundation to research and test non-medical developments in healthcare.

"Yeah, I'm not sure you need to give that much away to do good," Lev said. "But I guess it's your money."

Abigail ushered us all out of the office, but as Noah and I followed the others, I slipped my hand into his. "Did I tell you today that I think you're wonderful?" I whispered.

The corners of his mouth flickered and he squeezed my hand. "I'm never going to get tired of hearing that from you."

My husband-to-be wasn't just an astute businessman and successful entrepreneur.

He was the best man I knew, my past, present, and future, and my very best friend.

OTHER BOOKS BY LOUISE BAY

Sign up to the Louise Bay mailing list to see more on all my books.
www.louisebay.com/newsletter

International Player

Being labelled a player never stopped me from being successful with women. Until I met Truly Harbury.

Truly was the first girl who ever turned me down.

The first female friend I ever had.

And she might just be the first woman I ever fall in love with.

When an emergency means she needs my help running her family's charity, I'm happy to introduce her to the glitz and glamour of the London business world—taking her to dinners, coaching her through speeches, zipping up the sexy evening gown I helped her pick out.

The more time we spend together, the more I want to convince her I'm not a man to avoid, that we're not as unsuited as she believes.

She sees herself as the book-reading, science-loving introvert while I'm the dangerous, outgoing, charmer.

She thinks I love parties and people whereas she prefers pajamas and a takeaway.

What she doesn't realize is that I like everything about her–the way her smile lights up a room, how her curves light up my imagination, and especially the way her lips taste when coated with tequila.

She's the first woman I ever fell in love with. I just need to know if she could ever love me too.

The Wrong Gentleman

I'm an all-or-nothing man—100 percent focused on whatever has my attention.

First it was serving my country in the Special Forces. Then it was building my business. Right now it's the hot blonde at the bar who's about to become another notch on my bedpost.

But women never keep my attention for more than a night.

Until I peel off Skylar Anderson's clothes and her mask starts to crumble, showing me glimpses of the girl she's hiding. She's funny, sexy and vulnerable and throws me out of bed before I can catch my breath and suggest breakfast.

When I start my last undercover job on a yacht, turns out, she's one of the crew. I try, but I can't look away.

Her high ponytail shows off her kissable neck that tastes like summer.

Her short uniform reveals the killer legs that were wrapped around me last night.

And her provocative smile? I know what that mouth is capable of.

I want to explore her body, discover her secrets and sail off into the sunset with her.

I might want to go all in for Skylar, but she should stay away from me. I've got secrets of my own and they can only bring her trouble.

A stand-alone novel.

The Earl of London

Love left me off its to-do list.

I date. I'm all for giving guys a chance. I've just never met *the one*.

Until on a spring morning in the English countryside, a tall, dark stranger emerges from the mist. Logan Steele is all tousled hair, hard chest and lips so perfect I want to reach out and touch them just to check they're real. I'm sure that's a thunderclap of chemistry I feel between us.

Did I mention he's an Earl with a self-made fortune?

A billionaire who works tirelessly for charity?

And he's so hot, watching him is like staring at the sun.

But like I said, love isn't rooting for me.

When I find out Logan Steele is out to destroy everything I've dedicated my life to protect, the chemistry disappears and the hope that had blossomed my chest turns to rage.

It no longer matters that he quickens my pulse just saying my name, weakens my knees with a single touch and that he might just be the greatest kisser that ever lived.

I might believe in love but Logan Steele is definitely not *the one*.

A stand-alone novel.

The Ruthless Gentleman

As a chief stewardess on luxury superyachts, I massage egos, pamper the spoiled and cater to the most outlandish desires of the rich and famous.

I've never had a guest want something I can't give them. Until British businessman Hayden Wolf comes aboard—all sexy swagger and mysterious requests.

He wants me.

And Hayden Wolf's a man who's used to getting exactly what he demands.

Despite being serious and focused. Demanding and ruthless. He's also charming when I least expect it as well as being devastatingly handsome with an almost irresistible smile.

But guests are strictly off limits and I've never broken a rule. Not even bent one. My family are depending on me and I can't lose my job.

Only problem is Hayden Wolf is looking at me like I just changed his life. And he's touching me like he's about to change mine.

A stand-alone novel.

Duke of Manhattan

I was born into British aristocracy, but I've made my fortune in Manhattan. New York is now my kingdom.

Back in Britain my family are fighting over who's the next Duke of Fairfax. The rules say it's me--if I'm married. It's not a trade-off worth making. I could never limit myself to just one woman.

Or so I thought until my world is turned upside down.

Now, the only way I can save the empire I built is to inherit the title I've never wanted-- so I need a wife.

To take my mind off business I need a night that's all pleasure. I need to bury myself in a stranger.

The skim of Scarlett King's hair over my body as she bends over . . .

The scrape of her nails across my chest as she screams my name . . .

The bite of her teeth on my shoulder just as we both reach the edge . . .

It all helps me forget.

I just didn't bargain on finding my one night stand across the boardroom table the next day.

She might be my latest conquest but I have a feeling Scarlett King might just conquer me.

A stand-alone novel.

Park Avenue Prince

THE PRINCE OF PARK AVENUE FINALLY MEETS HIS MATCH IN A FEISTY MANHATTAN PRINCESS.

I've made every one of my billions of dollars myself— I'm calculating, astute and the best at what I do. It takes drive and dedication to build what I have. And it leaves no time for love or girlfriends or relationships.

But don't get me wrong, I'm not a monk.

I understand the attention and focus it takes to seduce a beautiful woman. They're the same skills I use to close business deals. But one night is where it begins and ends. I'm not the guy who sends flowers. I'm not the guy who calls the next day.

Or so I thought before an impatient, smart-talking, beyond beautiful heiress bursts into my world.

When Grace Astor rolls her eyes at me—I want to hold her against me and show her what she's been missing.

When she makes a joke at my expense—I want to silence her sassy mouth with my tongue.

And when she leaves straight after we f*ck with barely a goodbye—it makes me want to pin her down and remind her of the three orgasms she just had.

She might be a princess but I'm going to show her who rules in this Park Avenue bedroom.

A stand-alone novel.

King of Wall Street

THE KING OF WALL STREET IS BROUGHT TO HIS KNEES BY AN AMBITIOUS BOMBSHELL.

I keep my two worlds separate.

At work, I'm King of Wall Street. The heaviest hitters in Manhattan come to me to make money. They do whatever I say because I'm always right. I'm shrewd. Exacting. Some say ruthless.

At home, I'm a single dad trying to keep his fourteen year old daughter a kid for as long as possible. If my daughter does what I say, somewhere there's a snowball surviving in hell. And nothing I say is ever right.

When Harper Jayne starts as a junior researcher at my firm, the barriers between my worlds begin to dissolve. She's the most infuriating woman I've ever worked with.

I don't like the way she bends over the photocopier—it makes my mouth water.

I hate the way she's so eager to do a good job—it makes my dick twitch.

And I can't stand the way she wears her hair up exposing her long neck. It makes me want to strip her naked, bend her over my desk and trail my tongue all over her body.

If my two worlds are going to collide, Harper Jayne will have to learn that I don't just rule the boardroom. I'm in charge of the bedroom, too.

A stand-alone novel.

Hollywood Scandal

HE'S A HOLLYWOOD SUPERSTAR. SHE'S LITER-ALLY THE GIRL NEXT DOOR.

One of Hollywood's A-listers, I have the movie industry in the palm of my hand. But if I'm going to stay at the top, my playboy image needs an overhaul. No more tabloid headlines. No more parties. And absolutely no more one night stands.

Filming for my latest blockbuster takes place on the coast of Maine and I'm determined to stay out of trouble. But trouble finds me when I run into Lana Kelly.

She doesn't recognize me, she's never heard of Matt Easton and my million dollar smile doesn't work on her.

Ego shredded, I know I should keep my distance, but when I realize she's my neighbor I know I'm toast. There's no way I can resist temptation when it's ten yards away.

She has a mouth designed for pleasure and legs that will wrap perfectly around my waist.

She's movie star beautiful and her body is made to be mine.

Getting Lana Kelly into my bed is harder than I'm used to. She's not interested in the glitz and glamour of Hollywood, but I'm determined to convince her the best place in the world is on the red carpet, holding my hand.

I could have any woman in the world, but all I want is the girl next door.

A standalone romance.

Parisian Nights

The moment I laid eyes on the new photographer at work, I had his number. Cocky, arrogant and super wealthy—women were eating out of his hand as soon as his tight ass crossed the threshold of our office.

When we were forced to go to Paris together for an assignment, I wasn't interested in his seductive smile, his sexy accent or his dirty laugh. I wasn't falling for his charms.

Until I did.

Until Paris.

Until he was kissing me and I was wondering how it happened. Until he was dragging his lips across my skin and I was hoping for more. Paris does funny things to a girl and he might have gotten me naked.

But Paris couldn't last forever.

Previously called What the Lightning Sees

A stand-alone novel.

Promised Nights

I've been in love with Luke Daniels since, well, forever. As his sister's best friend, I've spent over a decade living in the friend zone, watching from the sidelines hoping he would notice me, pick me, love me.

I want the fairy tale and Luke is my Prince Charming.

He's tall, with shoulders so broad he blocks out the sun. He's kind with a smile so dazzling he makes me forget everything that's wrong in the world. And he's the only man that can make me laugh until my cheeks hurt and my stomach cramps.

But he'll never be mine.

So I've decided to get on with my life and find the next best thing.

Until a Wonder Woman costume, a bottle of tequila and a game of truth or dare happened.

Then Luke's licking salt from my wrist and telling me I'm beautiful.

Then he's peeling off my clothes and pressing his lips against mine.

Then what? Is this the start of my happily ever after or the beginning of a tragedy?

Previously called Calling Me

A stand-alone novel.

Indigo Nights

I don't do romance. I don't do love. I certainly don't do relationships. Women are attracted to my power and money and I like a nice ass and a pretty smile. It's a fair exchange—a business deal for pleasure.

Meeting Beth Harrison in the first class cabin of my flight from Chicago to London throws me for a loop and everything I know about myself and women goes out the window.

I'm usually good at reading people, situations, the markets. I know instantly if I can trust someone or if they're lying. But Beth is so contradictory and confounding I don't know which way is up.

She's sweet but so sexy she makes my knees weak and mouth dry.

She's confident but so vulnerable I want to wrap her up and protect her from the world.

And then she fucks me like a train and just disappears, leaving me with my pants around my ankles, wondering which day of the week it is.

If I ever see her again I don't know if I'll scream at her, strip her naked or fall in love. Thank goodness I live in Chicago and she lives in London and we'll never see each other again, right? A stand-alone novel.

The Empire State Series

Anna Kirby is sick of dating. She's tired of heartbreak. Despite being smart, sexy, and funny, she's a magnet for men who don't deserve her.

A week's vacation in New York is the ultimate distraction from her most recent break-up, as well as a great place to meet a stranger and have some summer fun. But to protect her still-bruised heart, fun comes with rules. There will be no sharing stories, no swapping numbers, and no real names. Just one night of uncomplicated fun.

Super-successful serial seducer Ethan Scott has some rules of his own. He doesn't date, he doesn't stay the night, and he doesn't make any promises.

It should be a match made in heaven. But rules are made to be broken.

The Empire State Series is a series of three novellas.

Love Unexpected

When the fierce redhead with the beautiful ass walks into the local bar, I can tell she's passing through. And I'm looking for distraction while I'm in town—a hot hook-up and nothing more before I head back to the city.

If she has secrets, I don't want to know them.

If she feels good underneath me, I don't want to think about it too hard.

If she's my future, I don't want to see it.

I'm Blake McKenna and I'm about to teach this Boston socialite how to forget every man who came before me.

When the future I had always imagined crumbles before my very eyes. I grab my two best friends and take a much needed vacation to the country.

My plan of swearing off men gets railroaded when on my first night of my vacation, I meet the hottest guy on the planet.

I'm not going to consider that he could be a gorgeous distraction.

I'm certainly not going to reveal my deepest secrets to him as we steal away each night hoping no one will notice.

And the last thing I'm going to do is fall in love for the first time in my life.

My name is Mackenzie Locke and I haven't got a handle on men. Not even a little bit.

Not until Blake.

A stand-alone novel.

Hopeful

How long does it take to get over your first love?

Eight years should be long enough. My mind knows that, but there's no convincing my heart.

Guys like Joel weren't supposed to fall for girls like me. He had his pick of women at University, but somehow the laws of nature were defied and we fell crazy in love.

After graduation, Joel left to pursue his career in New York. He wanted me to go with him but my life was in London.

We broke up and my heart split in two.

I haven't seen or spoken to him since he left.

If only I'd known that I'd love him this long, this painfully, this desperately. I might have said yes all those years ago. He might have been mine all this time in between.

Now, he's moving back to London and I need to get over him before he gets over here.

But how do I forget someone who gave me so much to remember?

A long time ago, Joel Wentworth told me he'd love me for infinity . . . and I can't give up hope that it might have been true.

A stand-alone novel.

Faithful

Leah Thompson's life in London is everything she's supposed to want: a successful career, the best girlfriends a bottle of sauvignon blanc can buy, and a wealthy boyfriend who has just proposed. But something doesn't feel right. Is it simply a case of 'be careful what you wish for'?

Uncertain about her future, Leah looks to her past, where she finds her high school crush, Daniel Armitage, online. Daniel is one of London's most eligible bachelors.

He knows what and who he wants, and he wants Leah. Leah resists Daniel's advances as she concentrates on being the perfect fiancé.

She soon finds that she should have trusted her instincts when she realises she's been betrayed by the men and women in her life.

Leah's heart has been crushed. Will ever be able to trust again? And will Daniel be there when she is?

A stand-alone novel.

KEEP IN TOUCH!

Sign up for my mailing list to get the latest news and gossip
www.louisebay.com/newsletter

Or find me on

www.twitter.com/louiseSbay
www.facebook.com/authorlouisebay
www.instagram.com/louiseSbay
www.pinterest.com/louisebay
www.goodreads.com/author/show/8056592.Louise_Bay

ACKNOWLEDGMENTS

Truly and Noah are very special to me. I've loved them both through this book and they really are meant for each other. Thank you for reading and I hope you enjoyed it!

Elizabeth . . . you were right, they were really friends to lovers rather than second chance. But you already know that you're always right! Thank you for your brilliant editing and fabulous friendship. "Blue thumb"

Sophie - you're an amazing assistant, mother and person! Thank you for being in my world.

Najla. I LOVE this one. I just need to write two more books for the other two proofs.

Bloggers, reviewers and everyone who helps spread the word about my books—thank you! You're the best.

Lenora, I want to buy you a Stranger Things t-shirt and I hope you find a man like Noah one day.

20677116R00173